Contents

The Cast	*xi*
Preview	*xiii*
The Motion Picture	17
Short Feature	238
About Sally Bolding	253

THE CYCLOPS WINDOW

THE CYCLOPS WINDOW

A View into Southern Life

Sally Bolding

LeveePressTwo

© 2003 Sally Bolding.
All rights reserved. No part of this book may be reproduced, stored in a retrieval system, or transmitted by any means, electronic, mechanical, photocopying, recording or otherwise, without written permission from the author.

ISBN: 0-9741709-0-9 (case-bound)
ISBN: 0-9741709-1-7 (trade paperback)

This book is printed on acid-free paper.
Cover design: OspreyDesign
Eye design created on computer by Susan Fossett
Book production and design: Tabby House
Author's photo by Sylvia Benson Frank

This novel is a work of fiction. Any resemblance to real life personages or locales is entirely coincidental.

Publishers Cataloging in Publication

Bolding, Sally
 The cyclops wondow : a view into Southern life / Sally Bolding. – 1st ed. – Pensacola Beach, Fla. : LeveePressTwo, 2003.
  p. : cm.
  ISBN: 0-9741709-0-9
  0-9741709-1-7 (pbk.)

  1. Segregation–Mississippi–Fiction. 2. Mississippi–Race relations–Fiction. I. Title

PS3602.O535 C935 2003   20033106871
813.16–dc21   0307

LeveePressTwo
330 Fort Pickens Road
Pensacola Beach, FL 32561

Dedicated to my husband, Harold Bolding.
And, with thanks to my helper, Susan Fossett.

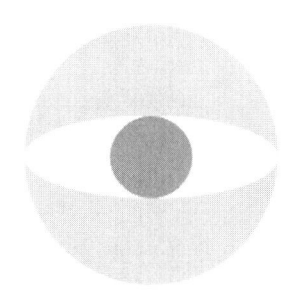

The Cast

Wash Bibbs   Arorah Hannah
Ladyree Soper Marshall   Mumford Marshall

N. Nathan Pankum

Also playing

Evelyn Haynes Buffton	child welfare worker, daughter of B. T. and Mattie Haynes
Red Ted Cockrane	high school classmate of Nathan Pankum
Max Durham	agronomist at Delta Branch Station
Claude Hannah (deceased)	father of Elia Hannah Marshall and Thor Hannah, lover of Arorah Hannah
Thor Hannah	son of Arorah and Claude Hannah
B. T. and Mattie Haynes	owners of the Homecooking Café
Dr. Tudor Jackson	minister of First Presbyterian Church
Mary Jefferson	called Mary Tomato Man, neighbor of Arorah Hannah
Tomato Man Jefferson	brother of Mary Jefferson
Dr. Jeff Johnson	black physician
Marsie Klingman	friend of Ladyree Soper Marshall
Dr. Prather Lewis	white physician
Elia Hannah Marshal	second wife of Mumford Marshall, heir and daughter of Claude Hannah

Sally Bolding

May Corday Marshall	younger daughter of Mumford and Elia Marshall
Spring Marshall	older daughter of Mumford and Elia Marshall
William Winston Milledge	(deceased) also called Will, national poet and late resident of Port City
Abner Owens	lawyer of Port City, Mississippi
Norwood N. Pankum	father of Nathan, owner of Pankum's Nursery and Greenhouse
Ruby Smith	employee of Abner Owens and girl friend of Norwood Pankum
Verda Soper	mother of Ladyree Soper Marshall
Hamilton Vance	Port City policeman

... and a cast of more, including:

The Borders	Billy, Mary Sue, and son, Junior, owners of white funeral home, and Junior's friends, Frankie and Herschel.
Adrian Oates	last lover of William Winston Milledge

Preview

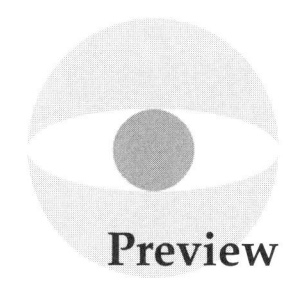

Turning west off of a Yazoo Mississippi Delta highway, two women drove onto a macadam road leading to an antique shop. On one side of the road, looking like a huge prehistoric insect, a mechanical cotton picker moved through the rows of this year's puffy white and green crop. They passed homes diminished by time, a long-closed service station, and new trailers in weedy yards.

Both women dressed well, their cloudlike hair expertly arranged. They held in careful check their appearance of about sixty years.

This morning before their shopping trip, the two women had attended a funeral.

"What a nice man to die at only sixty-something," said the woman who drove. "He shouldn't have retired. Men retire, and two years later, that's it."

"Nathan Pankum just wanted to make sure his grandson got his bank presidency," said the other woman. "And that grandson is too young for my thinking—and, God knows, I hope not for our money."

"Never saw the Presbyterian Church so full, and overflowing with flowers."

They reached the antique shop. In the dilapidated downtown, all the stores near the shop had long ago gone out of business. The shrinking community around it had to drive miles for groceries.

The women emerged from the car with ready handbags. They entered the antique shop.

The owner sat behind a long counter reading a mystery. He looked up and nodded at his customers. A Blue Plate Special advertisement marked the counter front indicating that the shop had once been a restaurant.

The owner returned his attention to his book.

"Blue Plate Special?" said the woman who had driven, her voice strong. She seemed tall now that she stood. "I thought you said this had been a fine restaurant."

"It was when I was young and dating. Afterwards, it went down," said the other woman, her voice moderate, her body now squat as it had not been when she dated.

They moved through the dim light in the dust and clutter.

The taller woman asked the owner, "Do you have any old painting? I'm looking for a good primitive."

"Over there," said the owner. He did not rise. He pointed to a stack of canvases leaning against a wall.

The women approached the stack.

The tall woman pulled one picture by one forward for inspection. She repeated, "Sunday painter's junk, Sunday painter's junk."

"I wouldn't know a primitive from a Picasso," said the other.

"Honestly, I don't see how your well-read, cultivated friends put up with you."

"I don't read what they read. I like movie-star biographies. So? I can still jolly well set a tea cart properly."

Both women lived in Port City, Mississippi, the largest town on the river between Memphis and Vicksburg. The squat woman's family was native to the area. The tall woman had come to Port City in her early middle years when her husband had been chosen to head a new industry there. He had hired the other woman's husband to handle public relations.

The tall woman abruptly stopped at one canvas. She scrutinized the painting's detail of a black man and a white man.

"It's signed S. Marshall," said the other woman. "It's probably Spring's."

The tall woman turned to the back of the canvas. On it Spring Marshall had written, *Wash Bibbs, scholar, saint. Mumford Marshall, my brilliant, funny, outrageous father.*

"I knew Mumford. Who is Wash Bibbs?"

"Wash Bibbs *was*," said the native of the area, "a servant of our poet, William Winston Milledge. Will Milledge died before you came. He was well-known in the whole country. Wash, born crippled, got horribly burned as a child in Will's kitchen, and Will educated him. You'd have approved of Wash's reading. Also, working in a garden, Will and Wash could bring a dead tree back to life."

The tall woman released Spring's canvas. "I don't want it. It's early work and not good."

The women continued on bypassing junk and ugly antiques, fingering pressed glass in search of signed cut glass, and turning over plates to check for origins.

The tall woman noticed some colorful shadows across a wall and turned to find the source.

"Look!" she screamed. "There against the store front. That stained-glass window."

Quickly she went to the window.

The other woman held back.

"Astonishing!" said the tall woman. "The color on that wall is the sun shining through the top part."

The other woman continued to hold back.

"H. B.," said the tall woman speaking of her husband, "will have a fit, but I'm going to buy it."

"Nooo," said the other woman.

"Why not?"

"It looked at me."

"Nonsense!"

"It was on the attic front of a house almost in the old downtown near the levee. It's shaped like a great big eye. When I was a child, I had to pass it to shop. I thought it looked at me."

"A scaredy little girl's imagination."

"Yes," she said, "but please don't buy it." She paused. "It won't fit in the car."

"Of course it will. I'll make it do."

"I won't ride with it."

"Nonsense! Ridiculous!"

The squat woman seemed to swell and then sink into the floor. Then she suddenly heightened and rushed out of the shop to stand in the sweltering heat on the cracked sidewalk by the car.

The tall woman stood her ground for a few minutes watching through the storefront glass the other woman outside sweating. Then she gave in and left the shop to join her friend.

They drove silently past the cotton fields and back onto the highway heading south toward Port City—without the Cyclops window.

A mile or so behind the women, visible through the store glass, the colors of the abandoned window heightened in the afternoon sun. The stained glass seemed a sleepy eye rousing from a dream, preparing a return to the dream.

The Motion Picture
First Sequence

The paperboy tossed a morning *Memphis Commercial Appeal* dated Sunday, March 9, 1947, between two thick oaks siding the walkway of the Cyclops House. The newspaper lay between the dark trunks of the only two trees in downtown Port City. The colored squares of its funny pages spilled out from black-and-white print. The one-storied house on the lot crouched behind the oaks, its overbearing roof heavy with a rising attic that lodged the house's single stained-glass window. Passing shoppers felt the eyelike window watched.

Climbing English ivy took fully two-thirds of the lower house and extended toward the attic. On the right, a new three-storied Sears Roebuck building loomed. On the left, low Town Creek ambled by, its banks eroding. Beyond the creek, the First Baptist Church and the boxy buildings of the downtown ran the length to the levee.

The white-owned downtown had long ago overwhelmed the fine old homes of the avenue. The river had swept away much in floods, but mostly new businesses had crowded out the residential blocks. The Cyclops House alone remained.

Inside the house, Ladyree Soper Marshall, called the Picture Show Lady because of her long tenure as an usher at the Majestic Theater, awoke. The room where she and her mother slept in twin beds was cold, but sweat soaked both the turns of her hair held rigidly by bobby pins along the base of her head and the pompadour set on top. Although awake, she kept still, fearing to rouse the anxiety that she felt somewhere lagging below her recent sleep. What had she been dreaming? She looked at her mother's wispy gray and blond hair, circling in soft tangles on the pillow of the bed next to her own. *She had dreamed that her dreams had been scrambled into her mother's*. The anxiety came alive.

Abruptly the alarm broke the silence of the room, the set hand of the clock rusted at seven, always the hour of the day when she began her routine.

"Cut off the alarm, Ladyree," said her mother, Verda Soper. Each morning the same querulous words followed the clock's ring.

Ladyree checked the alarm in an automatic move and rose to stretch her legs toward her worn and formless slippers. She felt quivery.

Her mother, an octogenarian, but with genes to carry her close to a hundred years, rested beneath a carefully sewn crazy quilt. Slowly, as if achy, Verda Soper sat up. Ladyree glanced away, knowing her mother's bridge lay in a glass of water on the bedside table. The old woman was pale like fragile china, but her partial toothlessness magnified the bold jut of her jaw and suggested the steel that her only child knew lay beneath the china appearance.

"Look at me, child," said Verda Soper.

Ladyree faced her mother. At once Verda Soper smiled—clownish, crow-footed, snaggle-toothed smile. The grotesquery of it always brought to Ladyree's mind a movie where a corpse had risen from its casket to smile with blackish, gappy teeth.

"Don't, Mother."

Verda Soper laughed. She put her bridge into place and patted her daughter's shoulder as she passed her bed. The early querulous sound was gone from her voice, and her face, first amused, was now content. Verda Soper left to go outside to pick up the newspaper.

This morning Ladyree decided to forego the routine of taking coffee with her mother. She waited until she heard her mother return to the house and cross into the kitchen to start making coffee. She continued waiting until she heard the hiccuping perk and smelled the aroma. She knew then that her mother was scanning news at the breakfast table expecting her to come. She would go instead to the "good room."

She paused before leaving the bedroom. On the dresser, an old sepia photograph taken of her years ago was framed in sweeping and knotted threads of silvered ribbon. The late William Winston Milledge, the town's only poet, had called her the beauty of her generation. Mumford Marshall, her ex-husband, had called her antiquish, a beauty maybe out of another age. It had been difficult to be objective about her looks, knowing then, as even now, that a Mississippi girl's appearance could be either life-giving or life-taking. Ladyree pushed her chin into her neck and felt accordion-like folds of skin.

She would soon be fifty years old.

The telephone rang.

"I'll get it," Ladyree called out. She answered the telephone in the hallway just outside the bedroom.

It was Marsie. Marsie was her oldest friend, who had married a local planter, had children, belonged to the garden clubs and the Junior Auxiliary. Marsie *belonged* in the community as Ladyree had expected herself to belong and did not. Good friend Marsie was to pick Ladyree and her mother up today for church.

"I can't pick y'all up, Ladyree. I feel terrible. I must have eaten something bad at the party last night."

"Oh, I'm sorry. It might be a cold. The weather's gotten chilled again so suddenly. I even started to put my plants out yesterday, but I remembered last year and didn't."

"No, just my stomach. Time and Tums will do it," answered Marsie. "What about last year did you remember?"

"Mother took my plants out too early. They almost froze."

"Damn, Ladyree. Your mother!"

"No, Marsie. You're wrong about Mother."

"She's stolen your soul."

"Stop, Marsie. Don't do this again."

"She prayed Mumford outta that house, made his life hell with her Bible."

"Don't."

"I won't shut up, Ladyree. I'll never shut up. She'll gobble up what little sustains you now, and she'll never die."

"Die? Oh, Marsie."

"She's even jealous of your plants. She didn't *accidentally* almost freeze them. She's jealous of your cats, too. If your salary at the Majestic where you flee into those movies didn't maintain her, you'd be out of a job. And I insist that if it weren't for Verda Soper, you'd be to this day with Mumford."

"That was long ago, Marsie. Too late. Lost," said Ladyree, a plea in her voice.

"Mumford loved you. You lost Mumford because of your mother." Something in Ladyree's breathing caused Marsie to trail her voice. "You lost . . ."

The haze, which had come and gone over the last few weeks to deaden Ladyree's sense of reality, returned. It was as if a thin roll of store-purchased cotton were wrapped around her head, clouding sight and muffling sound. "Lost Mumford. Lost my baby. Lost," repeated Ladyree, the haze thickening.

Marsie was silent a few moments. "The baby?"

"Oh . . . ," said Ladyree, "No babies. Never. I meant those I might have had." Ladyree changed the subject. "Tell me about your family."

"Let's don't talk about family! You break my heart. You don't have a family. I've got to go. I already feel like hell. Bye." Marsie hung up.

Ladyree passed the kitchen door on her way to the "good room."

"You want coffee?" her mother asked, still seated at the kitchen table.

"No," she answered still hazy and moved on in slow-motion.

The "good room" was a room of light in the shadowy old house. Years ago Mumford had helped her strip paper from three walls revealing beneath aged pine planks, had helped her sand light the dark varnished woodwork. The fourth wall was a spellbinding line of high windows. At night it let in the moon and starlight, and in day, sunshine for her own well-being and for her plants that abounded in the room. She had given the plants names of film stars. She liked the fact that the windows faced north towards Memphis, reminding her of the world outside the Mississippi Delta, a world she knew only through Hollywood.

She watered Gary Cooper, Humphrey Bogart and Vivian Leigh. She approached the window nearest the armoire where she stored cat food. There a fat prism, a crystal testicle, hung on a string. She twirled it. From the right it captured morning sun making the room into a rainbow kaleidoscope. Outside, she saw that her mother had left the kitchen and had gone into the back yard.

Through the window Ladyree saw Verda Soper holding a fishing net that had belonged to her father years ago. It was attached to a broom handle. Behind the cat-feeding bowls, cornered within lattice, house and steps was CAT.

CAT, Ladyree's favorite cat, was back. She had not seen CAT since last December when she had put a Christmas collar with a tiny, tingly bell around his furry neck. Over the intervening months she chastised herself for not realizing that CAT was too free-spirited for collaring. At times over the months, Ladyree thought she heard a faint tingling from the little Christmas bell above in the high ivy, but she was never sure. She had grieved for CAT. CAT was back, but what was her mother doing?

The Cyclops Window

Ladyree heard CAT snarl. Verda stepped toward him, net held high. CAT hissed and ran. Verda slammed the net down with all the energy her eighty-plus years could muster. CAT was caught. CAT turned, his claws snagging in the net. Verda pulled the net in the direction of Town Creek, CAT turning in the web of fish net, snarling, hissing repeatedly, wild.

"I got you!" said Verda, audible through the window panes.

CAT rolled his body, gathering power in his spasmodic twistings. The aged net broke and began to disintegrate from his force.

Verda struggled with the handle to recapture CAT, but the net was too old. CAT sprang away, taking the net in his claws as he fled.

Verda raised the broom handle and beat the bushes where CAT had vanished, but to no purpose.

The scene had immobilized Ladyree. Now breathing evenly again, she considered what she had witnessed. Why did her mother dislike cats and plants? Why, when she had never harmed her cats to Ladyree's knowledge, did she pick CAT to molest? Was it because she thought since CAT was already missing that Ladyree would not notice? Ladyree made a mental note to let her mother know at once that she knew CAT was home.

The thunderous sounds of "Faith of Our Fathers" shattered the Sunday morning hush over a stilled Port City where few worked on the Lord's Day and the Blue Laws kept stores closed. The First Baptist Church had installed in its steeple Port City's first modern chimes. So near, now, they seemed to shake the Cyclops House like a small earthquake.

Ladyree called from the window, "Come in, Mother. It's church time. I'm driving us this morning."

On the drive to First Presbyterian Church across town in their immaculate, angular, navy 1939 Buick, Ladyree told her mother that she knew about CAT's return.

"I wish the church were still downtown like the Baptists'," said Verda Soper, passing over Ladyree's remark about CAT.

The First Presbyterian Church was located on the old golf course greens of the Port City Country Club until the club had been moved to a less populated area and greatly expanded. The church had been rebuilt in the architectural style of the Old South and was part of the town's post-World War II construction boom.

When they arrived, Ladyree left her mother among old friends gathered for the usual pre-church coffee hour to search for a bathroom in the still unfamiliar church. Returning to the coffee hour, Ladyree became disoriented and opened one door by error. She stood fixed in the frame of this wrong door. What she saw astonished her.

The room, flooded with sun from a skylight, was lined with small pots on wooden horses and planks, pots of what seemed to be corn sprouts. Just as incredible, Mumford Marshall stood with the First Presbyterian's minister, Dr. Tudor Jackson, over several pots at the far end of the room.

Mumford glanced at her. After a bare instant of attention, he continued his talk with the minister. Mumford was a jolly giant, with a bald dome, big, even features, a mouth full of huge teeth—still very animal, as he had been in his handsome prime of youth. Since he never came to movies, Ladyree had not seen him up close in years. One day not long ago, when she had shopped at the Pankum Nursery and Greenhouse next to Mumford's land, she had spotted him striding across the distant fields towards his home . She had seen, or imagined she saw, his expression of good humor that day. That expression was known to her to mask the workings of his quick, imaginative mind. She knew also that if he stumbled or, if a splat of dropping from an overflying bird hit his shoulder, the volatile temper below the pleasantness could erupt with a fury.

Ladyree heard Mumford speak across the room. "You mean to tell me, Tudor Jackson, you pray over this damned corn, and it grows more than that over there you don't pray over?"

"Absolutely," answered Tudor Jackson, a reedy, neat man, gray templed, an other-worldly glint to his eyes. "I read about such an experiment and tried it. It works."

"I don't believe you," said Mumford.

Tudor Jackson laughed. "Come back next week and see."

"How do I know you'll pray?"

Tudor laughed again. "You'll just have to believe I don't lie."

"Well, I guess you wouldn't, preacher. Norwood Pankum has a special greenhouse for experiments. I use it. You should try it." Mumford swept his arms around indicating the room's makeshift arrangement. "Better than this."

"I was just planning to do that," the minister answered. "Stay for church, Mumford."

"Nawh. Wouldn't want to tempt the wrath of God. Elia's gonna get me into heaven anyway. She's here, and I think she prays." Elia was Mumford's second and current wife.

The men passed Ladyree going out the door. Mumford nodded, looked at her carefully, grinned uncertainly, nodded again and passed.

Ladyree swayed, touched the doorjamb for support. *He had not recognized her.* Mumford Marshall, her ex-husband, had not recognized her.

The sermon was starting by the time Ladyree regained enough composure to enter the sanctuary. She found Verda Soper in her usual pew up front. Tudor Jackson spoke.

"My sermon today will be based on Malachi 4, Verse 1. 'For, behold, the day cometh that shall burn as an oven; and all the proud, yea, and all that do wickedly, shall be stubble: and the day that cometh shall burn them up, saith the Lord of hosts, that it shall leave them neither root nor branch.'"

"I don't like that verse," whispered Verda Soper to Ladyree.

"Because you fear fire," responded Ladyree, in an aside.

"Shhh." Verda Soper put a finger to her lips, the proper mix of piety in her expression.

Tudor Jackson continued in a more moderate vein. Ladyree fidgeted.

"I'm going, Mother. I need to be at the Majestic early. You go home with Mary Clara, eat dinner with her." Before Verda could protest, Ladyree left the pew. Up the aisle she tiptoed, trying to be invisible as she made her way out of the First Presbyterian Church of Port City. Mississippi.

Early at the Majestic Theater, Ladyree sat alone in the great empty cavity of the dark theater, staring at its blank screen until the other employees and the moviegoers began to enter. All afternoon she felt she moved slowly as in that cotton cloud. She could not follow the plot. She could not recognize the movie stars. An important preview of a coming attraction did not register in her mind.

Ladyree returned to the Cyclops House at dusk. She could see in the dim light that the erosion on their side of Town Creek had worsened, and she made a mental note to buy some kudzu at Mr. Pankum's nursery. She found it odd that such a detail had broken through her numbness. Inside, she found her mother and friend, Mary Clara, going over the Sunday church service.

A huge Bible lay in Verda Soper's lap. Across the print of two upturned, oversized pages rested her perfect hand, its blue veins mapping her bloodless skin like a river and its tributaries. A whiff from dried flower petals, a mingle of lavender and roses, scented the air in the shadowy room already illuminated by the soft and indistinct yellows of incandescent lamplight.

"Ladyree," said Miss Mary Clara, "your mother is so lucky to have a lovely daughter like you to look after her in her old age." Mary Clara, always pleasant, with a face round and wrinkled like a melting lollipop, moved her fat and aged body in the rosewood frame of a Victorian chair. The chair creaked, like the pop of a knuckle.

"You're going to break that chair, Mary Clara," said Verda Soper before turning to Ladyree. "God sent you to me, child, in the years of my menopause—"

Ladyree interrupted. "To look after you, Mother, in your old age. Is that God's purpose for my life?"

"Some people have no purpose that I can see," said Verda Soper.

"What are you reading, Mother?" Ladyree lifted the Bible from her mother's lap. She located Malachi 4, Verse 1, and read, "'. . . and the day that cometh shall burn them up, saith the Lord of hosts, that it shall leave them neither root nor branch.'" Ladyree replaced the Bible. "It's cool, Mother. Why don't I fix a fire here in the parlor beside you?"

Verda Soper scrutinized her daughter.

"Your mother thinks that verse is bad," said Miss Mary Clara.

"Nothing in the Bible is bad, Mary Clara," said Verda Soper.

"Excuse me, Mother, Miss Mary Clara. I am very tired." She left the two old friends.

After Miss Mary Clara had gone, Ladyree suppered on light food with her mother in a veil of silence. Ladyree ate little. Verda Soper retired as soon as the meal ended.

In the "good room," Ladyree stood fixed before the windowed wall, her eyes steady on a wind-swaying tree beneath a streetlight just off the back property line. Beside her an empty coffee cup and a silver spoon were balanced on the sill. Inside, light shone from a wall lamp attached to the jerry-built armoire and from the open fire she had lit. Fire soothed Ladyree as much as it disturbed Verda Soper.

Ladyree remembered the summer spent with her mother's mannish friend, Alita Cameron, who had inherited remote acreage outside Ocala, Florida,—acreage with an old two-storied house, a barren orange grove, trees, moss, snakes, blind mosquito invasions and loud night-creatures. Alita Cameron was trying to turn the unprofitable land into a Christmas tree farm, working and managing it herself. Ladyree found herself in this unearthly wilderness with her mother's friend that summer when her own world had tumbled away.

Mumford had left the Cyclops House, wanting her to leave with him. A week later she learned she was pregnant. She chose not to tell him because of pride and because she did not wish to force his return since she felt certain of his love and believed he would eventually come back. She yielded to her mother's pressure to leave Port City before showing her pregnancy.

Ladyree fantasized that she would flee and Mumford would rescue her. As the days in sweaty Florida heat mounted, and she heard nothing from Mumford, she became ill. She lost the baby. Her Ocala doctor was disdainful of her, certain she was unwed. Alita Cameron was incapable of comforting her. As soon as she was able, she fled back home to what she accepted as mother-love.

"Mother-love?" she whispered now in the "good room." The thought occurred to her that Mumford might have tried to contact her that summer and been thwarted. No, it could not be true.

The fire glow in the grate became lost in gray ash. Ladyree reached for the poker, tipping the silver spoon from the sill onto the floor. At the same moment, the light bulb in the lamp popped, burned out, and the room darkened, heightening Ladyree's sense of being far away from all that was near. On the floor she searched for the spoon, like a crab on some ancient beach. Her extended hand wavered. In her mind she had been a dutiful daughter, but to her mother she was no more than a nurse in old age. Her mother's vow of love meant nothing.

Spoon in hand, Ladyree rose. And Mumford's love? So long ago. He did not even see her now. Light now shone only from the street. Inside, the room was dim. She pulled the spoon toward her and touched it to her cheap print dress aware as she did so of her protuberant middle bulging from the two flaps of her yawning, worn cardigan. Did she wonder that he did not recognize her?

She was just a sweet-looking, middle-aged woman, past style, past sex, past life. The spoon, Prufrock's coffee spoon, measured out the futility of her life. With her other hand, she touched a monstera plant, a green jungle in a flower pot and closed her eyes, seeking in vain to be someone else—a character in a movie.

With a sudden move she lifted the silver spoon to her heaving breast and started to lash out at the monstera. She felt her stomach turn and twist sounding faintly like a muffled scream. My insides are screaming, she thought. She stopped her action toward the plant. What did she feel? Anger? Her sense of fogginess had masked a triggering anger. The fog vanished. Anger? More than anger? Power inside her pulsed, burgeoned, made itself known. She checked herself. She did not wish to be cruel to her plant. Cruel? Now in dark, not blinded by sunny glare, she realized it was sunlight itself that had been cruel. It was the same great light of her childhood that had promised so much with its shimmering loveliness, only to trap her now in her worn print dress.

She raised the silver spoon again to blast the monstera. Anger? No. *Hate*. And she did not hate the plant. She dropped the spoon, her arms tight at her sides, her breast rising and said aloud, *"It's Mother I hate."*

Later, in bed, she remembered the movie of the day. And, more important, the *preview*.

Gone with the Wind was being reissued and would soon play at the Majestic.

Second Sequence

In black Port City, Mississippi, blacks rose early to hurry a late planting of jonquils, hoping for one last hard freeze in the year. They covered the bulbs in cold earth next to the ground-level, tatty boarding of their homes, loosening extra soil for the later seeding of vegetables and spring flowers. Such work had to be done before full daybreak, before regular jobs. Already, the sun still asleep, a bus had turned off Redbud Street, Port City's black thoroughfare, loaded with workers to prepare the fields outside the town for spring planting. The jonquil gardeners returned inside to rooms warm with wood or coal fires.

Soon again, female domestics opened the simple doors and began to walk slowly down Redbud, calling as they did, to rheumatic elders sitting in chairs and blanketed on their open porches along the way.

The women walked to work where they cleaned, cooked noon dinners, listened to whites discuss all but blacks who served them and might overhear at their noon tables, and returned home in fading light with brown grocery bags of leftover food and at week's finish with a little money.

About the time that the black women started their servants' jobs, the black men walked their same path past Redbud's jerry-built restaurants with adjoining living quarters, mom-and-pop businesses, churches, and a nightclub where the great Bessie Smith had sung and where knifings were overlooked by Port City policemen. They walked past all this on neglected sidewalks patterned in chinaberry tree shadows from the soft, beginning sun. These lucky men walked to jobs as service station attendants, janitors and similar employment.

A small group of other men, handicappers among them, waited on the corner near the nightclub to chance for an odd job offered by passing whites who knew the corner. Turning onto Redbud Street was the Cadillac driven by a black doctor, who worked in a compelled frenzy among his people and preached a crazy sermon of poll-tax-law repeal and black vote.

Around ten o'clock an all-white invasion of welfare workers appeared on Redbud and its surrounding streets and alleyways to check aid recipients. These women were either just out of college and passing time before marriage or older widows, needy in a man's world without a man. They carefully identified themselves as welfare workers, fearing no harm with crime so rare in Port City, but mindful of the unwritten law that no black divulge the location of another to a white without precaution.

Arorah Hannah was staring at a wall in her back room kitchen when she heard a bold knock at her front door. Her house, built on a wide alley abutting Redbud, was a three-room shotgun house—a house where one bullet could enter the front and pass through all rooms before exiting the rear. Arorah had installed locks on every door. As she progressed through the heavily shaded, dark rooms, she unlocked and relocked each door. She stood within the cavernous frame of the front door after unlocking the final time, and faced a young white woman.

"I need to verify the residency of Mary Jefferson next door," she said to Arorah.

"The Tomato Man's sister?" Arorah asked. Mary Tomato Man helped Arorah when she became lost, and chased away the pesky boys who taunted her. Only Mary Tomato Man would do no harm to Arorah Hannah.

The white girl said impatiently, "The record says her brother does sell baskets of tomatoes. I guess he's her brother and not a boyfriend. I just need to know if you've known her to be here all year. We have to ask. We don't want her getting two checks, one in Chicago and one in Mississippi." She paused, as if she had said too much. She spoke again emphatically. "Has she lived next door all year?"

Arorah looked puzzled.

"Oh, never mind. It's only a formality. Sign right here . . . or make your mark," said the white girl who smelled of Toujours Moi perfume and Ivory soap.

Arorah looked puzzled.

The welfare worker smiled with little-girl charm and pushed the clipboard and pen toward Arorah.

"Come in," said Arorah. The girl shrugged and followed.

Inside, Arorah locked the door behind her and turned to the young woman. A naked bulb above them revealed the talc, whitening Arorah's face like a mask spotlighted within the dull gray of the room. Under the stark light Arorah became suddenly ghostly and grotesque. The young woman swayed, backed further into the room and took a second look at Arorah Hannah. Arorah Hannah, thirty-two, her body a slim sparrow's, her breasts pointy beneath her shimmery blouse, moved with the grace of an ancient maid with a vessel on her head, her beauty heightened strangely by the absurd talc. From a swing of keys belted at her waist, she took a key to turn the lock.

"Come," Arorah said to the frightened girl still swaying in semi-shock, the clipboard lengthening one limp arm, the pen and papers in the other hand. They progressed into the depths of the house, Arorah locking each door behind her as they went. In the middle room, the girl remained dazed, but once in the kitchen, her senses revived and some of her poise was restored. The welfare worker placed the form and clipboard on the middle-of-the-room table and urged Arorah again to take the pen.

"Sign right there so Mary can get her check," said the girl. She dropped the pen. It fell on the table beside a paring knife. The sight of the knife made the girl's lower lip tremble.

Arorah picked up the pen and signed "Mrs. Claude Hannah." The girl frowned and reached to scratch out the "Mrs." but glanced up and met Arorah's steely eyes. Arorah unconsciously fingered the paring knife. Seeing the gesture, the welfare worker fumbled with the pen, paper, and clipboard, and stumbled to the back door. She slammed her body against it, shaking its old, ungiving wood.

"I will show you out," said Arorah. She unsnapped the lock on the middle-room door. The girl found her dignity and remained calm at Arorah's side until arriving at the front door. There Arorah hesitated, searching for the correct key. The young woman dropped her papers. They swept across the floor in different directions. Flustered, near tears, she stooped to an awkward squat and gathered them into a wrinkled disorder.

"Silly girl," said Arorah as she freed the door. On the porch the young woman spun around at its edge to give Arorah an expression of hate before rushing to her car. The car stalled, died. From the porch a stilled Arorah watched. The engine coughed. The car bucked, then smoothed, and broke away.

The welfare worker's displeasure did not threaten Arorah, but across the alley a group of black school boys watched her as she had watched the young white woman. They pointed at her and laughed. While Arorah's lover, Claude Hannah, white and a power in Port City, lived, no one had dared question her pale face powder. With his death, however, Arorah had whitened her face more and the neighborhood boys had begun to taunt her. "Arorah Hannah, Lost Banana," they chanted.

Arorah turned in the door frame to look at the boys sideways. She never looked at them directly. Once inside, she placed the paring knife within her purse. The boys were out to get her.

Anger marred the pretty brow of the young welfare worker and stirred in her fresh bosom as she drove from Redbud Street. She passed the Picture Show Lady's house, glancing at its odd stained-glass window before turning onto the blue gravel parking lot of the Mississippi Department of Public Welfare. Her tires made scratchy sounds on the loose pebbles, crushing and scattering them. Outside the car in the late, but still chilly, morning air she made her way toward the department entrance. She had determined to report her experience with Arorah Hannah directly to the agent, the formidable Miss Taylor, sister of Port City's mayor.

Miss Taylor, an Amazonian woman, ruled the department with intelligence and an iron hand, clad in velvet, the metal dulled and fabric worn by lapses of sudden sentiment. Despite her brother's being a politician, she had no firm grasp of deception. Each election she collected her staff and, without finesse, marched them to the polls to vote for her brother, always astonished the next day by the resulting chide in Port City's newspaper.

The young woman hardly looked at the building she entered. In the 1930s, initially housing the WPA, the building had been a whitewashed shack built by trusties on a small lot between a magnificent iron fence surrounding the old courthouse and a new jail. A few years earlier, during World War II, the fence had been donated to the war effort to be melted down for weapons. The unfenced grounds allowed the sprawl of one ugly white-painted addition to the department after another.

The girl entered the building. Inside the roomy waiting area, flimsy partitions vibrated with the babble of interviews within. Those waiting sat in segregated rows and whispered.

The Cyclops Window

The young woman saw Miss Taylor at once. She dominated the waiting area, rising like a huge, sculpturesque pole by the front desk with three other people. The girl recognized them as Catherine Vance, receptionist, her husband, Ham Vance, a policeman, and Evelyn Buffton, child welfare worker, the only educated black employee of the department, the others, sweepers or maids. The young welfare worker rushed to Miss Taylor, interrupted, and blurted out her story.

"Wait. Let me finish the business at hand," Miss Taylor said restraining the girl.

"But she had a knife," the girl continued.

"Arorah Hannah is harmless," insisted the black Evelyn Buffton.

"Yes, Evelyn" agreed Miss Taylor, "but I don't like that knife. Now let me finish my business, young lady."

Miss Taylor returned to the child welfare worker. "Evelyn, I know we need a colored rest room. We can't afford one. I sympathize that you must go to the courthouse to use the colored bathroom as the clients do, but I can't do anything about it."

"The trusties could build it in the closets next to the white rest rooms and use their pipes," said Evelyn Buffton.

"They're raising Cain now about trusty labor. I just can't, Evelyn. I'll do it when I can," said Miss Taylor.

A someday-is-better-than-a-no-day expression on her face, Evelyn Buffton excused herself and left.

Miss Taylor now addressed the Vances. "Catherine, I can't replace you at the desk today after all. You and Ham'll have to put off going to shop in Memphis."

Ham Vance nodded and spoke of the young welfare worker's matter. "If it's OK with you, Miss Taylor, I can check out Arorah Hannah."

"No, Ham, I don't want the police at this point," said Miss Taylor and returned to the girl. "Now you, young lady, come to my office and tell me all about it again. Be calm. All will be well." The big Miss Taylor led the small young woman away as if she had a child in hand. Ham Vance watched the sway of the girl's comely body, not thinking of her immaturity until Catherine Vance caught his look. Catherine Vance would not make love naked or without a sheet over her body.

"I gotta go," he said to his wife.

Outside in his patrol car, Ham Vance, a big man near Miss Taylor's size, thought about the beautiful Arorah Hannah, and the dead Claude

Hannah. He had hated Claude Hannah. He had reason, but always he had held his hate to himself. Vance jerked the car into gear and drove away into the direction of Redbud Street. He would not incur Miss Taylor's displeasure by contrary action. He had ambitions. He, just a police officer now, had begun a base from which to vie for the mayoralty of Port City in the next decade. No, he would not act, but he would check on Arorah Hannah. A time would come when he could avenge an old wound.

Third Sequence

"I don't remember your mother," Norwood N. Pankum said to his son.

N. Nathan Pankum Jr. dropped the breakfast eggs.

His father looked down to the splatter across the kitchen linoleum. "God! What's the matter with you, Nathan?"

Nathan stooped and pushed a cupped hand towel toward pebbly eggs, a tilted, yellow-smeared plate in the other hand.

"What's the matter with you?" repeated the elder Pankum.

Nathan jumped to his feet, leaving plate and eggs on the floor, swung his hands wildly in a waste of energy, an erratic dog paddle, a semicircle at hip level. "I can't please you. That's what the matter is." He stepped toward his father but kept his arms close-in.

Norwood Pankum met his son's forward step, an arm rising. Nathan, as tall, but less fleshy, retreated. Norwood checked the lift of his ready-to-strike arm. He advanced, stopped abruptly, waited interminably in the boy's mind, then turned and strode from the room.

Nathan relaxed his jutting chin and his stiffened body. Staring at the door where his father had disappeared, he absently pinched an acne pimple and wiped the pus from his fingers across a paper napkin. He fidgeted, undirected. He stooped once more to finish the clean-up of the ruined eggs. When he completed the task, he paced the length of the room several times, his face a mask of adolescent melodrama and deep pain. All at once he left the room, seeking a source of psychic relief, seeking his father, knowing and fearing the outcome, seeking it like a mindless homing pigeon.

Norwood shaved before the bathroom mirror, white foam peaking on his face like a cotton beard. He might have had a Santa Claus look but his eyes were cheerless.

"Do you want me to cook more eggs?" asked Nathan.

Norwood lathered more soap onto his face, turning his chin one way and another, mute, mimelike.

Nathan matched his father's silence. He watched Norwood, splay-footed, standing before the upright pool of silvery wall above the lavatory, maneuvering his sharp razor with great care over his soap-slippery skin. Nathan, disregarded, perhaps dismissed, his question unanswered, studied his father trying to feel his way toward the sense of the situation. Nathan was always trying.

To the boy Norwood Pankum seemed as sophisticated as Cary Grant, the debonair movie star. Many mild-mannered Deltans prospered more than the owner of Pankum's Nursery and Greenhouse. Many who prospered less were more mannerly. But Norwood, bred in Mississippi's rustic piney woods, had succeeded in business and acquired polish living in the culture of the Mississippi Delta. He put his razor down precisely. Norwood bragged on his tidy personal habits attributing them to the vigorous scrubbings of his mother during his youth. He admitted to feeling superior to the dirt farmers of his beginnings. Greenhouse work was less sweaty than plow or tractor grind. And now he worried less over pennies and small silver.

Norwood finished his shave. He rinsed away the foam with faucet water and covered and wiped his damp face with a white towel before patting on lotion. The sweet smell of Old Spice drifted to Nathan. Norwood stepped on the nearby scale. His frame was average and tended toward weightiness from middle age and inactivity, yet because food and its tastes were unimportant to him, each morning the scale registered the same.

Nathan, his own eyes the black-olive eyes of his dead mother, caught the eyes of Norwood, which were a washed-out blue.

"Do you want me to cook more eggs?" Nathan tried again.

"No." Norwood combed his shadowy, straw-colored and gray hair carefully over the bare scalp of his crown.

Nathan searched his father's face. He could no more read his thoughts or expression than he could Wash Bibb's, whose facial scars hid all emotion. The boy finally turned away, unsatisfied, resigned, sad.

Down the sunless hall, Nathan stopped to lean on a wall. His father did not remember his mother? How could that be? Had his father loved her? Did he love her son? He paced the hallway, careful to keep the sound of his steps from Norwood. At last he opened the door to the outside and headed for the river.

He crossed the fields out back and hiked the levee toward its top.

On the levee slope, wild onion spikes shot through winter's dead grass reaching for spring sun. As Nathan went, his feet leveled the gray-green spears leaving a track behind and enveloping him in the scent of the early weed. Behind him a panorama of Delta fields spread in watercolor shades of sepia and coffee tones, the approaching spring secreted in the drabness.

Next to the Pankum Nursery and Greenhouse, one still-fallow, still-mud field away, lay the home of the planter Mumford Marshall. Before the Marshall home and the Pankum nursery, across the highway, which followed the line of the levee, on Mumford's second plantation, One O'clock, three Indian mounds broke the flatness of the rich-earthed fields. A mile west in the distance at the side of the highway where the levee turned north, Nathan could spot the white dot of the city limit sign and the junky start-up of Port City's outskirt businesses.

As he crested the levee, a cold breeze swept his body. He shivered. The chill that had come over him during his first Delta winter had never quite left him. It lingered in his bones and rose at the least provocation.

That winter, a few weeks after the first anniversary of Japan's World War II surrender, Nathan had come to live with his father from the rolling piney woods where amenities were plainer and blacks fewer and the Mississippi River far away. The Delta extended from Memphis to Vicksburg along the great river, its western border. Unlike the pine country, its rich alluvial soil, accreted from the river during centuries of flooding, lay tediously flat. The flatness was unrelieved except by the manmade levees and the occasional burial mound of the Tunica or Chucchuma Indian tribe whose bloodlines were all but lost. That winter had been followed by a brief spring and a long summer of cruel sun ending miraculously in a September-October bumper crop. Cotton had exploded from bolls in row after row, and in lesser fields, viney soybeans had turned silver-over-green in the breathy winds of first autumn.

The Mississippi Delta was a singular whereabouts, and in it, Nathan, a foreigner. Grandmother Pankum, his guardian since the death in his infancy of his mother, had grown too old for the responsibility of her only grandson. Norwood, a stranger to caretaking, had assumed the task of completing Nathan's rearing. Nathan thought of himself as a stumbler in a rearranged world.

Atop the levee Nathan sat. The smell of downed onion spears

broke around him again. The river sent its boiling currents up to roughen its surface. The sun touched the water like light on cellophane making it sequiny and grand as it passed steadily south toward New Orleans. Already the river was swelling with the first melt of northern snow.

High and away, the world was silent and still. All sound had been stolen, and the wind had been sucked away as if by cloud-spirits. Nathan wrapped his arms around himself for warmth.

He recalled his father's words. "What's the matter with you, Nathan?" Nathan did not know. He felt *odd*. A terrible word, odd.

Even in the piney woods he had differed from other boys. He did not have the usual two parents. Not even one.

He was certainly not homesick. He cherished only a single sweet memory in those hills in his childhood times. Once his wrinkled, bony grandmother had held him for a long time. He had lingered with her, warm body to body, until she finally grew impatient and pushed him away.

Was it true about the coppery and muddy river below? Wash Bibbs, the black man with the burned away face who labored in the greenhouse and nursery and who often seemed to recognize Nathan's pain, said it was true. That the river was God.

Other people believed God was in the sky. Nathan thought of his grandmother and her tattered family Bible. He thought of Sunday school and her church, its clapboard construction brilliant white in high Sunday morning sun.

"Just you know," the preacher had said. "Them tall pines outside around this church point to God Almighty, and he is watching." Nathan could almost smell the cedary needles matted beneath the pines outside while hearing the fearsome sermon begin.

Could his grandmother's God help him? Could the Delta God in the river help? Nathan wished to be good, not odd, not bad. Maybe, he thought, if he didn't masturbate, God would help, but even as he thought this, he felt a swelling in his groin. When it had subsided, he started a prayer.

"God? Wherever you are . . . in the river? In the sky? Make me good."

The silent river moved downstream. The swift and mute clouds rolled overhead. A slow-motion wind came from the unknown to ripple the onion spears before returning to its source. The magic of life stirred unseen like the wind.

"Amen," said Nathan.

He stood and glanced behind him to the fields. There Mumford Marshall strode from his home toward Pankum property. It was Saturday, no school, and time for Nathan to work. He started his descent, catching his balance between downward leaps, quickening to a forward rush just before level ground slowed him. He followed Mumford Marshall into one of the greenhouses.

Three damp greenhouses adjoined by breezeways, the drier store where the cash register rang amid stacks of clay pots and general goods, and an attached roomy, but Spartan, living quarters, formed the Pankum undertaking on a bare thirty acres, a swath of breedy land between highway and levee.

Bedding plants on planks raised by wooden horses and small scrubs shaped the most spacious Greenhouse One into long aisles where customers could wander. Norwood used Greenhouse Two for seedlings. The smallest, Greenhouse Three, still vast, had special uses.

Currently in the smallest greenhouse, Norwood concentrated on developing a new orchid, something he had dreamed to do for several years. In a far corner of the greenhouse, Tudor Jackson, the Presbyterian minister who had just brought in two rows of corn shoots, prayed over one row to promote its growth, carefully neglecting the second row as a test. A third experiment was one of the ferments of Mumford Marshall's active brain.

Nathan entered Greenhouse Three behind Mumford Marshall. In the outdoor-like room, earth smells permeated air misty with water droplets. Sunlight warmed, fell from the screen and clear plastic roof, filtered through raised greenery down into a filigreed pattern of shadow and light. The flickering sun and the abundant plant life made the room feel like the forest floor of a deep jungle.

Norwood and Mumford met beside Mumford's kudzu plants. Mumford dug a kudzu root out of the dirt, brushed it, and chewed on it. "They use this damned root for hangovers in the Orient," he said after spitting the root out into a nearby waste bin.

"You got a hangover, Mumford?" said Norwood.

"Naah, but I get 'em once in a while." Despite the fact that Mumford had studied Greek and the classics at Webb School in Bell Buckle, Tennessee, and at Vanderbilt, his language was careless. Most Delta planters, not afraid of mongering Delta power, feared primness, feared sounding like Port City's late poet, William Winston Milledge. Most spoke as Mumford did mingling good grammar with field labor vernacular.

"Kudzu is good for erosion—if it doesn't cover you while you're planting it." Norwood spoke with more care than Mumford. He was too newly successful in the Delta to be lax about his grammar.

"Listen, Norwood. We cover our levees with this damned vine, and we won't have any more 1927 floods." Floods and yellow fever years had marked Delta time for generations. Now yellow fever was past and floods were a lesser threat, but a threat still.

"It is a mighty vine, Mumford, but . . ." Norwood stopped. Was he being too argumentative?

"Mighty vines for a goddamned mighty river. You weren't here during the '27 flood. We need an answer to the river."

Norwood knew about the great Mississippi River Flood of 1927. He had heard about the break at Klingman's Bend above the town and about Port City's levees being covered with Red Cross camps. Flood waters strewn with dead animals and humans had stretched from Illinois to the Gulf, and Port City had taken the brunt of the disaster.

"I don't want to argue with you, Mumford," said Norwood. "I just think kudzu won't solve the flood problem, that's all. It has huge roots. It could make holes in the levee just as well as making it strong."

"Damn you, Norwood!" Mumford's face grew red with anger.

Norwood backed away. Nathan retreated to the wall.

Mumford stamped. Then he noticed the space around him was empty. The red in his face slowly faded. He grinned. "It's okay, Norwood. I'm so angry 'cause I think what you say may be true."

Norwood reapproached. Nathan relaxed.

"You should talk to Max Durham, Mumford," said Norwood. Max Durham, an agronomist, ran the Delta Branch Station popularly called the experiment station. "He says kudzu will cover the South before it's over with." The Delta Branch Station had been set up in 1904 to combat the first boll weevil invasion and now was used as state-owned acreage for agricultural research.

"I hadn't thought about those damned big roots making holes," said Mumford. "Maybe they won't do that."

"Maybe," said Norwood with caution.

"We gotta set up something better to keep the river out of our fields. It thinks 'cause it gave us this land, it can come and get it back.

The Corps of Engineers misthinks they've got the river tamed. I think it's damned unwise to underestimate the power of the river," said Mumford.

"Me too," said Norwood before catching himself.

"Me too, Norwood?" said Mumford, grinning. "Now, you know what I say: Never be a me-too man."

"But I agree with you about the river." Norwood was getting testy himself. A me-too man? Damned Delta planters thought they knew it all. "About kudzu on the levees? No. Even the new weed killers developed from what they used during the war don't faze kudzu. Planting something uncontrollable even for erosion could be a big mistake. And planting it on the levees without knowing what it'll do is a mistake."

"That's what I'm doing in here. Trying to find out what it will do," said Mumford.

May Corday Marshall flounced into Greenhouse Three, a pink candy among the vegetation and dirt. "Daddy," she said and danced around Mumford.

"Shoo," said Mumford, distancing himself from his wiggly, cheery child.

"Daddy, I need money."

Mumford preferred his adopted grown daughter to May Corday, who had come as a surprise long after Elia had convinced him that, for some reason he did not understand, she was barren.

"You always want money. You'd think I was raising money trees and not cotton."

She grinned and put her palm up. Someone had sent her a new-style crinoline petticoat from New York to fill out her rose gabardine skirt above old-style bobby socks and saddle shoes. Nearby Nathan stooped to water low-rowed plants. He peeked up her skirt.

"Daddy!" May Corday had seen Nathan. She jumped away. "He looked under my dress, Daddy!"

Mumford laughed.

Norwood jerked Nathan up from the floor. "You embarrass me, Nathan."

"It's okay," said Mumford, still amused. "I might'a done the same thing at his age with someone else's daughter. Just natural."

May Corday began to sniffle.

"Sex, sex, sex, May Corday. Get used to it," said Mumford.

"Waaaa," wailed May Corday.

"Here's some money. Now run along." Mumford patted her shoulder.

Taking the money, lip trembling, she fled.

"Nathan," commanded Norwood Pankum, "go help Mr. Jackson." Nathan obeyed immediately.

Mumford, the thought of his daughter now recessed into the back of his mind, spotted Tudor Jackson for the first time in the expanse of the greenhouse. The minister responded to Mumford's wave before bowing his head again in prayer over the row of corn shoots.

"He says praying makes those plants bigger. Horsefeathers!" said Mumford.

Norwood nodded. "Doing it for some North Carolina college."

"A college?" said Mumford.

"Yes. A department of . . . parapsychology."

"Parapsychology. Hoodoo," said Mumford. He thought a moment. "A good college?"

"I think so," answered Norwood.

"Well, I don't rule anything out. The world is mysterious."

Norwood frowned. People's actions mystified him, but not the world.

"Gotta go, Norwood. Gotta check my buffalo ponds. Buffalos got too many fish bones in them to eat well. A sweet fish like catfish would be better except for the name. I can't see a lot of people eating cat anything."

"Ponds doing well?"

"Naah. Buffalo project is about like kudzu project—close to no good."

"You're spread too thin, Mumford," said Norwood.

"Yeah. The buffalo fish and the kudzu probably oughta go," said Mumford, "especially since I got something else really big in my sights right now."

"Mumford. Something else?" Norwood had experienced before the sudden enthusiasms of Mumford Marshall.

Mumford read Norwood's expression. "You got up on the wrong side of the bed this morning, Norwood. This is not an unexplored enthusiasm."

"What's not an enthusiasm?" said Tudor Jackson coming upon them.

"Hey, Preacher, how's the praying?" said Mumford in better humor.

"Fine," said Tudor Jackson who preferred being called Tudor, Mr. Jackson or Dr. Jackson rather than Preacher. But Mumford was Mumford.

"Norwood thinks I'm spread too thin, thinks my new project is too much," said Mumford "I listen to Norwood, but it rankles me that he doesn't trust my judgment. My new project is big, Preacher, and I've got the marketing figured already."

"The marketing?" said the doctor of divinity.

"Marketing. Who's gonna buy it? How you gonna get it to 'em. You can raise anything in our fields. Raise sweet potatoes, but how you gonna sell 'em? Bring a wagonload to town on Saturday night? That's no good. But, by God, Preacher, I've got the answer this time."

"I'm not a farmer," said the minister. "What answer?"

"The answer to crop diversification in the Delta. We're too cotton dependent. Bad cotton. Bad year. I've told you and everybody else we've gotta diversify. And rice, rice, by damn, is gonna be an answer. I talked to those farmers in Jennings, Louisiana, rice country. I've studied our water tables. I want my first fields diked and water pumped into them from the Bogue Phalia by next spring. We got lotsa creeks to pump, lotsa water below. And I'm gonna build a rice dryer—" Mumford suddenly stopped. His ebullience died.

"Something the matter, Mumford?" said Tudor Jackson.

"Yeah, it costs too much to keep my places going." He preferred the plain word places to plantations. "My rice is gonna cost. Progress is expensive."

"I've heard you say often, Mumford, you have to spend money to make money," added Norwood.

"I believe it."

"I thought, with your wife's inheritance from her father, you wouldn't ever have to worry about tight money again. Surely Claude Hannah left a good bit to her," said Norwood.

"Damned right. Humph," said Mumford. He abruptly turned away. "I gotta go home. I got to talk to somebody."

He strode toward the doorway and left, his mind turned inward and no longer aware of the greenhouse or the fields outside.

Fourth Sequence

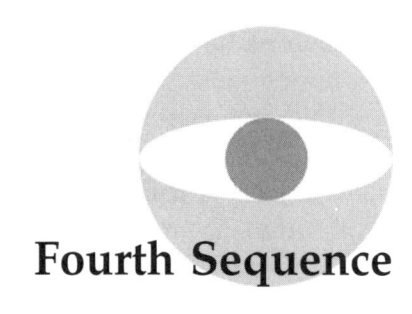

Mumford Marshall opened the front door to the Southernish house his wife had designed and built at his expense. She had planted first for the setting of the house a grove of magnolias now thriving, their evergreen only darkened by past winter, their branches curving low and reaching high, the whole creating an out-of-place beauty rising in the colorless flat fields, naked and unsowed. Just inside the door, he stepped left and down into what he called the front porch and what his wife had named the verandah until they had glassed the area and she had renamed it the solarium.

Elia Hannah Marshall, Mrs. Mumford Marshall, sat at a table arranged before a glass wall. The view behind her seemed a green and sun-shadowy backdrop, too realistic, too carefully arranged. She cautiously nibbled at a tiny corner of toast patting away the two crumbs left at her thin mouth with the cloth napkin in her left hand.

"You don't eat enough to nourish good red blood," said Mumford suddenly aware of all the little details about Elia that annoyed him. His irritation made him mindful of how he had felt toward her last fall after he had lost money on his Buffalo fish pond and she, at the same instance, had inherited Claude Hannah's estate. She had not offered to help or to allow him control of the new money.

Mumford sat down beside Elia. He toyed with the silverware at a place setting ready for the next meal.

"I thought we'd eat out here for lunch." Elia prided herself in serving the new lunch instead of the old midday dinner. The sunlight through the glass walls told Mumford it was still far from noon.

Mumford nodded. Okay. They returned to silence. Mumford was woolgathering.

He had married Elia for two reasons. Her family was moneyed, and he wanted, God knows why, he wanted children. After his marriage to Ladyree Soper, a marriage by heart, he had told himself to make this one by head. He wanted a bed partner, children, to be settled. Elia even then owned the 800 acres adjacent to the 600 he had owned and rented out. It was these 1,400 acres he had increased to the 5,000 of MM place and One O'clock across the highway. Both were plantations, called places, unless old history determined a grander name.

Children. Two girls. Mary Spring Marshall. Adopted. The product of an old love of his he had traced down through an unbelievable obstacle course. And May Corday Marshall coming long after he had accepted Elia's unexplained inability to bear children and so endangering Elia's life that all thought of a try for a boy was unthinkable.

He punched the handle of his teaspoon down flipping it back. He repeated the action.

"Don't play with your silver, dear," said Elia as if to a child.

He nodded. Okay. Okay.

Two girls. Just as well. Being a father was not what it was cut out to be. It was a consideration. It was an encumbrance. Your genes got carried forward, but you paid your dues.

May Corday. That incidence this morning in the greenhouse. Damned Delta *ladies*. Full of pose. Sex. Good stuff. Elia probably had not taught May Corday even to spell the word. May Corday, his child, but dumb. A streak in Elia's family. Jennie, Elia's mother, was not too swift. Well, maybe May Corday could get by on cheerfulness. She didn't have beauty, or brains but, by God, she could be cheery.

He heard light footsteps and saw a moving blur in his side vision. While he had thought of his youngest, his oldest daughter, Mary Spring or just Spring, had entered the room through the archway that connected it to the house proper. She held a rough drawing up for his inspection.

"What's that?" he asked.

"I was just thinking about trying to do your portrait." She turned the paper toward herself and studied it. "A drawing doesn't really do you justice. You're a colorful man and should certainly be done in more than black and white. Color. Maybe brighter colors than I usually use." She thought another moment. "Yet color may present a problem, too. You lend yourself to caricature, not portraiture."

"I lend myself to reality," he snapped. "I lend myself to the elemental. If that's a problem, so be it." He liked her brains except when they intruded on him. He did not like having his daughter understand too much about him. It wasn't fitting. "You got a beau on top of dirt now, girlie?" Spring Marshall was twenty-five years old, too old to be unmarried in the Mississippi Delta.

"She's too bookish," said Elia.

"She's too arty," said Mumford. "I don't understand you. I didn't understand William Winston Milledge, either. My own daughter, arty."

"Are you two through depicting me as wrongful? Books and art are good, and you two are shortsighted and limited," said the daughter.

"Hush. We like art and books, Spring. Hush, you two. I like a peaceful house," said Elia.

"Humph," mumbled Mumford.

"Your dress is pretty, Spring. Don't you think so, Mumford?"

Unlike her young sister, Spring had beauty and brains. The lavender of her simple shirtwaist dress enhanced her coloring, her opalescent skin and snow-blond hair.

Spring grimaced, her father's grimace, her mouth and teeth as even, but smaller and better proportionally. She turned abruptly exiting the room without further words

"I don't understand her," said Mumford.

"You don't try. She could be your own blood. Just like you."

"No." He paused. Elia did not know that she *was* his own blood. "I guess she has learned from me."

"I hope not too much." Elia took another small sip from her chilled glass. "Iced tea?" she asked.

He nodded.

Elia motioned to Sally Mae, a black servant who dusted in the living room through the archway, to bring him tea.

"I have something to talk to you about, Elia," said Mumford.

Sally Mae, considered a good servant, entered the verandah and quietly, almost without discernible motion, as if by legerdemain, expertly placed the iced tea before him. From the room with its mix of names, verandah, glassed-in porch, solarium, from the much-used, multifaceted room, Sally Mae disappeared leaving none of her essence, disappeared like breath from the soft wind of a lonely and passing ghost.

Elia looked at Mumford expectantly. "About?" she asked.

Mumford delayed. He squeezed lemon into his tea, the tickling and circling of its ice now the only sound and motion in the room.

Elia ran a good house, he thought, despite all her attention to social matters. Even the social matters helped by providing business talk with other men and leveling out his own disregard for certain amenities. Now that he needed money, however, he wondered if her social power added to her new wealth might not give her an edge over him. Most Delta women avoided outright power. Elia was always something of a blank wall to him. Damn women, Elia and her socialite friends, all together, power lovers or not, used power for sure when they could within the bounds of home. Yet he did not feel vulnerable. He doubted anyone knew his current financial weakness. You didn't weigh in against something you did not know about. But he must be careful in handling Elia.

"About?" repeated Elia, "About what do you want to talk?"

Mumford studied the neatly prepared table. He didn't like what he saw. There was something too orderly about Elia. She had always wanted him to be more orderly, more predictable. "Umph," he said aloud. In all this order there was something *steely*. That was it! She was part machine, like a combine, and he did not want to get chewed into her mechanism.

"Elia," he said, "you've got too much Mississippi Chemical. I think you should put something in city bonds."

"Now, Mumf, Daddy liked to encourage industry in the state. And let's leave things alone until I can understand what I've got."

Mumford rose like a sudden storm. He was a big man. He knew at once he should not let anger take him, but he proceeded. He threw his thick napkin into the middle of the table catching in the sweep of the cloth two individual condiment shakers at the side of his plate, spilling salt and pepper and destroying all neatness. Elia winced. "Goddamn it!" he continued. "I know already about these things, and I will not have you wear the pants in this family."

"Now, Mumf, you told me you'd sold my initial 800 acres and then lost the money on one of your harebrains, that's what Daddy called them, harebrains, and he told me not to let you do that again, and I'm not going to."

"Your Daddy's gone and if you want to sit at my table and feed off me, you're gonna have to let me handle the money. You don't know a damned thing."

"Now, Mumf," protested Elia, "I don't know anything, but I can learn."

"Why learn? I know. You see what I did to 1,400 acres. I more than doubled that."

"Doubled it more except that you sold my 800."

"Your 800? My 5,000."

"Then why my 800?" she said.

"You don't know a damned thing. If I got run over by a velocipede tomorrow, you'd be a rich widow."

"I'm not poor now."

"Humph. Well, you'd be damned better off, that's for sure," he said.

"Mumf, you've made and lost, made and lost."

"Don't Mumf me. It's irritating. I may have made and lost, but I've made some damned good progress in getting these stodgy planters in this area diversified, raising something besides cotton, someday irrigating the land, now fertilizing it with anhydrous ammonia, in general getting them up on their haunches and out of their ruts into some real farming, and that's more than your damned father even thought about."

"Mumf!"

"Goddamn it!" He shoved his chair. It tipped and fell.

"Mumford! You always disturb everything!"

She heard the door slam.

Outside Mumford strode through the careful gardening beneath the drooping magnolias until he reached clearing and the rugged fields. Still furious at Elia, furious at himself for losing control, he felt better with the warm, bumpy dirt beneath his feet and with full sun and free air touching his body. In his mind he said, Goddamn Elia, his usual oath, safe enough for mixed company. Goddamn Elia. He shook his long, tough, muscled limbs into the air as if to let the Sunday school God in the sky know the extent of his anger. If Elia were a man, he would box her. He shook his arms skyward again and stomped his big feet flattening the ground with footprints as he went. He stopped at the levee's edge, stood a moment grinding his magnificent teeth before sitting down on a raised irregularity of the levee's slope.

He looked out over the fields. He became calmer. Like Wash Bibbs said, this damned Delta owned him. The fields. The river over behind him. He stripped grass away from the soil and grasped a handful of dirt. Jesus, he must use control, use *judgment*, not emotion with Elia. Damn mistake, mistake, just now at the table. He needed Elia's money in order to get his new rice project off the ground and continue his kudzu operation as well as run both places. Damn. Damn. He wanted to make his 5,000 acres into 50,000 acres, unheard of now, 50,000 acres before it was over, make through his operation a

Rockefeller-J. P. Morgan fortune like the ones he had read about as a boy. Wanted to leave his mark on the whole Delta before he was in his grave.

50,000 acres, rice, kudzu . . .

Why he would eat dirt on Elia's plate if he had to. Everybody, he had learned, had to eat dirt sometimes. Yes, indeedy, he would eat dirt if he had to for 50,000 acres.

He started to get up and head back to the house, but he sat down again. The idea of eating Elia's dirt displeased him mightily. He would think a little more. Maybe he could figure something else. Time went by. He touched his tongue to the dirt in his hand before releasing it earthward. He grimaced before he got up and returned to the Southernish house.

It was still not lunchtime. Elia was no longer on the front porch. He met May Corday coming down the steps into the living room.

"Where's your mother?" he asked.

"I don't know, Papa," she answered tossing her ringleted hair and offering her happy smile.

Humph. She never knew anything. Dumb May Corday. Maybe cheerfulness was not enough.

He found Elia in the kitchen going over the week's menus with Sally Mae. He wondered why Sally Mae affected him as Elia did—just as much a blank. Maybe she mirrored Elia for some reason. Maybe to please. Anyway he knew neither woman.

"Elia, honey, let's talk," he said.

"Let me finish, Mumford," she responded not looking up from the menus.

No longer Mumf? Well, just you wait. "Sure, honey. I'll go sit on the porch until you're through." He tried to grin at her, but she did not see. Just as well, she might have noticed what she called devilment in his eyes.

On the front porch, the chair had been righted and the table reset. His iced tea glass, he reflected, had probably already been scrubbed and returned to its row in a cabinet. He seated himself in a nearby wicker chair and waited.

In a few minutes, Elia came in and sat on a matching rattan and wicker sofa adjacent to his chair. Through glass behind Elia, the grounds of sun and shadow and green remained as perfect as an artificial flower. The view bothered him. Careful, he said to himself. Elia's thin lips curved. Not her best teatime curve, he thought.

"Elia, we're going to have to cut down on some expenses."

"Mumford, you know I don't throw money away. I manage, you know."

"Well, you're gonna have to cut back. I lost money on my buffalo fish ponds."

"Your latest peccadillo."

"You're gonna have to be more modest in your spending."

"You lost money. Papa said you would."

"Your papa never thought anything I did would make money and, by damn, I've made more money than he ever dreamed of."

"Papa left a fortune."

"Papa left the same fortune he got from your mother Jennie's Papa."

"Well, he kept it."

"Couldn't farm. Rented it out."

"Rented it out and invested it and made money," she countered.

"You're getting too big for your britches, Elia. We got *more*, not the *same*. More. Not like your Papa."

"If we've got more, this idea of yours to cut back makes little sense," she said.

"Cut back, I say. It's my money we're using. Cut back. Get rid of one of your servants. Sam doesn't do anything in the winter months. You don't need a house manservant to keep your yard all year. You don't need him chauffeuring you in the winter. Drive your own damned car, fix our supper at night and keep Sally Mae half days. Cut down on all these steaks and fixings we eat too much of. You run a man crazy with these expenses. And this damned D.A.R. meeting you're planning at the house with all those costly refreshments. Let someone else have the D.A.R. What do you think I have? A money plantation? You and May Corday think alike."

Elia's composure faltered. "Mumford, I can't change all of this." She was alarmed.

Mumford thought he saw a resemblance to May Corday as she frowned. Maybe there was just a vacancy behind all her little niceties. He was beginning to believe that her kind of steel might be penetrated.

"I won't do it!" She had rallied. "I won't make these changes."

"Well, by damn, then you pay for them. You pay Sally Mae, you pay Sam. I ain't gonna do it. Don't expect any household funds from me. You're an heiress now. You control your funds, and you expect me to support you like I've always done. The Hell with you, Elia. The

Hell with you." Mumford got up. He smiled, delighted. He had found a little money at least, but best of all, he might sabotage her orderly, superficial world—until she said uncle.

After Mumford had gone, Elia sat at the table a long time. She waved away Sally Mae's attempt to serve lunch. Elia looked to her right side and watched through the glass as Mumford walked in his fields. "To Hell with you, too, Mumford," she said.

Fifth Sequence

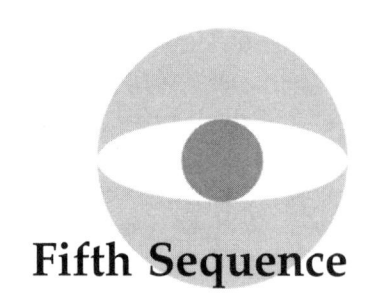

Arorah Hannah was lost.

One tree seemed familiar. Then in her brain, a negative sent her spirits lower. Trees were like people, similar but all different. She felt terror striking in her heart. What will become of me?

It was getting late. The sun was descending west; the temperature was lowering. Then someone, their front shadowed and obscure, dying sun on their back, was coming toward her on the sidewalk. Who? The someone came closer.

Bless Jesus. It was Mary Tomato Man. Mary Jefferson, Mary Tomato Man, would always help. Arorah smiled.

"Come," said Mary, a slim, dark caramel-colored woman in her mid-forties, her penetrating expression becoming tender as she reached for Arorah's hand.

As the two women approached Redbud Street, Mary's brother, called the Tomato Man, came toward them. He carefully avoided the wider cracks in the neglected sidewalk. In each hand he held by hook a tray fabricated in layers and filled with baskets of ripe tomatoes.

"Sister Mary, who's that good-looking woman you with?" he said. The Tomato Man knew that he was considered a handsome man.

Arorah let go of Mary's hand and moved back. As long as Claude Hannah lived, the Tomato Man had never smiled or spoken to her. Now always he smiled.

"It's okay, child. My brother ain't gonna hurt you."

The Tomato Man put both trays down and lifted a basket of tomatoes. "Here, Miss Arorah, you take these. I grow the finest tomatoes in Port City—all year 'round," he bragged.

"No," said Arorah backing farther away.

Mary Jefferson took the basket. "You go on," she said to her brother. He smiled again at Arorah, picked his trays back up and continued on his way.

The Cyclops Window

It became evening quickly. The green in the trees became black, the light now gray. At Arorah's door, Mary Jefferson gave her brother's tomatoes to Arorah. "They're okay," she said and was gone.

Inside, locked up, the shades drawn and the lights on, Arorah was not so sure the tomatoes were okay. In the kitchen she placed them on the table. She would watch them for a while. She wondered if roaches ate tomatoes. Arorah believed that the rife and indiscriminate roaches of Port City had a special sense enabling them to escape poisoning. She decided that no roach would eat a poisoned tomato. She would wait and see.

Four days later after seeing the Tomato Man talking to the pesky boys gathered across the alley, Arorah hurried into her home carrying a sack of groceries and locked herself in until she reached her kitchen. There on the table, the tomatoes had turned a mushy-looking red. Black spots grew around their stem circles. Arorah made dough balls of onions, flour and boric acid to control pest problems, but a few survived, and none approached the shriveling tomatoes on the kitchen table.

"Poison," she said aloud convinced the Tomato Man had bad things in mind for Arorah Hannah.

Hours later in bed, her eyes open, a nightmare came and went, came and went, preventing sleep. At dusk she went out the kitchen door and stole toward the homemade greenhouse of plastic and stakes next door behind the Tomato Man and his sister's house.

Carefully she pulled the opening of nailed stakes and stapled plastic to her and went inside the makeshift greenhouse. Inside light was dim. At once she stumbled, tangling the long nightgown Claude Hannah had loved over a hoe crossing the ground, falling.

"Shhh," she said to herself.

She must not wake anyone. But, she thought, she must do it, must kill the poisoned fruit. Light was coming fast. She got up quickly brushing the dirt clinging to her gown. She liked being clean.

Before her she now saw three long rows of tomatoes in varying stages of growth.

She began with the little ones. She had worn her heaviest shoes. Down! Down! Down! The young shoots were broken into the rich soil. Down! Down! Again and again. The young shoots would now not harm her.

The big plants were weighted with red and green fruit. She pulled the red tomatoes off their slender branches and crushed them into the dirt, their juices running and leaving pale, sandlike seeds against the earth. The green tomatoes were harder to destroy. She took the Tomato Man's hoe and attacked the whole plants until all were irretrievably broken.

Sun-up had come. The plastic turned pink like the cherry caramels sold in wrapped squares for a penny apiece at the Homecooking Cafe off the alley on Redbud Street. She must go.

She could not find the opening. All the plastic and stakes looked alike. Lost. And lost within the Tomato Man's greenhouse among the plants she had killed. She panicked. Nooo. Then she saw a section of greenhouse plastic flutter like an insect wing from a morning breeze. The opening. Bless Claude in heaven.

Once outside she saw the Tomato Man coming out of his back door.

"Miss Arorah, what you doin' there?"

He did not seem angry.

"You like the tomatoes? I'll bring you some more," he called after her before heading for his greenhouse.

Arorah reached home and locked up.

Soon she heard a banging at her back door.

"You come out, you witch, bitch. You come out," the Tomato Man screamed as he beat the door.

Arorah heard Mary's voice.

"Come on. Stop. She ain't right. She can't help it. She's got no one now. You can replant."

"Replant!" he screamed. "What we gonna eat on 'til they regrow?"

Arorah had done what she was supposed to do. She had been brave. Fear faded from her beautiful face. A smug look of false strength took it.

Mary was talking. "I got my job at the building. I can feed us a while. Two more offices want me to clean. You come on. You can't do nothing acting like this."

"Ara . . . Ara . . . Arorah," he sputtered before shouting her name again and again.

An angry Arorah would open up. She unleashed the chain to the back door opening a crack. Through it she saw the Tomato Man's enraged, nasty face. She spat.

"Don't do that, Arorah!" said Mary now at the opening.

Arorah spat again and quickly shut the door reengaging the chain.

Suddenly through the door, Arorah heard a loud, manly laugh.

The Cyclops Window

"You got more spit than I did," the Tomato Man said.

"I didn't know she'd do me like that," said Mary, hurt in her voice. "Spittin' on me. And after all I've helped her."

"Oh, come on, Sister Mary. We'll replant like you say," said the Tomato Man consolingly. "You got to learn to keep your good heart in the family."

They moved away.

A few days later, lost as inevitably she would be, Arorah knew that Mary Tomato Man would not help this time. She sat on a broken curb. Where was south? Where was north? East? West?

If only Claude were alive, she thought. Pray, God, let him come down from heaven and help her. Her mind dwelled on her dead lover. She thought of the good, early days as she looked up and squinted at the sun above the tree line and at the blue and white sky where heaven must be.

The year Claude came for her, she had been twelve and he, thirty-seven. Claude had fallen in love with her after watching her from time to time wade through the rain-filled gullies of the fields beside her grandmother's cabin out on Jennie Hannah's place. Jennie Hannah was the white and legal wife of Claude.

But the clear recall of that early time dimmed as the raw wound of losing him in recent time overtook her.

Claude had been sickly. He had preferred her nursing to his wife's. Arorah awoke one morning in bed at Claude's side. He was cold, stiff. She kept him all day, holding him, talking to him. At dark when he had not moved, Arorah recalled Claude telling her to go to Mary Tomato Man if trouble came.

Mary stood with Arorah while the men from the funeral parlor wrapped Claude in a sheet, placed him on a stretcher, and rolled him out of the house and put him into their ambulance. The black funeral home owners, black aristocrats, had driven him to the back door of the white funeral home. Arorah never saw Claude again.

The next week a lawyer came. The house was hers. A small check would come each month. Nothing more, he claimed.

But now, lost, lost, Claude did not come from heaven to help her find home. She rose from the curb. She must find her own way home, go inside, lock up. She opened her purse, touching the paring knife before withdrawing the talcum. She had forgotten her puff. She dumped the powder into her palms and threw it on her face, strewing it like spilled flour over her skin. Whiteness would keep her safe.

Now, again, she asked, was that way east? West? The sun was west. The levee was west. And east? She remembered that the water tower was east. It stood tall, bolted to its side a siren which had screeched and awakened the town in the early hours, signaling D-Day during the war and now sounding whenever tornadoes threatened Port City. She looked up to locate the great water tower on stilts lifting up above the trees. Yes. There was east. She crossed south to north. Redbud Street! *The alley. Bless Jesus*, she thought. *Bless Claude in heaven.*

But she was not safe.

"Arorah Hannah, Lost Banana." The young black boys ringed her. "Arorah, Hannah, Lost Banana."

The Tomato Man watched from his porch.

The boys danced around her.

Oooh. She drew the paring knife out.

The boys kept the circle, but stilled.

A woman rushed up. "Don't cut my son," she screamed.

The Tomato Man bounded from his porch, breaking to the center of the ring of boys. "Get back, boys," he said. He grasped Arorah's wrist. The knife fell. He shook her to the ground. "This time you go to Whitfield."

"Noo," said Arorah.

Mary Tomato Man came.

"Go call the police, Sister Mary," said her brother.

"She tried to cut my boy," the woman said to the growing crowd.

Reluctantly Mary obeyed and went home to call the police. When she returned, she helped Arorah to the steps of her house.

"I shouldn't help you. You spit on me, Arorah," said Mary.

"I know. I'm sorry," said Arorah. "Let me go inside. I'll lock up."

"No," commanded the Tomato Man from afar.

"They'll poison me like my grandmother said they did my mother if they take me to Whitfield," said Arorah to Mary. "Let me go inside," she begged.

Mary shook her head.

A patrol car pulled up, and a policeman handcuffed Arorah and shoved her into the back seat of his car.

Arorah flailed at the sturdy wire and glass encasing the back seat. "But I'm white," she wailed. A dab of white talc dropped from her

lovely and distraught face. Was there no longer safety in whiteness?
    In the driver's seat, Ham Vance drove slowly away from Redbud Street. He began to hum.

Sixth Sequence

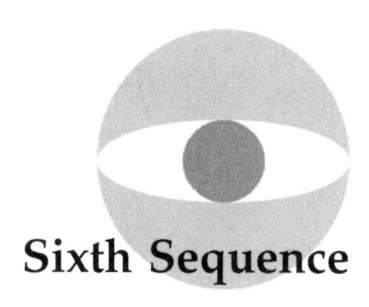

The Majestic Theater, source of abracadabra in a drab cottonland, cooling summer's nasty heat, its rowed seats soft and not church-pew hard, stood tall and proud today near the low downtown by the river's edge.

The movie had not yet begun, and the screen on the stage was a huge, gray sheet without life. Small starlights at the end of each row gave enough light to reveal the vast cavity of the theater with its small balconies rounding on the side walls and two large balconies facing forward, one for white couples to love in, and above it, the black balcony. All the theater was an Italian villa seemingly in moonlight secreted away from damp winters or sweaty summers outside. Here Port City had been to Oz with Judy Garland, danced with Fred Astaire, and today would be with Scarlett O'Hara at a plantation barbecue.

In the lobby, the Picture Show Lady greeted afternoon moviegoers like a party hostess about to serve tea. It was her old bright way. Her weeks of being burdened by the hazy feeling of being separated from reality ended as with a wand's touch when a bold plan had taken hold of her, bringing with it clarity and energy. Her body too rounded, gray strands through her dark hair, Ladyree smiled nevertheless like a girl at the white ticket holders and tore their tickets in half. The black ticket holders were filing into the highest balcony of the temple-like theater from a different entrance.

Ladyree let another employee handle the final ticket taking, and she ushered last-minute guests into the theater. The movie began. Words flashed across in Technicolor. Ladyree, after seating someone, looked back over her shoulder to catch the first few moments of the movie and the last of what appeared to be a poem.

The saccharine words started *Gone with the Wind*, or *GWTW* as the Majestic employees knew the movie. Ladyree remembered its initial release in 1939. Hollywood's glamorous Old South had raised then the spirits of all Southerners, still ostracized, downtrodden, barefooted, by the old war. Only a few pockets of the New South were prosperous like the Mississippi Delta where black fertile land and black laborers made money from cotton for its white half of the populace.

The prosperity had created culture in an area where the Old South had barely existed. The Old South had sent to the Delta only its overseers, adventurers, and slaves who worked the rich riverbottom land and endured its oppressive heat and the diseases thriving in its swamps. But the Old South lived in the Georgia of the motion picture. *GWTW*, history by Hollywood, myth and truth mingled, drew many to Southern theaters.

"Don't know why we should care about being expelled from college. We'd have had to come home before term was out anyway," says Brent Tarleton to Scarlett O'Hara, his twin brother Stuart beside him.

"Why would you?" says Scarlett.

Stuart Tarleton answers, "The war, goose! The war's going to —"

Scarlett interrupts, "If you boys say 'war' just once again, I'll walk into the house and slam the door! Pa talks war morning, noon, and night, and all the gentlemen who come here talk war and Fort Sumter and secession and Abe Lincoln till I could scream! And this war talk's just ruining every party I go to. There isn't going to be any war!"

In the background the columns of the verandah of Tara rise. Nearby a cape jasmine bush blooms. There is more talk of tomorrow's barbecue and ball at Ashley Wilkes' Twelve Oaks.

Ladyree, having seated the moviegoers, stood at her station behind the waist-high ledge separating the foyer and the theater's dark. The dark was cut by a sword of light drawn from the far-back projection room.

Ladyree readied herself to be Scarlett, to leave Delta surroundings dominated by monotonous fields—fields she loved, but thought unexciting because their drama seemed to live only in the slowly changing seasons. She readied herself to be Scarlett, but today she failed to fall into her usual fantasy.

Sally Bolding

A vexing, a missing piece to her bold, new plan kept her from surrendering to the world at the end of the light knifing the dark, kept her from owning the charm and youth of Scarlett O'Hara. Yet she was awake to the movie. An old, unsurfaced remembrance nagged at her making her feel that the missing piece of her plan was lost somewhere in the movie script.

Two late moviegoers, two lovers, appeared.

"We want to sit far back," whispered the young man, his hand at the girl's waist.

She seated them carefully avoiding the light shaft. She was mindful of the frequent shadows on the screen of late moviegoers mingling their lives of Sunday dinners and cotton fields into the screen's make-believe.

From her station she watched the nearby lovers cuddle. How long ago was it that she had been in Mumford's arms?

She concentrated on the movie.

On the screen Scarlett O'Hara roams Ashley Wilkes' splendorous Twelve Oaks. Scarlett, delicate looking, tough, lively, commonsensical, loves Ashley, polished too fine, his head full of Grecian thought.

Attending the barbecue and approaching ball also are Melanie Hamilton, Ashley's unannounced wife-to-be, unbelievably altruistic, and Rhett Butler—wicked, magnificent.

Ladyree felt an untoward craving to see not this scene but a later one. She wanted to see the Atlanta fire scene with its spectacular blaze of running red lines on barn-like buildings, all against the night skies of the southern city. The flames of burning buildings would fall in crumbling skeletons to ash around Scarlett, Rhett, Melanie.

Fire. Ladyree loved fire. Why did Verda Soper feel terror at the mention of fire? Ladyree did not know. No matter. She would burn her up. *And burn as in an oven.*

Vengeance might belong to God, but she, Ladyree Soper Marshall, would help Him. In the Presbyterian faith there was belief in justice. She would have justice. She had determined to burn Verda Soper up.

And burn as in an oven.

The pictures on the screen continued to flip by at a rate surpassing eye-time blending magically into a whole.

On the screen, in an elegant library, during the Twelve Oaks party, Scarlett tells Ashley that she loves him.

"I'm going to marry Melanie," Ashley answers, his voice kind.

"You're afraid to marry me. You'd rather live with that stupid little fool who can't open her mouth except to say 'yes' and 'no' and raise a passel of mealymouthed brats just like her!" says Scarlett.

She slaps Ashley. He bows and leaves the library. In a fury, Scarlett seizes two china vases and flings them into the fireplace. She is astonished to see Rhett Butler rise from a high-backed chair at hearthside. Rhett Butler and Scarlett O'Hara meet.

Then the Civil War breaks out. Heartbroken and reacting to Ashley's marrying Melanie, Scarlett weds Melanie's brother. Both grooms go to war.

The two lovers rose from their seats, cutting off Ladyree's view of the screen. As they made their way through a full row toward the aisle, they stumbled over knees and forced other more polite moviegoers to stand.

"We'd rather sit in the balcony," the boy whispered as he passed Ladyree.

Ladyree followed them quickly.

The balcony was closed.

The theater manager often allowed his family to come free to watch sparsely attended movies during weekly afternoon hours. Recently on such an occasion, his daughter had begun an unmarried pregnancy in the balcony. The manager, fearful of bringing more scandal to himself and family, had consequently closed the white balcony. Unwed motherhood was a great social disgrace. Too late and unable to find a doctor or a back room abortionist, the manager had sent his daughter to a home for unwed mothers in Knoxville, Tennessee, far away where after the birth, an adoption would be arranged. Rumors and gossip had made the situation known despite his great efforts at secrecy.

Ladyree was about to tell the couple that the balcony was closed when she decided not to stand in their way. She unhooked the large velvet cord blocking it off and allowed them to go up the marble steps. She would let them have a time for their joy in the dark, unpeopled mezzanine but would check later to ensure that they limited their loving. They made her think again of Mumford.

Mumford Marshall, always the man with whom she might have lived happily ever after. Mumford Marshall, pioneer farmer, crazy Mumford Marshall who talked of a mechanized cotton picker, growing rice, raising fish, and even of industry. Crazy in cottonland. During their marriage he had grown cucumbers and they had manufactured Green Gold pickles. But the cucumbers grew so fast in the breedy

Sally Bolding

soil that harvesting was problematic. Picking the new crop before it was full grown seemed an unreasonable thing to do for both white managers and black laborers, and Mumford would not wait long enough to straighten matters.

"Did you ever see a fella walkin' down the street eatin' a pickle and spittin' out seeds?" he had joked, ending the operation before returning to his library of robber baron biographies and Horatio Alger stories to dream another dream of glory in the Delta.

Ladyree kept abreast of happenings through her mother's gossiping, where Mumford's name when used was always associated with the Devil, through what she overheard in the lobby of the Majestic, and through whisperings over the dark theater rows. Ladyree had learned last week that Mumford had some new use of the mighty vine kudzu stirring in his ever-working brain. Mumford—always the man with whom she might have lived happily ever after.

Ladyree thought of his second wife, Elia Hannah Marshall, daughter of the late Claude Hannah and Jennie Hannah—Elia, who belonged, as did Marsie, in the world of garden clubs and children's birthday parties. Elia was a handsome woman in her early forties. Ladyree coveted the two Marshall daughters, one adopted and too old to be Elia's natural child and a second, younger girl born to Elia. Spring, the elder girl, was twenty-five, her time to mate shortening. The dates she brought to the Majestic were usually bachelors-always-to-be or older widowers. Spring was pale, delicate, vapor in the sun. The oil paintings she created of compress workers with black bodies rippled by sweat-shiny muscles shocked Elia's garden club friends. Ladyree remembered Spring in Shirley Temple curls, always playing the game of movie stars, always Alice Faye, always making Ladyree think of the child she had lost.

Ladyree shook her head to right her thoughts. All this did not matter. She would never belong, be a mother, be again in Mumford's arms.

She whispered loudly to herself. "It does matter!" She would make it matter.

And burn as in an oven.

On the screen, General Sherman threatens Atlanta. Scarlett, who has lost the young husband she never loved, has gone to Atlanta to stay with Melanie who carries Ashley's child, and her Aunt Pittypat Hamilton hoping to keep abreast of the man she still loves, Ashley. In Atlanta the famous blockade runner Rhett Butler pays court to the black-weeded widow Scarlett at a bazaar. He dances with her in her hooped black skirt and scandalizes the other Atlantans and old Dr. Meade.

Old Dr. Meade. Something clicked in Ladyree's mind.

Rhett says to the widow Scarlett, "In India, when a man dies, he's burned. And his wife is burned with him."

"How dreadful," says Scarlett.

"For myself," says Rhett, "I think it's a more merciful custom than our Southern way of burying widows alive."

Later Scarlett witnesses an amputation within the horrors of a makeshift hospital for the war wounded. Melanie becomes heavier with child. Atlanta's situation grows graver and graver under General Sherman's bombardment.

Ladyree left her post to check on her balcony lovers. Going up the marble steps, wide as if leading to a throne room, her flashlight flitted spiritlike onto the cool, dark columns of the banister. As she approached the landing, she saw the lovers coming down. Their clothing disordered, she doubted if she had caught them in time. They smiled at her sheepishly as they passed on the steps, entered the lobby below, and exited towards the avenue outside.

Ladyree stood on the top tier of the balcony, then settled herself in a seat on the balcony's back row to await the fire scene.

On the screen, Melanie's time has come. Scarlett sends Prissy, a slave servant, to find old Dr. Meade to deliver the baby.

Something rings in Ladyree's mind. *Doctor. Old doctor.*

The doctor is at the depot hospital with the wounded and will not leave them to deliver Melanie's baby. He sends Prissy back.

Scarlett goes to Dr. Meade herself. The camera shows a panorama of the railroad yards covered with the bodies of wounded Confederates lying in the heat and sun as Scarlett makes her way through them.

"A baby?" says Dr. Meade. "Are you crazy? I can't leave these men for a baby! They're dying! Hundreds of 'em."

In Ladyree's mind . . . Scarlett needs a doctor . . . old Dr. Meade. *Burn as in an oven . . . old Doctor Meade . . . old doctor.* OLD DOCTOR.

Ladyree sprang from her seat, rushed into the outside hallway of the balcony to the absent manager's office. She unlocked the door with her employee key, entered the office, picked up the telephone on the desk, asked for the residence of Dr. Prather Lewis.

"Dr. Lewis," she said.

"Who is this? I was napping."

"This is Ladyree, Dr. Lewis."

"Ladyree? Oh, yes, lovely Ladyree." Only old Dr. Lewis still called her lovely. "How is your mother?"

"She's fair. She missed you last Sunday." Ladyree surprised herself. Her voice was as steady as her mother's inner steel. "You won't forget to visit us next Sunday, to come for refreshments in the afternoon?"

"Forget? I do not forget. You are mistaken, Ladyree."

"Of course, you don't. Just an expression. Mother says you're the most intelligent doctor in the Delta. She has a crush on you."

"Nonsense. We're both too old for that."

"You'll come Sunday?"

"Yes. You'll make the cake my poor wife used to make, won't you, Ladyree?" Doctor Lewis had been shaken badly last fall by his wife's death from heart failure.

"Of course," said Ladyree.

Downstairs, back at her station, the vexing problem of her plan solved, she absorbed herself in the Atlanta fire scene.

Atlanta burns.

Scarlett has delivered Melanie's baby herself. Rhett passes, offers to rescue them from the marauding outlaws in a horse and buggy. The fire is spreading over the city.

It was no make-believe fire. The entire back lot of a movie studio had actually been torched. A huge, real fire blazes in the night sky on the screen.

Scarlett, Rhett, Prissy, Melanie, and her newborn ride in an archaic wagon behind a single horse, all before the magnificent, terrible burning. The Yankees are coming. The Yankees are coming.

Atlanta, in pell-mell disorder, is being ravaged by unpoliced scavengers sacking the remains of the city. Atlanta burns, burns. The back lot crumbles in a blaze, hot orange, real, menacing. Melanie's baby cries. The wagon sways in the hell of Peachtree Street. The cannons blast in the background. Sparks fly. The horse balks near a stockade of ammunition threatened by fire. Behind the actors, a full shot of burning warehouses.

Rhett says, "Easy, boy, easy. Come along, now." The horse remains unmovable.

Rhett calls to Scarlett, "Give me your shawl! Quick!"

Scarlett hides in the shawl, afraid, but after a moment's protest, hurls it toward him in a sweeping move. Blinding the horse with the shawl, Rhett pulls horse and wagon toward an opening within the blazings.

Scarlett screams, "Rhett! Rhett! Not that way!"

Rhett answers, shouting, "It's our only chance. Between those cars. Before all blows up!"

And burn as in an oven, Ladyree Soper Marshall was thinking when Nathan Pankum came to relieve her of her usher duties. Nathan worked part-time when not at school or working in his father's greenhouse. The long movie necessitated a second employee shift. Ladyree would see the last part of the movie another day.

And burn as in an oven, Ladyree thought again as she walked away from the theater, the movie within still rolling.

And burn as in an oven.

Seventh Sequence

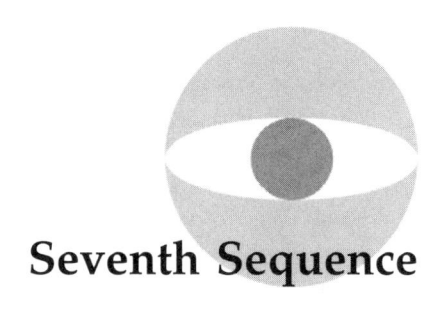

Nathan Pankum felt his whole existence centered around sexual fantasy or nightmare.

His bedroom was dark, the window shades down, the early evening light dying in the squarish room. The shapes of the linear furnishings had blackened and were beginning to blur into the gray spaces of the room.

In his bed, Nathan climaxed himself, waited, climaxed again. Where was love? Would there be more than this?

In the hallway, he heard his father's voice speaking into the telephone. Nathan rose. Slowly he cracked his door.

"Hell, I can't do that, Ruby. I don't live alone anymore," said Norwood Pankum. "We'll have to go across the river and get someplace again." He waited. "Damn, Ruby, don't be a pest. I got enough problems. Both the Episcopalians and my mother's Baptists would be down on me with a teenager here. Bad enough we risked it before he came."

Nathan slowly closed the door. The thin spear of light across the floor vanished. The dark claimed him. He felt . . . empty. A loneliness lay deep in some hollow within him. All of a sudden, the room became a black box, close, coffinlike.

When he was small, he could not tolerate being enclosed, but he had conquered the tendency for the most part. His grandmother had complained that he was sickly and weak, sniffling all the time with his allergies and flowing sinuses and fearful of heights as well as enclosures. In response, he had hidden his snifflings, and after a while, he could not remember when, the mucus drip at his nose had dried and his nostrils cleared. He hid his phobias, and his pretenses had made them subside. Only rarely, unannounced, did he feel his early peculiarities stir.

But now new things had come to haunt him as he went about his daily ways. The first winter he lived in the Delta had been a particularly cold one. He had shivered the entire season. When spring warmed the days, he continued shaking.

"It's like a blasted nervous tic," his father had complained to Wash. Hearing this Nathan managed his shivering as he had his sniffles, but afterwards his bones began to feel cold. Even now he could feel them chilled, but he had accustomed himself so to the bother that he was but little concerned.

Nathan, his back at the wall, slid down to the floor beside his bed and held himself with his long arms in a tight ball trying to make himself warm and strong.

He heard his father leave the house. Away in Wash's quarters a muffled sound of music ceased as Wash apparently cut off his radio. The house was ghostly silent. The tomblike room closed in tighter on Nathan, the space around him seemingly narrowing, the air sucked away. He jumped up and shoved open the door.

He opened a hall window. Far out front of the nursery, traveling the highway, sparse traffic could be heard moving by, making a card shuffling sound, quick to come, quick to go. He distracted himself by trying to distinguish the whiz-bys of cars from trucks, of big cars from small, of big trucks from small. But the game was no good, and he stopped.

He ambled to one room from another depending for guidance on the few lights his frugal father had left burning until he reached the breakfast area just off the kitchen. He flicked on the overhead light. A naked bulb mercilessly spotlighted tacky linoleum flooring and a cheap dinette before a double window, unshaded, and blackened by night. Nathan blinked from the glare quickly turning on a table lamp before cutting off the power above. Better, he thought, yet the stark lighting had revealed much in the room to him.

The black woman who cleaned the nursery and their adjoining quarters said you could tell that only men lived in these rooms. No doodads for one thing, she had said. The room was uncluttered, orderly, empty of all save the necessary—no doodads.

Two things struck Nathan in his short scrutiny of the small room as out of the ordinary. His father had left a plant from his orchid experiment on the dinette table to catch the next morning's sun. The orchid was pregnant, its stem slightly bulged like a woman's belly. And, a cabinet door stood ajar.

Nathan approached the opened cabinet. It was where Norwood Pankum kept his liquor supply. Nathan widened the crack of the door. Tall bottles in Sunday finery stood congregated—churchgoers—or maybe bowling pins with rounded bodies and heads. Nathan took out a bottle to examine. The lamplight caught its moving amber fluid. The liquor seemed jewellike reminding Nathan of the old brooch his grandmother Pankum always wore in the lace at her ample bosom. The depth of his teetotaling grandmother's disapproval of the bottles had she been in the room crossed Nathan's mind. It would have been too great for measure. Norwood Pankum had come far from the Piney Woods. Nathan Pankum had never had alcohol even over Christmas fruitcake.

Nathan removed more bottles from the cabinet to the dinette tabletop. Some were clear. Most were varying shades of amber similar to the first bottle's color. One bottle held a lovely green liquid.

He stepped through the archway that separated breakfast area from kitchen and from a shelf near the sink took a stemmed glass. At the table again he opened a bottle of crème de menthe and lifted the rim of its neck to his nose careful not to slosh or spill the beautiful green liqueur swimming behind the curve of glass. He drew its fragrance into his nostrils pulling back at once from the smart of its minty smell. The bottle held the glamour of Hollywood as the screen of the Majestic did, held what must be in the world somewhere, maybe someday, but not here and now, held the promise of grown-up and better times. He watched the pour, a swirling grace falling through light, as it filled his glass. His misery was forgotten.

He took his first sip of alcohol. It burned, then cooled. Strong. He liked the mint and the sweet. He dropped a cube of ice from the refrigerator into his glass stirring the crystal white into the green to dilute the drink. Better, he thought, of the taste. The cool-hot liquid went down and soon soothed him. He finished the drink and two more.

Outside the double windows the moon appeared. Outside bright moonshine struck the levee horizon, a white line streaking the dark. Atop the rise Nathan saw a figure seesawing—the clubfooted Wash Bibbs.

Nathan started to fill his glass with more crème de menthe, but, spotting a shotglass in the liquor cabinet, he thought to change to something brown colored. He would pretend to be Gary Cooper at a western bar and drink something in a shot glass. Whiskey? The crème de menthe had released something playful in him. He smelled the whiskey, but it did not appeal to him. He smelled brandy—like candy, he thought. Brandy-candy. He filled the shot glass with brandy. No room for an ice cube. "Okay," he whispered. Down the hatch. He gulped it away.

Aaah. He stood up, jumped from one foot to the other, lost his balance, banged his hip into the table. Aaah. He sat down and in a moment felt better. *Not better. Wonderful*, he thought.

Through the windows he caught sight again of Wash Bibbs. He considered joining him. Wash Bibbs was the only one who seemed to care for him. He liked him, too, he thought. Indeed, he would visit Wash in the moonlight on the levee.

He pulled his father's woolly sweater from a large nail near the closetlike hall between kitchen and outside. While maneuvering his arms through sleeves and exiting the door, he stumbled. The cool air hit him from behind and, unlike most times, when it would have reminded him of the cold at his bones, invigorated him. He felt extremely well. He walked, then climbed toward Wash.

"Wash," he said as he topped the levee, moonlight directly in his open face and bathing him with its goodness.

"Nathan?" said Wash Bibbs. The stark moonlight traced the ugly ruts of Wash's burned-away face. He had only a dribble left for a nose. One eye was too wide, too much white and highlighted now by too much moon, the other eye narrow. The night hid the pink facial scars spotting his black skin. Wash Bibbs, a man of few words, a book always in his back pocket.

"Here," Nathan answered as if responding to a roll call. Nathan stumbled again, this time over a clump of tough Johnson grass. Wash steadied him.

"Nathan, you've been drinking."

"Nooo," said Nathan. He and Wash sat in grass, the grass a combination of sticklike winter residue and soft spring growth.

Wash said nothing. Nathan prepared to present himself as sober. The effort dampened his euphoria.

Wash spoke at last. "See how beautiful all this is?"

Nathan now glum, disoriented, looked about him. The river reflected a silver sequined distortion back to the perfect moon, river and moon the visual center of the evening. Here, high, cool, the town lights were a distant glow and traffic on the highway too faraway for sound. Nathan's mood continued to be glum. He remembered being in a church alone.

But his mood was unstable. The pimply, hypersensitive Nathan, primed on crème de menthe, grew poetic. "The moon is like an eye ... like God's eye maybe ..." His voice trailed. Had he spoken too much?

"The eye of a goddess, I think," said Wash. "The moon is female tonight. Our river, always male."

Swooning winds, soft currents circling invisibly, stirred the air around them. Wash stood and faced the mighty moon-polished river. "The Delta owns its people," he said. "A little God may be in their Bible Belt churches, but below this levee, there is a real God. You can see him swifting on down to New Orleans. He isn't invisible. He gives his land, his Deep South Israel, to his Deep South chosen people, and when he's angry, he floods the land, showing his fury like any self-respecting God."

They lapsed again to silence. The river darkened as clouds on the horizon drifted forward and high. The moon disappeared.

Nathan's inhibitions loosened by alcohol, he asked Wash a question which had often occurred to him.

"Why do you call me by my first name?"

"Do you object?"

"No, but I thought maybe you felt I was unworthy of being called—"

"Mr. Nathan?" Wash's face was unreadable, masked in his scars.

"Yes."

"I mean you no harm, Nathan. White people think prefacing their name is black courtesy. Mr. Milledge use to say that good manners were only commonsense thoughtfulness. I think this practice is thoughtless and denies dignity to another human being."

Wash reached down and grasped Nathan's hand pulling him to his feet. "Let's go back, Nathan. No more to drink. Your father wouldn't like it. Drink some milk before you sleep."

Nathan nodded.

When a few minutes later he returned to the kitchen, he went directly to the refrigerator for milk as Wash had suggested. He added sugar and vanilla to a glass of milk and took it to the bottle-laden dinette table.

On the table he had left the stopper off of the brandy. The smell of vanilla and brandy mingled and pleased. He poured a little, then a lot, of the browny liquor into his milk concoction. Candy-brandy only better. He studied the bottles. Between sips, he opened and smelled vodka. It looked as innocent as water. Its smell seemed negligible. He poured a little, then a lot, into his mixture, adding more milk, vanilla, and brandy. The vodka seemed to do little for the flavor. The mix remained tasty. Again he began to enjoy himself.

Of a sudden, he recalled with pleasure his secret fantasy. He had overheard—he was always overhearing, always listening—two grammar school boys arguing over the strength of the comic book character Superman. Did he have the strength of ten men? A hundred men? A thousand men? Once the boys were gone, Nathan wondered what he would do had he the strength of a thousand men. Now tonight the fun fantasy reran on the screen in his brain. He would be the star high school football player. He would be more popular than the quarterback Red Ted. Red Ted would actually be in awe of him as he flicked away players and leaped over the goal line. If Spring Marshall's car became mired in mud as it had last season, he would pick up the car and carry it to where she wanted it. She would smile at him. He would be modest. Norwood Pankum would be proud. "My son," he would brag. Nathan took another swallow.

"The strength of a thousand men," he said aloud. His father would give him a loving bear hug. "Loves me. Loves me not," he said and playfully plucked a petal from his father's prized orchid. "A thousand men, ten thousand men, a hundred thousand men." Only a few petals were left on the bulging stem of the pregnant orchid. "The strength of a MILLION MEN," he screamed. The orchid was now naked of petals.

He heard a car enter the parking lot in front of the nursery. He listened as it drove into his father's space, the space sandwiched between the living area and a tin roofed garage used to store soil supplies.

Nathan jumped up, quickly put the bottles away. He slammed shut the cabinet door, but it swung back ajar striking the drink in his other hand. The drink dropped to the linoleum, shattering sticky milk and glass. In alarm, Nathan rushed to the kitchen sink for water and rag. Swirling around to return, he felt dizzy, then sick. Bad sick. He fought to continue the clean-up hitting his hip on the table edge again. The pain of the blow cleared his mind enough for him to determine reaching the garbage pail in the kitchen where just in time he vomited.

He lifted his head from the pail to see his father standing in the doorway, a woman by his side. He watched as his father's expression changed from astonished to grim.

"Are you sick, boy?" the woman asked.

"Sick, Ruby? He's drunk!" shouted Norwood.

Sick. Sick. Nathan sank to the floor into a fetal curl, his arm shielding his face, his eyes tightly shutting away reality.

He could feel the woman hovering over him. "He's sick, Norwood, honey," she said.

"Watch your skirt. He'll look up it," replied Norwood. "I told you we should have gone across the river tonight. Now what do we do with this on our hands?"

"Sick, honey," she repeated.

"He's drunk. Drunk. Look at this mess on the floor, and he's vomited in the kitchen bucket. I'd just scrubbed it out with soap and water."

"I'll clean it up," she said. Nathan heard her lift the pail, heard the back door open, close, open again after she had carried out the bucket. Now she was once more close.

Norwood had made no noise while she was gone, but Nathan knew his look without seeing. He felt a sharp blow on his thigh. Norwood had kicked him.

"Don't, honey," said Ruby.

"BASTARD!" Norwood yelled. Nathan realized his father had rushed to the dinette table. "Look! Look what he's done to my orchid!"

"Oh, honey!"

Nathan vomited again on the floor. A moment went by. Suddenly Nathan's head was being cut from his body. His shirt tightened and pulled at the neck. Norwood had grabbed his collar. A violent tug. Nathan felt his body lift.

"Norwood, honey, wait. I'll clean it up."

Nathan was being dragged. He kept his eyes closed, stayed limp, played dead.

"What you going to do, honey."

"I'm going to lock him in the soil supply garage."

"He's too sick to know what we do, honey. You don't have to do that," she protested.

"HUSH!" he screamed at her. "I'm going to lock him up there forever. Nathan, you hear me? *Forever.*"

Nathan felt his feet hit steps as they exited the kitchen. Still he did not resist nor speak nor open his eyelids. He felt himself shoved, pushed, shoved. He heard a door swing open, felt himself released and falling, heard the same door swing shut and the loud click of its locking. The ground he fell upon was cold, but the last vomiting had been merciful. He slept before his father's footfalls died. Sweet oblivion.

Nathan's stomach seemingly spun in one direction before jerking toward another. He opened his eyes to the dark within the garage. How long had he slept?

He groped about in the little space not stacked up with bags of potting soil searching for something to use as a bathroom. He found an empty container. After relieving himself, he stood thinking that he might feel better upright. He felt worse. He sat again leaning his back against a wall of loose boarding. The moon had returned from behind the clouds low toward the horizon and sent its beams through the small spaces of the boarding making tiny lines on the dirt floor beside him. All else was a deep dark. The ceiling, a cover of corrugated tin, blocked all other light. The blackness overhead seemed something unknown and ready to fall and press him. His old fear of being enclosed flooded up from long ago compounding his sickness.

He panicked. He must get out. He beat the boards behind him, his adrenalin surging. The boarding took his attack, gave nothing.

"I do not have the strength of one man, let alone a thousand," he said, his voice low, a tremble.

He battled now to calm his panic.

Outside it lightened. Dawn. The sun came up. He could see rosy light in the fields. Still the ceiling held the oppressing blackness.

He was so thirsty. He found a faucet in a corner, the spigot curling from the ground like an umbrella handle. He drank, his mouth upturned, his hair touching earth. He drank too fast. The water came up and sputtered out through his mouth and nasal passage. He drank slowly and retained the water. It seemed to slosh in the cavity of his stomach, but the cool ground water was merciful.

He slept again fitfully. When he awoke the sun was higher. His stomach felt better, his head more firmly on his body but—the panic held within struggled too much.

Of a sudden, he screamed, "HELP." He thrashed on the floor like an epileptic. "HELP."

Someone rattled the door. "Nathan. What is it?" It was Wash.

"Get me out!"

"I'll get the key," said Wash.

When Wash pulled him outside, Nathan's teeth were gritted and tears rolled down his contorted face. "I hate . . . ," he began. He was a little mad.

Wash held Nathan for a moment to calm him. "No, Nathan," said Wash. He pulled away. "Look at me." He pointed to his burned, scarred face. "This is what hate looks and feels like on the inside."

Nathan wiped his tears.

Eighth Sequence

Mumford Marshall strode across his fields toward the Pankum Nursery. He was looking for Wash Bibbs.

He glanced toward the levee where he knew Wash to be this time of morning. On the levee slopes, the east had reflected a faint pink causing Mumford to seek its source. A rising sun blazed and spread the color of cooked salmon low across the eastward sky. Mumford paused a moment before turning back. He saw Wash descending the levee at a hobble and a catch. Wash quickened to a rush of wayward limbs just before level ground.

Mumford's attention on Wash's possible fall, he himself stumbled and fell into a furrow. He righted his big body, brushed his kneecaps, and shook his fist at the furrow below and the sky above.

"God damned dirty trench!" he exclaimed. He blamed the furrow and God in the sky for his misstep finding no personal fault. Mumford tried never to hide a major truth from himself, but a minor one was fair game.

"Wash! Wash, you gotta help me," Mumford called.

Wash stopped in the field, the levee behind him, and waited. When Mumford reached him, he spoke, "How?"

"Come on into the greenhouse," said Mumford.

When Mumford and Wash entered Greenhouse Three, Mumford went immediately to his two rows of kudzu cuttings.

"Look at this stuff, Wash. You think the damned solution Max Durham made up has retarded any growth?"

Wash limped closer for a better scrutiny. "I don't think so."

"Neither do I. Damn. Damn. Umf. You gotta help me, Wash."

Wash said nothing.

Mumford fussed and made unintelligible mutterings as he inspected each plant in both rows. Wash began to sweep the concrete squares of the floor. Grass growing from all the cracks between the squares made Wash's work difficult.

The sun was now higher, and its light through the Boston ferns hanging below the clear ceiling created a pattern of leaves across the gridded floor. Only the larger shadows of Wash and Mumford broke the design. Earthy smells penetrated the moist air around them.

Mumford interrupted Wash's sweeping. "You gotta help me figure out how to control this kudzu, Wash."

Wash took a few more sweeps, was thoughtful, silent.

"Damn, Wash, say something."

"I don't know how to retard kudzu," said Wash.

"Nobody does now. But, Wash, you got a second sense with plants and a lot of knowledge. You tell me how."

"I don't know," repeated Wash.

"Preacher Jackson prays over his corn, thinks prayer will make 'em grow better. You think if we talked to the devil over ours, he'd do something?"

Mumford recognized the funny rattle that was Wash's chuckle.

"Guess not," said Mumford. "You never know who or what might smite you." He continued, "You gotta help, Wash. Nobody knows plants like you and Norwood and Max Durham do and like Will Milledge did."

"You tell me how I can help you, and I will," said Wash.

"You know what I'm trying to do?"

"Yes."

"If I could keep floods out of the Delta, floods like the '27 one, and get these damned planters to grow something besides cotton during my lifetime, I'd be happy to let it go. You shouldn't hang everything on one nail, on one crop."

"Your aim is good," said Wash.

"Well, help me then. If we could control the kudzu and grow it on our levees they'd resist any fury of the river to get its land back."

"You'd have to consider those big kudzu roots making holes in the levees," said Wash.

"Another problem. One problem at a time," said Mumford.

"One problem?" said Wash.

"Well, two. I'm gonna grow rice next year."

Wash continued to sweep. Mumford took out a Lucky Strike cigarette, sat on an upright tree stump used as a stool, lit up and puffed white smoke into the damp air. He grew reflective as he often did in Wash's company. His relationship with Wash was singular. Wash himself was singular.

"The flood, Wash? What happened to you in the '27 flood?"

"I was young. I built a dam around Mr. Milledge's flower garden," said Wash.

"Umf. Well, we had more to save than flower gardens."

"Mr. Milledge was chairman of the flood relief," said Wash defending his former employer and his mentor.

"Of course, and I don't mean Will Milledge just saved flower gardens. I meant no disrespect to Will Milledge's memory. I may not have admired all his practices," Mumford meant his homosexuality, "but there was plenty—and everybody agrees—to admire about Will Milledge."

"Yes," said Wash.

"Bitter with the sweet. Hadn't been for floods we wouldna' had these rich fields."

"No," said Wash.

"I remember, too, Wash. I can hear the fire whistle blowing when word got to us that up on the river the levee had gone. Madness. People running for high ground, upstairs, attics, on roofs, on the levee. I rushed out to One O'clock in a beat-up boat with a two- and-a-half horse-powered motor. Thanks be to the Choctaw or Chucchuma Indians for burying their chiefs and their stuffs into high mounds. I gathered my people and what livestock I could on the mounds. We watched bodies of people and animals, broken houses, and trees with naked roots wash by below the mounds. We felt helpless to do more. Nature is a humbler."

"Yes," said Wash.

"Later in town, the water wasn't like a burst or a rush like it was at the break or as swift as out on One O'clock. It just sort of trickled in and deepened. But people were afraid."

"Yes," agreed Wash.

"Always had floods. Use to measure time around here in flood years and yellow fever years. But '27. Umf. The Red Cross practically moved here, tents all over the levee and Indian mounds, anyplace higher enough in the country to escape water. There were so many people who needed to be sheltered and fed on such a little ground. Ol' Herbert Hoover himself shortly before he became president came to see about us. Nobody'd ever heard of the Mississippi Delta 'til then. Don't know us now, I guess, but then we got a lot of national attention. No flood like it in the country before or after."

Mumford rose, put out his cigarette, and pulled at one of his kudzu plants.

"What about my kudzu, Wash?"

"I don't know. I've never seen a plant so hardheaded," said Wash.

"I bet Ol' Will Milledge woulda' known."

"Maybe. If there was anything written about plants, he had read it," said Wash.

"Damn. I bet there're some old dusty books in his library about weed control. We're treating kudzu like a modern weed with these new weedkiller poisons. Herbicides, Norwood calls 'em. Treating kudzu with 'em trying to wound the damn vine, not kill it. Ought to be a lot of old treatments for weeds like burning but better. Ought to be something else. Weeds been around since Adam."

"The people at Mississippi State and the Experimental Station have probably done all that research," said Wash.

"Experts! I distrust them. They think they know everything. Nobody knows everything. I'm talking about old methods, not their new methods they can't see behind. Wash, you go to the public library and get those old books. You're always reading. You know plants. I'll pay you good."

Wash did not speak.

"What you say, Wash?"

Wash still did not speak.

"What is it?" asked Mumford.

"Mr. Marshall, black people can't use the public libraries in Mississippi."

"What? I never thought about it."

Wash flinched.

"Bet the black public library ain't much, either," said Mumford.

"There is no black public library here," said Wash.

"Oh?" Mumford scratched his bald dome. "That's a pity for you. Damned planters running away black people to Memphis and Chicago and California. Don't they know we need your labor? I've told 'em we oughta' treat you better. I built a school on the place last year and got a lot of flack. We gonna have to go to Mexico like Will Milledge's father went to Italy for extra labor if we're not better."

Mumford grew silent. Wash was quiet and inscrutable.

At last Mumford spoke. "What you reading now, Wash?" Mumford gestured toward a book tucked as always into Wash's back pocket.

"I read a little poetry every morning on the levee before I work."

"Kinda like a prayer before beginning the day? Like my mama always done." Mumford had lapsed deeper into Mississippi Delta vernacular mindful of his outburst on Delta labor and reaching for a friendlier tone.

"Yes, kinda like a morning prayer."

"Let's see your book," said Mumford. Wash handed it to him. "Walt Whitman."

"Yes."

Mumford flipped through the pages of Whitman's poetry. From time to time over the years, Mumford had been a regular in Will Milledge's home and knew that Will Milledge had educated Wash matching his own instruction by private tutors and later at Sewanee. Mumford's own classical education had faded as the years of disuse had grown.

At Vanderbilt, Mumford and his friends managed to attend early classes in overcoats covering the tuxedos worn while partying into early hours. Other students influenced by a faculty of poets followed a more rigorous approach to education. Yet he had been touched by a milieu in which poetry flourished—Crowe, Tate, Warren, and Jarrel. And, then, because he had excelled in public speaking, he had developed a prided skill in poetry reading.

Mumford settled on the poem "Song of Myself." "Gee, I remember this one," Mumford read aloud.

"I wish I knew what that damned kudzu is." Mumford skipped lines. Mary Spring Marshall entered the greenhouse and stood at the door and listened in disbelief as Mumford continued reading the poetry.

"Well, I hope so, Wash. Luckier, I mean, and what you think this damned kudzu was before now? Something or someone tough, I know for certain."

Wash shook his head and made his chuckle sound. Mumford noticed Spring.

"I didn't know you'd ever heard of poetry, Daddy," she said.

"Well, I have!" snapped Mumford.

"You read very well," she said.

"What do you want?" he demanded.

"Money, of course," she answered.

"You always want money. Just like May Corday."

"Of course. Shall I grovel for it?"

"No, but you could thank me."

"You haven't given it to me yet," she said.

Mumford took two one hundred dollar bills from his wallet. "That enough?"

"More than I expected." She put the money away. Pointedly she said, "Thank you."

Mumford made a grumbly sound. Spring nodded at Wash and left.

"Big Delta Daddy, made of money, that's what I am, Wash." Mumford handed Wash his book of poetry. "Thanks."

"It was good to share poetry with someone, Mr. Marshall."

"Yeah. Gotta go. Some damned fool's misplaced a tractor on One O'clock. Can you imagine misplacing a goddamned tractor? Those things cost like the devil."

"Your tractors are pretty big," said Wash.

"Damned right. Helping a friend train his son in farming, and the damn fellow keeps mislaying tractors. He's too young and spoiled to think about making a living. Last time he let a tractor roll into a 'grudge ditch'—a dredge ditch."

Mumford turned to leave.

"Wait, Mr. Marshall," said Wash. "I may be able to help."

Mumford stopped.

"Adrian Oates is still at Mr. Milledge's," said Wash.

"Adrian Oates?"

"Milledge's lover," said Wash.

I can check Milledge's library. He used a special mixture to stop grass and maybe I can find it in his gardening books. We can try it if I can find it."

"Great, Wash. Much obliged. I knew I could count on you to help me." He reached for the door pull to exit, but he stopped again, his expression reflective, and once more faced Wash. "You know about Walt Whitman and those plants and people and that reliving stuff. I don't much cotton to it, but I don't rule out a thing. Nobody, especially know-it-all experts, have the answer, or even sometimes, the questions."

"I agree," said Wash.

Mumford left.

On the way to One O'clock, Mumford mulled over Spring's fate. He was ambivalent about the fact that Spring was smart. A lot of Delta men liked their women dumb. A lot of smart Delta women painted their toenails and pretended sweet dumbness until they were widowed and promptly became the tough matriarchs of their families. Yet he was proud she had gotten *his* brains.

He turned his new Studebaker, already dusty, onto a gravel road leading toward the section of land beginning his place. Rocks popped against the bottom of the car.

He wanted Spring to marry one of those son-of-a-bitch offspring of some good Delta planter, Delta Brahman as some of the newspapermen in the Jackson state capital called them. Some of those son-of-a-bitches were like this ass, this son not of a planter but the banker Townsend, who expected him to teach the ass of a son how to farm when the ass kept losing tractors. He had looked at this son of a banker with his own place rented out as a prospective bridegroom for Spring, but this last incident had forced him to abandon such a notion. Spring was definitely too bright for the bonehead despite his papa's banking interests and land. Townsend had probably turned the boy over to him because he couldn't do anything with him. Nobody can do anything with dumbness. And Spring. She was too smart for her own good. He wished he had sent her to Ole Miss instead of that high-priced school in Virginia where they made her study too much.

He wished, too, that she would play more bridge, accept more dates, stop that damned Department of Public Welfare job and all that painting and reading and concentrate instead on getting a husband like all the other daughters did. And good looking. Spring was damned good-looking and ought to be able to catch anything she chose. His fear was that she would wind up being outside the good life in the Delta like Ladyree.

He found some comfort in thinking that you could be an eccentric woman if you were rich. He would try to see that she was rich, but he would not do it at the expense of playing safe in his farming practice. He wanted his own life to count. He was certain that this was his first responsibility.

He had said to young Nathan Pankum last week that every man should uphold his own time, and when Nathan had asked how, he had told him that that was Nathan's question to answer. And Spring likewise would have to do her own answering and upholding. If he could help, he would do it, but not by neglecting his own duty.

Thank goodness for May Corday. He would never have to worry about her marrying. "Damn," he said aloud when he thought that he might have to rely on dumb May Corday's genes for all his grandchildren.

"God damn," he repeated his ever-present oath, polite enough for unguarded use. "Damn." Talking to Wash and reading Whitman had made him too thoughtful. The tractor. Time to act, not daydream.

On One O'clock, its three Indian mounds rising near, Mumford found the errant tractor in the ditch as he had suspected. The tractor slanted like a grocery buggy having rolled astray down a slope and into water.

He tramped through the weedy growth outlining the ditch mindful of rattlers and moccasins and entered the mud at the foul water's edge before jumping into the tractor seat.

Thank God the damn engine didn't get wet. He turned the key which had been left in the ignition. The engine groaned, then made an horrendous grinding noise as it struggled free of the ditch and backed onto firm Delta land.

Ninth Sequence

Along the highway in front of the Pankum property, Wash Bibbs flagged down a Greyhound bus. As always he sat at the very back because the white bus driver arbitrarily could move the seating line dividing black from white, the back for the blacks, the front for the whites. Once when May Corday Marshall had a birthday party group transported by bus from town to the Marshall home, he had been ordered to stand causing pain in his twisted foot as the bus bumped about and a deeper pain in his soul.

Riding along, reminded of the incident on May Corday's birthday, he thought further about the recent time in the greenhouse when Nathan had peeked up her skirt. Nathan had been wounded unmercifully by his father. There was little Wash could do about it except to treat him kindly, maybe even fatherly.

Fatherly? Wash was not without his dreams of being a father. He would have liked to educate a son, read him "Jabberwocky," tell him stories of history as Will Milledge had to him. He would build in such a boy a love of poetry. Sharing Walt Whitman with Mumford Marshall had reminded him of the poetry readings in the Milledge household. Wash shook his head. He would never be able to bring to a son or a daughter his love of poetry. He would never be a father.

Since Lois had died, he had lived a monastic life. Lois, the older woman of his teen years had enjoyed his young body despite his crippled leg and the mishmash that was his face. Wash felt himself stir in his loins as he remembered Lois's body and quickly began to concentrate on the passing scenery of fields where the brown mounds of turned dirt were rising between furrows and were touched now with a faint promising green. Who would want ugly, ugly Wash Bibbs?

The bus came into the Port City station. Wash did not enter the black waiting room, but headed directly for the old neighborhood. Soon he began to pass houses, once kept and always spruced, now with screens out and broken toys and litter in their yards. Pieces of automobiles sat by worn but still runnable cars parked on the rutted berms of the potted macadam streets. These were poor white homes in a neighborhood that had once been Port City's finest. It had begun its decline before William Winston Milledge's heart failure and death.

The whole area seemed for sale or for rent. Stucco, once white, now gray, cracked. Bushes, overgrown, malformed, needed pruning, and grass grew wild and high where not matted with old leaves. Down one dilapidated street the home of the poet rose. It pained Wash to see the house shabby, but its grand size and clean architecture, like a small French chateau, still pleased.

Wash opened the wrought-iron gate of the old brick wall leading to the back door of the house where blacks in his youth had come for Will Milledge's generosity. He hobbled up the familiar steps to the porch, inside its side walls latticed and screened, its facing wall framing the kitchen door.

Wash stood a moment. He remembered the smells of yeasty rolls rising on trays in the sunny windows of the kitchen. He remembered the marvelous aroma of the rolls when they were table ready after a last minute in a hot oven.

"Eat your rolls while they're hot. Don't wait," Will Milledge would say to his guests in the dining room. But Wash and the other servants would eat later in the kitchen around a huge wooden table with big claw feet after they had removed the dirty dishes from the whites' table in the other room. On the kitchen counter he could see and smell the crispy fried chicken draining, leaving dark spots of grease on the brown Kraft paper of a grocery bag.

Wash hesitated longer savoring memory, turning away from the back doorbell to look past the lattice and screen of the entrance door. Outside past the brick walk leading through the garden to the servants' house where "Cook" had first lived and later Lois, over the high bushes on the property boundary, he could see on the alleyway the rising chimney of the shotgun house that had been his own home. But his real home he felt was the chateau-like residence within the kitchen doors.

Wash rang the doorbell. The white Adrian Oates came. He embraced Wash.

"The garden's not as good as when you and Unk kept it, is it, Wash?" Adrian swept his arms toward the brickwalled garden behind them. A slight catch in his throat broke his words.

"No. Well, hello," said Wash.

"Good to see you, old fool. How've you been?"

"Well."

"Is the job okay?"

"Working with plants. I like plants," said Wash.

"Wish I could hire you to fix our garden. Unk must be rolling in his grave about it."

"I guess," said Wash. Adrian, Will Milledge's lover of many years, always called the poet Unk or Uncle. Adrian had been a teenager when the relationship had begun. It was long after Wash had been burned in the kitchen where the two men now stood. Wash could never recall the day he burned.

Adrian looked away. "Sorry, there wasn't enough money to send you to college like Unk wanted to happen after his death. He thought the estate would be mine, and it's not going to be that way. The litigation is going against me."

"I'm okay. I have the plants. I'm even taking an interest in cotton. Never cared much for it, but it's all around the nursery."

"You didn't like cotton 'cause you were afraid you'd haf' to pick it like every other black bastard."

They laughed together. Wash's full laugh was a kind of huff-huff noise. His rutted face trembled. Only Adrian could talk to him so.

"I need to use the library. Looking for something on weed control or kudzu vines," said Wash.

"Unk had everything. You go look. I'm gonna finish getting dressed."

Inside the library, a big room walled in books, their cases grand and high, it smelled of old wood. The library was furnished in simple but elegant antiques. Two small statues of armored knights flanked a magnificent fireplace. Big windows let in ample light. Memory again overwhelmed Wash.

The two overstuffed armed chairs that had been pushed together to make his bed while he recuperated from his burning now were apart and sided a lyre desk near the fireplace. Wash remembered raising his head to look over the chair arms at Will Milledge as he wrote his poetry each early morning. He remembered that at 8:30 A.M. the poet would interrupt his work and cut on the turntable of his Magnavox to listen to a Beethoven symphony. The grand music signaled for a servant to bring him his breakfast on a silver tray. Will Milledge would put a biscuit and jelly on his coffee cup saucer and give it to Wash.

One day at breakfast time, the poet had asked him, "Can you read?" And the boy Wash, in his new uncertain and strange surroundings, his body seemingly strapped to his soul with crusty, shrinking and healing skin, had managed a nod.

Will Milledge had begun Wash's education by reading him nursery rhymes far too young for Wash but which Wash had never heard.

One day Will Milledge had said, "Wash, you're going to have a bad time because of your burn and lameness. But you have a good mind, and I'm going to show you how life can be rich despite being different. I know from my own experience." Will Milledge had reached then into his bookcases for the books his own tutors had used to instruct him long ago in order to draw the lines of Wash's education along those of his own. Later when Wash's health improved, the poet took him outside to garden in the deep, dark soil in back of his grand house to share his favorite pastime. There Wash learned to emulate the poet's tender regard for nature.

Now, so much time later, Wash searched the bookcases for books pertinent to his errand. He found two—one on Oriental vines, one on killing weeds. He also chose several of Will Milledge's gardening journals handwritten by the poet. Adrian who was not a deep reader had little disturbed the Milledge library. Wash's hands were dusty after his search.

"Can I take these?" Wash asked Adrian when he returned. Adrian was dressed impeccably, his thin body carrying his clothes well, his silver hair neat, his face still smooth and boyish. The older Adrian remained a beautiful man.

"Sure. No one will miss them. In fact, take what you want or at least what you can carry."

Wash added a book of Lewis Carroll's letters to the little girl who would suggest the character of Alice and a book of T. S. Eliot's poetry to his small stack. It would have been difficult to carry more, and he did not wish to create further problems for Adrian. "Thanks."

"You know, Wash, I'm gonna have to sell the house. The contents are up for grabs—and Unk would have used the word grab—but the house is, thank God, the only part of the estate that the cousins couldn't get back."

"I'm sorry it's to be sold," said Wash. The house meant much to both men.

"I tried to get the city to buy it as a memorial to Unk, but they wouldn't."

"Any offers?"

"An Oriental who is gonna make apartments out of it. I see the rest of the street and grieve 'cause all this elegance will go. The garden's already gone." Wash acknowledged this with a wag of his head. Adrian continued, "I've had someone in to clean once a month. It's too big for me, but it's all I can afford. I live in two rooms upstairs and the kitchen. We'd both be better off if Unk had been a little more careful with legalities. I'm an old, poor fag. There's nothing worse." Adrian laughed and patted Wash on the back. "I wonder Unk didn't make you a fag, Wash, but he didn't. Nothing worse than an old, poor fag than an old, poor nigger fag, pardon the word, ol' dear."

Wash did not laugh, but he took the remark in stride. It was just Adrian's way. "What are you going to do?"

"I have a friend in New York. Actually, he was Unk's friend. He's got me a job as a night clerk at the Barbizon Hotel for Young Women at Lexington and Sixty-third. They won't let men in any place but the lobby, and they know I won't harm the poor dear girls. 'Course they'd never let on to know that I'm queer. Too genteel for that."

"No," said Wash.

"Will you come visit me?" said Adrian.

Wash did not answer. "Good-bye, Adrian, and thanks." They embraced and Wash departed.

Down the shattered street Wash went, books heavy in hand, his heart as weighted by memory. He passed the Port City Cottonseed Oil Mill. A truck of seed had just come in to be weighed on a huge scale constructed within pavement beneath a kind of porch roof, drive-through arrangement giving the mill a service station look. From the cylindrical storage bins, light-gray and tall and behind the building, a strong smell from the processing of seed into oil flowed out into the streets, the smell identical to and as powerful as roasting ham. Cottonseed oil mills were one of the few industries in the state owned by Mississippians and not Northerners.

Adrian's New York and Northern relocation led Wash to reflect on industry. There were fields to work in but few factories within the whole of the South in which to find employment. After Will Milledge's death, Wash had considered moving to Memphis, Chicago, Michigan, Indiana, or California. Many black people were leaving for good paying factory jobs, but Wash felt his physical limitations and a loss of his association with his late employer which still gave him some protection in the community would make a move foolhardy and costly. Wash also was cautioned by the memory of his father's difficult leaving of the South.

Periodically during Wash's boyhood, Julius Bibbs had left the Delta for Chicago. He returned many times homesickened and with tales of unfamiliar indignities. "We have all sorts of indignities here," Julius Bibbs had told his son, "but at least we know what they are." Sometimes, the elder Bibbs would call Will Milledge collect for fare home from Chicago. Milledge would send it. "Mr. Milledge likes me, but in my place," his father had said. Wash suspected that his father drank too much away from his family, away from Wash and his mother, Marie, adding to his problematic travels. In the end, after all the backing and filling, Julius Bibbs stayed North disappearing from his family after a few years. During that time Wash's mother had sought to find her husband, failed, but eventually disappeared North herself leaving Wash in the care of Will Milledge.

Wash passed an alleyway with a house similar and as small and ill-kept as the one in which he had been born and partially reared. The alley smelled of spring flowers suddenly proliferating, flowers a cheap luxury, cheaper than the fancy dresses of the whites and the beef on their tables. Other alley smells whiffed into the air above the broken sidewalk over which Wash made his labored steps—sidemeat searing and sizzling in an iron skillet before sending up its aroma and overcooking vegetables being overwhelmed by steaming, boiling, cheap cabbages. The black and white areas were kept separated for the most part, but sometimes their boundaries blended. Wash passed the end of the black business thoroughfare, Redbud Street, which butted into the old white neighborhood.

In the early days of the year, Wash had gone to B. T. and Mattie Haynes' black restaurant and mini-grocery on Redbud for a rare meal out. When B. T. and his wife, Mattie, servant and cook for many years to a prominent Port City citizen, found themselves unemployed after his death and after many decades of serving him, they opened their business. A white banker who had eaten Mattie's cooking over the years and a meager five hundred dollar bequest in their late employer's will made the venture possible. As a sideline, the couple filled baskets with hot foods, many individual dishes of vegetables, meats, spoonbread and potato casseroles, hot homemade rolls and corn bread sticks, varied desserts, for white households. From eleven until twelve midday, B. T. carried these baskets out to the cars of waiting whites while Mattie served blacks in the big front room. Until a few years ago, B. T. had delivered the baskets by horse and buggy down the alleyways separating the white homes. Upstairs the Haynes lived and rented rooms for blacks who were not welcomed at white hotels. Wash had had a good meal there recently on a still-very-cool spring day, like today, but something had occurred to him that day that blocked out his memory of the details of Mattie's famous cooking.

After the meal, he had crossed Redbud Street and had seen the beautiful Arorah Hannah. He recognized that she was bewildered. She was sitting on a curb made of earth.

"I'm lost. Help me," she had said to a passing boy.

"Arorah Hannah, Lost Banana," the boy had answered, dancing a circle around her before going on.

Wash went to her immediately. "Ma'am?"

She raised her head and a look of horror erupted on her face. "A demon!" She had scrambled up from her squat on the curb and begun to scream.

The boy who had taunted her returned. "That way, Arorah Banana," said the black boy. "You live that way." He pointed.

Arorah had looked wildly at Wash before running in the direction indicated by the boy.

Later when Wash passed his reflection in the glass window of a business, he had thought that he should have known better than to approach her so. He wondered too whether being invisible, disregarded, might not be less painful than being grotesque.

Thinking back on the incidence with Arorah, Wash clutched his books in his arms and hastened as best he could to the bus station.

Tenth Sequence

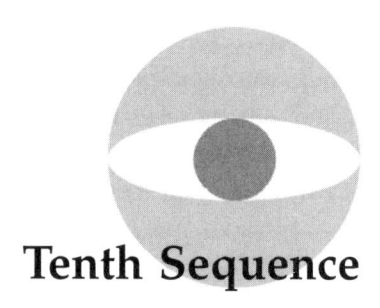

And burn as in an oven.

In the dark house, in the light room, in the "good room," Ladyree Soper Marshall repotted a small ficus tree. Outside the room's wall of windows, the hush of Sunday prevailed. Soon Dr. Prather Lewis would arrive for his afternoon visit for coffee and cake. Finished with their doings, Ladyree's hands slackened and fell. Her fingers were roped in bands of Delta dirt, and the print of her hands was impressed still in the fresh soil around the ficus. She wiped her hands clean with a ragged tea towel and reached to spin the prism in the window for its rainbows. The prism tapped a pane, making a thud, a note from an out-of-tune piano, in the quiet of the Sunday afternoon. The aroma from a baking devil's food cake swelled into the room from the kitchen.

Her work done, Ladyree left the "good room." She checked the cake in the kitchen, cutting off the gas oven . . . *and burn as in an oven* . . . before entering the parlor where Verda Soper read her Bible. Ladyree stopped to sprinkle water over the parlor fireplace. The fire popped, spit, died from orange to gray. She picked up the poker. A tiny cinder bounced from the grate and landed on the skin of Ladyree's hand.

"Ouch," she said.

"Be careful!" said Verda Soper, looking up sharply from her Bible. "And don't raise your voice so. It isn't charming."

Ladyree paused. "Mother, why do you fear fire?"

"My own mother feared fire. Her home burned when she was a child," answered Verda Soper.

"Is that the only reason?" asked Ladyree, certain there was more.

"Well, there are worse things than house fires."

"Like what, Mother?"

Verda Soper remained silent for a long minute. Ladyree waited.

"Well, there's hell and . . . ," Verda hesitated, then continued, "you know. . . . No, you don't know. . . . I actually saw Wash Bibbs afire." Two deep lines formed a tight frame around Verda Soper's thin, colorless lips.

"Is that why you don't like Wash?"

"No, I don't like Wash. I don't like you hiring him to work in *my* yard, *my* home. You spite me."

"Not so. We're lucky to have someone as knowledgeable about the yard and my plants."

"Your plants! Hang your plants!"

"Mother!"

"And he's a reminder."

"A reminder?" said Ladyree. A frowning Verda Soper waved her perfect hand in the air dismissing the question. "A reminder?" Ladyree insisted.

"I see, when I look at Wash, see him scooting on his crippled legs toward me . . . afire. He was . . . afire!" Her bloodless hand, delicate, trembled, the veins atop it pulsed. "Will Milledge claimed Wash a saint. Saints are for Catholics. I'm a Presbyterian!" Disapproval tainted the old woman's words. The Delta was run by Episcopalians and Presbyterians, the Delta, where few Catholics lived, far in spirit from the Catholicism reigning in New Orleans down the river. "A saint? Wash Bibbs? The only saintly man I can remember from my schooling was Savonarola—and they hanged him and *burned* him up."

"The fire, Mother, tell me about it," Ladyree continued.

Verda coughed, seemed to strangle, stared at the ashes of the dying fire.

"I was helping in Will's kitchen," said Verda Soper, "His cook had the flu, and he had a dinner party scheduled."

"Speak louder, Mother. I can't hear you."

"Yes, well, that day Marie, Will's servant, was ironing and cleaning spots with mineral spirits. Wash, her little boy, was playing at her feet, his foot clubfooted, legs bow-bent and crossed on the floor. He was playing with everything. I took the mineral spirits away once. The cooking oil was full in my skillet, too hot, little comma-like flames hopping on the grease surface. The skillet oil sputtered and spotted my clothes and sprinkled Wash. I turned away.

"I looked down, saw Wash, saw the spilled mineral spirits we used for dry cleaning, volatile as gasoline, saw the fire leap from the skillet to him. Then he was a huge flame. You could barely see his arms and face in the blaze. I . . . I . . . A spot fell on me, a small flame at my belly.

"It was so quick. Wash didn't move. He couldn't believe it, didn't understand. Nobody believed it. I didn't help him. I put my own flame out. He moved toward me as he burned. Horrified, I moved away, my eyes fixed on him as he burned. I couldn't believe what I saw.

"Marie whooped, grabbed a rug and rolled Wash in it, snuffing out the fire. I stood there. Will came running in. I . . . I . . . I . . ." Verda gasped. Ladyree did not move.

"The spot on my belly hurt so, but a thousand times less than . . . ." She took a deep breath. "It could have been both of us. My foot almost touched the mineral spirits. We were so near. I . . . I was already afraid of fire."

Verda Soper paused, then continued. "He could have killed me, burned me up, too."

"Wash?"

"Yes. Everytime I see him, I feel nausea. I do not see his ugliness. I *see* fire. Wash should have died. I prayed he would. I wish him dead *today*. Only Will saved him, made him live to haunt me. And, you, you hire him to haunt me. I know you do."

"I hire him because he's good and because we were friends as children before we got too grown-up to be equal friends," said Ladyree.

"You hire him to spite me."

"If I have, I don't know it."

A knock at the front door broke Verda's monologue which had again become barely audible. She struggled to regain her usual steel-steady self.

"You go to the door, Ladyree. It is Prather. Let me have a second to myself."

Ladyree delayed. She still had the fire poker.

"Put the poker behind the tilt table where it's not visible. Go on. Neither Prather nor I have years to wait." Verda's impatience signaled the return of her control.

Dr. Prather Lewis's knock shook the door to the Cyclops House again.

At the entrance Ladyree greeted the old doctor. The spring sun touched his oily white hair that tended to stick together in tapers. The same sun highlighted the wrinkles, splotches, and broken veins of his pale, ancient face. His once imposing stature had become puffy like overripe fruit, and the shape of his belly could be determined, hanging like an empty bag within his trousers. His multicolored tie was a widower's mismatch to a conservative suit chosen by his late wife. A spot of egg yolk dotted the tie.

"Forgive me for keeping you, Dr. Lewis. I was putting out the parlor fire now that the cold seems over."

"Don't believe it. I feel low temperatures still in my flesh. The cold will be back," he said.

"Do you think? Well, come in. Mother's eager to see you."

He sniffed the air. "Devil's food?"

"Your late wife's best cake."

"Prather," said Verda from her chair when he entered the parlor. "Come sit nearby."

There were two chairs near. Dr. Lewis glanced from one to the other. He wavered, then chose, drawing himself up to what he assumed was magnificence to cover a momentary confusion.

"Mother, I'll get the cake. Coffee or something stronger, Dr. Lewis?"

"Coffee. Sherry doesn't agree with me anymore," he said.

In the kitchen Ladyree watched the hot coffee perk against the hollow glass knob of the coffee pot lid and listened to the burpy sound of each eruption of liquid. It perked only at breakfast or for company.

The kitchen was comfortable and homey. It occurred to Ladyree that such familiar things had fooled her into feeling a mother's love where none existed.

She took the just-right cake from the rack within the oven. *And burn as in an oven.* She cut the cake into precise pieces.

As she served in the parlor, she set her careful plan into motion. "I hate to bring this up, Dr. Lewis, but Mother really needs to tell you about her troubles." She paused. "And . . . I know it isn't polite to talk of such things while eating and drinking, but . . ."

"What? What?" said Prather Lewis. "Verda's hemorrhoids acting up?"

"Prather! Ladyree! Not in the parlor over cake and coffee!"

"Nonsense! You Delta Belles claim you aren't born with an intestinal tract. You wouldn't have all these hemorrhoidectomies if you'd been more interested in bowel movements."

"Prather!"

"I've had so many hemorrhoidectomies lately. Terrible ones. My dear wife wouldn't submit to one. She might be here, cooking her own cakes, if she hadn't been so damned dainty about the whole natural matter. The poisons should be emptied daily. Affects the whole system, maybe even the heart. It's too much strain that causes hemorrhoids. And it doesn't help that you Delta Belles call constipation and diarrhea a stomachache."

Verda Soper's perfect hand toyed with the thin handle of the china cup. She did not eat.

"Those young doctors at the clinic say surgery is too hard for me now, but who is to take care of you older Delta Belles when you've never taken proper care of yourselves that way?"

"Are hemorrhoidectomies dangerous?" asked Ladyree.

"No. Nothing to them."

"I've never feared any treatment in your good hands, Prather," said Verda Soper.

"Mother's only afraid of fire and hell," said Ladyree.

"Hell is nonsense," said the old doctor. "There's no hell. We get our hell here on Earth. Hell's a Hollywood thing just like all that propaganda you ladies read once a week under the hair dryers at the beauty parlor in those movie magazines. Those magazines are printed in California, and California is full of kooks, vitamin nuts, and hoodoos. Consider the source. There is no hell, I repeat."

"Prather! The Bible's a good source," said Verda Soper, her mouth prim.

"You can't take the Bible literally, Verda. There's no one, not even God, who'd burn somebody up for eternity."

"Oh, Prather, let's not talk about being burned up."

"Mother," said Ladyree, "make an appointment with Dr. Lewis."

"Not yet. I'm not sure it's necessary," said Mrs. Soper.

"Dr. Lewis, you must insist on seeing Mother."

Before the devil's food cake had been eaten, Verda Soper agreed to an appointment with Prather Lewis on the next day.

As the old doctor began to take his leave, he patted Verda on the shoulder and said, "I'm going to make you good as new. Once I take those hemorrhoids out, you'll be young again."

"Take them out?" said Verda.

"No, you take out gallstones and appendices," said Dr. Lewis.

"You took my appendix out years ago," said Verda Soper.

"And your gallstones?"

"No, I still have my gallbladder," answered Verda Soper.

Dr. Lewis seemed confused.

"Yes. That's right. Just a joke, Verda," he said at last. He changed the subject. "I'm glad Ladyree has the day off and can bring you tomorrow."

Ladyree saw him to the door.

"You take out gallstones," he repeated to Ladyree, his facial expression a little puzzled, a little sad. He wandered down the walk of the Cyclops House to the street.

Ladyree watched him, satisfied.

Eleventh Sequence

Elia Hannah Marshall raised a glass of iced tea from a crystal coaster on the breakfront in her dining area. She carried the tea across two rooms to the verandah in order to sip it while taking in the warming air of the morning. Ice turned and touched the glass sides making the tinkling sound of tiny bells. Elia's back was ruler-straight, her small body thin and uncurved like a reed. She moved herself, young and strong in her middle years as she was, like an elderly patrician woman afraid of breaking fragile bones. Maintaining her posture, she sat in old wicker painted new. A slight breeze from a window opened at the ceiling disturbed her black and silver hair moving strands at her forehead across her milky skin. With a delicate lift of one manicured hand, she neatened the errant hair.

The wicker of the porch chair had been repainted its gleaming white during the recent annual refurbishment of Marshall House as Elia so grandly called her home. Elia turned her head to look out over the grounds. She lectured the new memberships of her garden club telling them that it took a good five years of steady work to accomplish a successful landscape. The grounds of Marshall House had had years beyond the necessary five and with the help of a crew of black attendants, the lawns she now surveyed from the comfortable cushion within the wicker befitted her presidentship of the garden club and her other social prominences.

Elia took her forefinger and pushed the ice in a circle to dissolve a pinch of sugar within the tea. As she did, she thought of what was uppermost on her mind. This morning she had an appointment with Abner Owens, Port City's best lawyer.

Conferring with him would be risky, but she had to have information before she could decide what to do about Mumford. She was determined to protect her inheritance from his rashness, and she realized that her ignorance of the farming operations she depended upon and of money in general weakened her position.

She had chosen Abner Owens to consult because he had probated her father's, Claude Hannah's, will. At the time he had successfully handled a strange and potentially embarrassing problem when a black woman of whom Elia had never heard figured too prominently within the will. Consulting a lawyer on her own would not ordinarily be an easy task for a Delta woman. Business, especially legal business, mostly fell within male purview. Yet yesterday when she had called Abner, she felt no unease. She had dealt with him before, and Abner was not fine, old people, for his money was new and possibly suspect. It helped Elia too that while Abner was tough and whip smart, his wife, a former nurse, catered to Elia often affecting a manner both obsequious and overly deferential.

Elia's social power was a source of pride for her, something she nurtured, something she valued on a par with the money she now sought to protect.

"Mrs. Marshall, the car is ready." Sam, Elia's chauffeur, had appeared.

The car moved slowly around the circular drive and veered left and onto the highway toward Port City. Elia rode in the back of her elegant new Packard. Sam in front wore a black suit, white shirt, tie, and cap. Mumford and Spring occasionally referred to Elia as La Grande Queenie, but their ridicule did not move her. Elia's mother, Jennie, who had never learned to drive, had traveled in the same way.

Gazing out the car window, not seeing the familiar rush-by of fields, Elia continued to think of her money concerns.

Claude Hannah had taught her that money was a medium of exchange. Some people exchanged it for comfort, for an elusive security, for various reasons in varied degrees. Elia feared that Mumford wished to exchange it for some kind of glory, an unfathomable desire to her, and she knew that he often dangerously disregarded money when it was necessary to fuel his aims. Her father had admitted his preference to exchange money for power. She herself wished it to support her own brand of power, social power.

Elia's father had been self-made, taking his wife's small farm-related assets and, contrary to what Mumford claimed, making them large and more diverse. Her mother was of old stock in a South where blood counted, since money was scarce. Elia's father's roughness made her wince on occasion despite her high regard for him. Her mother probably overschooled Elia in her own socially lopsided values and

Sally Bolding

Southern niceties to compensate for Claude Hannah's low beginnings. Hannah accused his wife of spoiling Elia, making her a "hothouse plant." He doted on his only child by his legal wife, but he often sought to toughen her, speaking and treating her like his equal. Elia thought of herself as tough, but believed at the same time a hothouse was necessary for her well-being. She had to protect her money, protect it from Mumford's rashness. Claude Hannah had taught Elia much about the value of money. She accepted his edicts. Never diminish your capital. Much in life, he had said, lets you down, not money. Now that he was gone, she must assume responsibility for the money. It fed her. It fed her social needs.

The car moved onto Jeff Davis Avenue, an old residential way where many of Elia's contemporaries had been reared and which was the main lead into the downtown next to the river. A cathedral ceiling of curved oaks extended over the street lined with comfortable homes. The grass median separating the lanes had been planted with spring bulbs as a project by Elia's garden club.

They arrived in front of the building where, on the top and third floor in his offices, Abner Owens practiced law. They slant-parked in front of Paxton's, which occupied the down level. Elia and her mother had both purchased their trousseaux at Paxton's, the oldest retail store in the county.

Elia greeted familiar people crossing on the wide sidewalk in front of the store as she headed for a door leading to the one elevator of the building. Her smile faded when Ham Vance suddenly exited the door. He stood aside for her, ducking his head slightly to half-hide a run of his eyes over the lines of Elia's body. No one else would have dared be so crude. She ignored him and brushed past him and into the elevator.

Before she entered Abner's offices, her annoyance at Ham Vance had dissipated. Abner's secretary Ruby showed Elia into the lawyer's office at once. He stood behind his desk reading a letter spread over the rich wood top of his desk. He was laughing. At once he looked up. Elia always was surprised at how attractive a man was Abner Owens, well-built, a good height, a large head heavy in premature gray hair, his features angular and strong. He was the only man Elia knew in Port City who wore custom-made suits. Abner came around his desk and took her hand.

"Elia," he said.

"Abner, how good of you to see me on short notice," she said.

"What made you laugh?"

He laughed again. "Max Durham sent me information about a soil test on some new land I got as a fee. Either he or that simple secretary of his signed the letter 'Friendly yours, Max Durham.'" He paused. "Excuse my unkindness, but I'm sure he dictated 'Friendly yours, M-M-M-Max Durham.'"

Elia smiled.

Max Durham stuttered. Abner still held her hand.

"Come. Be seated." He led her to a comfortable chair. Abner Owens was a courtly man. Sometimes, Elia believed, he exaggerated his mannerliness to play a game with himself for his private amusement. Today she perceived no self-mockery.

He released her hand at last and returning behind his desk and to his chair, he fronted her and searched her face with his black, burnt-like eyes. "Well, my dear, what can I do for you?"

She looked down to her lap, his eyes having distracted her, and drew in her breath. "Abner, I want to be as candid as I dare. I have two things to discuss with you—one about my own situation, the other about a college roommate of mine whom I've kept up with all these years."

"I see," said Abner Owens, nodding, his attention strong, his eyes steady.

"My father's money is now my responsibility."

"Not Mumford's?"

"No. I realize that my father and Mumford have always handled the money, though differently, but now that my father is dead, I want to do the managing of his money myself. I want to learn—let me repeat, to learn—to invest, to move investments, maybe even to farm myself. Most women do not bother. I think this is a mistake."

"You are right."

"My father balanced moving his money around. Bonds, farm land for real estate, a few stocks. I don't know all the details really."

"He was right to diversify. I hope he delved into no commodity trading. Commodities are agrarian in nature. We are an agrarian society, but commodities are too risky despite being in our purview." Abner Owens had lost some money in commodities last week.

"I barely comprehend your words, Abner. But I was always a fair study, though I often hid the fact from my beaux."

"Well, Elia." He studied her. He stretched back in his chair. "I can help you invest if Mumford will not."

"I do not want you or Mumford investing for me. I want to do it—whether unseemly for a woman or not, Abner." She spoke his name with emphasis. "Can you suggest a path toward my goal?"

"Mumford's teachings?"

"No. And I want my plans unknown to him."

"Would you be willing to learn from me?" he asked. "I once was a low-paid teacher."

"Yes, I do want someone to teach me, you or someone you'd recommend. You, if it will not impose on you. I would pay you your hourly fee."

He ignored her mention of a fee. He laughed. "I had no idea your mind was so clearsighted. You always have seemed so . . . cool . . . and simpler. I'm glad there's fire there."

"Fire?"

"In your mind, of course," he said.

"Yes."

"Well, let me think for a few days on the matter."

"I do not wish to impose. . . ."

"No imposition. I will present a very lucid plan after much thought. Now, Elia, the other matter?"

"Coffee first, please, Abner."

He buzzed for Ruby to send in coffee. While waiting, Abner and Elia chitchatted. How was his son, Dalton Owens, doing in school? Elia spoke of May Corday's going to high school soon.

Mary Tomato Man, who cleaned Abner's offices and those nearby, brought in and served two cups of steaming chicory coffee before quickly exiting.

"I brought this back from New Orleans. I hope you like chicory," he said.

She nodded. She was ready to speak of the other matter. Divorce. Divorce was rare in the Mississippi Delta. Grass widows, as divorced women were called, had no certain place in Delta society making old acquaintants uncomfortable. Grass widows seemed to Elia to be not only religiously compromised, but . . . déclassé . . . of questionable repute. But money could solve many problems.

Elia spoke each word circumspectly. "My roommate . . . ," she began. "It is a delicate matter, Abner."

"I understand. It is in confidence. A lawyer knows about confidences."

"Divorce is an ugly word in our world, Abner," she said.

"Mumford was divorced," he reminded her.

"Yes, but people have forgotten, and they are more forgiving of men. Consider Ladyree. She has always been so odd. Divorce is especially bad for women."

"Has been since Henry VIII," he said. "Go on."

"It is . . . I think the word might be seedy." She went on with her fabricated story. "My roommate's husband drinks. Her life is hard. She has asked me to find out about divorce law should she have to resort to an extreme."

"She's your age?"

Elia nodded.

"Children?"

"Two. One underage."

"Is her husband wealthy?"

"To some degree." Elia feared she had revealed too much. She remained silent for a moment. Her mythical roommate must be similar but different from Elia Hannah Marshall. "They have land in Arkansas. There's a nice home." She paused again. "Would she retain the home? What of their land? Most, not all, is in his name. She knows too little as most women do."

"It may not matter whose name it is in. If he is a sot, there are sympathetic grounds for a divorce. You can never tell for sure before a chancery judge, but usually she gets the home, the children, alimony, child support, some property settlement."

"Grounds? Property settlement?" said Elia.

"Well, his drinking constitutes good grounds. Is this well-established in the community?"

"No. She has managed to secret it pretty well."

"That's unfortunate. The property settlement could be less—especially if it's the man's living and his means of providing wife and child support."

"And, other grounds?" asked Elia.

"Is there another woman?" he asked.

"Well, no. . . . A woman? Another woman? Would that help . . . my roommate?"

"Indeed, Elia, I'm surprised you wouldn't know this."

"The law is a strange animal to me. That, Abner, is why I am here." She smiled at him. "I must go." She stood. Abner quickly stood. "May I call you if I need more information for my friend?"

"Of course," he said.

Abner saw her to the elevator. Before they parted he said, "I'll call you soon about your lessons." He bowed his head slightly to one side and grinned. "Bring me an apple next time."

As the Packard moved through the downtown, it passed the home of Mumford Marshall's first wife. The eyelike window of the Cyclops House seemed to watch the automobile. Below the stained glass, Wash Bibbs cut away at an overgrowth of English ivy.

Twelfth Sequence

A young black man carrying a suitcase exited a black-owned taxicab on Redbud Street. His skin was the color of coffee with milk, more milk than coffee. In his face, his eyes were African, his nose was a blunt-featured white man's and his wide mouth a mixture of the races. His tall body was slightly stringy, just growing into thicker muscles. His clothing was out of place, eastern and prep school. His name was Thor, so named as a newborn by the poet William Winston Milledge because he was born to a clap of thunder and the kink of his still-wet hair was tinged with red like a Norse god's. His name was Thor Hannah.

He knocked on his mother's door in the near alleyway. Spring weeds had overcome Arorah Hannah's yard. Thor's knock sounded low as if against a hollow, studless wall.

"She ain't there," yelled a young boy across the alley, the toe of his shoe toying with the dust of the ground.

"Where is she? Do you know?"

The boy did not answer. "You talk funny. You look funny," he said at last.

"Do you know where she is?" he said.

"Ask Miss Mary," the boy said and ran off.

"Miss Mary? Where?"

"Next doe'," the boy yelled back.

Hearing nearby voices, one strange to her, Mary Tomato Man came out onto her porch. "Who are you?"

"Thor Hannah. I'm looking for my mother."

"She's gone. Gone where you can't get her."

"Gone?" He approached her porch.

"Come sit," said Mary Jefferson. They took the two seats on the small porch. Her home was a duplicate of Arorah Hannah's shotgun house. Both were built at the same time as white real estate for black renters who paid weekly. On Sunday afternoons, the owners in their long cars would stop in front, honk, car engines humming, and wait, and the renters would come out to bring forth their meager dollar bills carefully wrapped around change. Both houses had later been installment-purchased at high interest rates, Arorah's through Claude Hannah.

"Why are you here, Yankee boy?" asked Mary Jefferson, Mary Tomato Man.

"I've been sending checks, since my father died, from a fund he made for me. She hasn't cashed my recent check," he said. "I want to see she's all right, and . . . I want to meet my mother now that I'm grown."

"Grown? You're just a boy."

"My father fought a war at my age."

"Claude Hannah. Well, you aren't white enough to help Arorah, I think."

The boy-man drew back. "I'm satisfied with who I am," he said firmly.

Mary Tomato Man studied him a moment. "You can't help much with that accent. You'll have to be quick-witted or quiet to get back north alive and not in a box car."

"I'll manage," he said. "Do you know where my mother is?"

"Jail."

"Lord God! What for?"

"Pulling a knife."

"Lord God!" he exclaimed again. "Where is the jail? I'll go at once."

"Stop! Listen! If you want to help your mother, you'll have to keep your head. You'll have to know what we know." She leaned toward him. "When white folks insult, remember it's not what people do to you, it's what you let what people do to you, do to you. You understand?"

"I'm not sure I understand what you're saying."

"I don't say it so well, but it's got plenty of sense."

He nodded after a minute.

"Keep cool. Stay alive," she continued. "Keep your mouth shut with that accent. Tone down those clothes. You can't help her or yourself by being dead."

Thor nodded again.

"You have a place to stay?" she asked. Arorah's house was locked tight and unsafe.

"No."

"Well, go down Redbud. There," she pointed. "Go to B. T. and Mattie's Homecooking Cafe. They've got rooms upstairs. Tell 'em who you are. They'll know."

Thor got up. "Thanks."

As Thor walked up Redbud Street carrying his suitcase and heading for lodging, he mentally compared his surroundings to those he had left in New Jersey. There since infancy, he had lived with a middle-class black couple with old but broken ties to Port City. Early on, Claude Hannah had made arrangements with the childless couple to protect his only son and prepare him for a fuller life than Port City offered. In New Jersey, Thor lived in a neat middle class neighborhood, had just graduated from an unsegregated school, and had been accepted by a quality eastern college for matriculation. In his northeastern environment, blacks and whites came and went. On Redbud Street, no white faces passed.

A now rare horsedrawn wagon clopped and rolled by making Thor think he had been thrown back in time. The sidewalks in New Jersey were neat. Those he treaded now were cracked and multi-leveled. A breeze lifted litter from a gutter and swept a rain of trash below him dusting his shoes before they crushed the rubble down. The few passersby seemed to move slower than people in New Jersey. In his mind, a word trick. He was grown-up, the passersby put-down.

In New Jersey, there was discrimination, but less blatant, and the effort to hide it diminished its danger. Danger, that is what he felt, something new to him and threatening him, something to beware of as his mother's neighbor had warned. He felt a rush of adrenaline at the thought, but his gait remained steady.

He reached the business of B. T. and Mattie Haynes. He entered their Homecooking Cafe. The tin ceiling of the big drafty room of the old building extended above fourteen feet. Seven scrubbed-clean tables with chairs, a now silent nickelodeon, a long counter before a double door into the kitchen filled the room. In a corner a few groceries were stacked on shelves and for sale. A black wood-and-coal stove centered the restaurant and warmed just enough to quell the lingering chill of an early spring. A slatted stairway crossed up the right wall. The Haynes had decorated the other walls with a chalkboard menu, Coca-Cola and cigarette advertisements, and an old picture of FDR.

An elderly man moved from behind the counter toward him in slow, firmly-grounded steps. "Can I help you?"

"I want a room," said Thor.

B. T. Haynes turned and led him up the stairway. Mattie Haynes met them at the top.

"Wants the other room, Mother," said the old man.

"I just cleaned it, Papa," she said. "Dr. Johnson's napping in the other room. Up all night with a sick lady. Don't make no racket, young man."

"No ma'am," Thor assured her.

The couple shepherded him to one of the three doors in the hallway and opened it.

Inside the room was spotless, smelling of the pine cleaner just used. It was simply furnished, a metal bed, a chair, a small table, and an old armoire once given to the Haynes along with discarded clothing and leftover food by their former white employers.

"That'll be two dollars in advance," said B. T. Haynes. "Give the money to Mother."

She took Thor's bills. She was a large old woman with skinny legs. She moved on them as if arthritic, below her shoes old, their forms lost to her knobby feet.

"We cook the most middle of the day," Mattie Haynes said to Thor. "But us and Dr. Johnson will have sandwiches suppertime if you want to join us."

"Thank you," said Thor. "But I got to go to the jail first."

"The jail?" said B. T. Haynes.

"My mother, Arorah Hannah, she's there."

The old man sat in the chair, his wife on the bed, Thor still standing. A draft from beneath the shade and through the net curtaining at the one window turned the small room's close air already being used up by the three of them.

"You must call Evelyn, Papa," she said.

"Yes." He turned to Thor. "You better let us get somebody to go with you. You may do harm. Evelyn, our daughter, works with white people at the welfare department. She'll know how to see you safe to your mama."

"I don't need help."

"You don't know the ways. You do what I say," commanded B. T. Haynes.

Anger flashed across Thor's face.

The Cyclops Window

"Now, boy, Papa and me know. Be smart, not angry," said Mrs. Haynes.

"You sleep, boy. You look tired," said the old man speaking now kindly. "We'll wake you for supper. Evelyn can take you to the jail in the morning. Too late now anyway."

Thor acquiesced.

At suppertime, Thor met Dr. Jeff Johnson. The doctor attacked his food with great energy. He was a small wiry black man of early middle years, the electric mat of his jet hair beginning to gray.

"The boy is Arorah Hannah's son come South from North," explained the old man.

"East," corrected Thor.

"East. Northeast. North to us," said Mr. Haynes. "Doctor Johnson tends us here in Port City, but he's got his own hospital in an all-black town up the road."

"An all-black town?" said Thor.

"Only one in America I know of," said Dr. Johnson nodding to B. T. Haynes as he left for the kitchen. "Do you vote up North?"

"Not old enough yet."

"You going to?"

"Yes."

"You know we can't down here?"

"Yes," said Thor.

"Going to, though," said Dr. Johnson between bites. "You going to college?"

"Yes."

"What you going to study?"

"I'm not sure," said Thor.

"You got good grades?" asked the doctor.

"Yes."

"Smart?"

"Yes."

"Modest, too," said the doctor, mirth in his voice.

"Not necessarily," said Thor.

"Well, you ought to plan to be a doctor, lawyer, professional. You like science? Chemistry? Biology?"

Thor nodded.

"Be a professional. Come down here and help us, help your

people," continued Doctor Johnson.

"Here!" said Thor. "Never. Sit in the back of buses, eat pork 'n beans, not vote! No, sir."

"You afraid?" said the doctor.

"Hell, no."

"Damn fool not to be," said the doctor. Thor grimaced. "Ought to come back here. You'll make your life count if you do."

Thor did not speak.

"You know much history?" said Dr. Johnson.

"A little," answered Thor.

"Well, young man, if you want to make your life count, be where the history is made. It is in Mississippi not up North where history's to be made."

Thor listened.

"The spotlight of the nation, you hear me? The spotlight of the nation will be on the South and especially on Mississippi in the next two decades. You'll do well to seize the opportunity to be part of this great history-making of your times, of your people." He paused, putting his fork down. "It's worth more than money, more than comfort, to make your life count. You agree?"

"I think so," said Thor.

"It will take courage. But you've apparently been given much, and you can give back, can help." The doctor's black eyes looked up from his food and seemed to burn into Thor's gaze. "Help, you hear, young man?"

"I'll think about it," Thor said at last.

"Good!" The doctor scribbled his name and address on a paper napkin. "You write me if you wish to know more."

Thor took the napkin. The busy doctor called over to thank the quiet couple standing at the counter who had provided his meal. He rose. "Got a meeting and a sick one, to boot," he said rushing away.

In the morning, Evelyn Haynes Buffton, the child welfare worker at the Mississippi Department of Public Welfare would come and take Thor to the jailhouse.

Thirteenth Sequence

Nathan hated. It mattered that his soul might look like Wash's face as Wash had suggested hate looked on the face of the soul, but he could not help himself. He hated the man who would not love him, he hated his own life, and he hated Port City High School.

This morning he passed the park across the street from the school where the afternoon football practice he often watched as an outsider was held. He wanted to dash across the way onto the school grounds and into the teeming high schoolers waiting for first bell. He wanted to dash into them wielding a mighty weapon and growling like he thought the Neanderthal man he had been made to study must have done in prehistory. He ached to hurt.

Before him the high school grounds, its worn grass crisscrossed by paths, held all of Port City's teenagers. On the playgrounds the students coalesced into a blur of flesh, saddle oxfords, and white socks, football and smart new Eisenhower jackets. A few "going-steady" couples, some rumored to be "going-all-the-way," distanced themselves from the mob.

Nathan hurried not to be late. The stress and physical exertion of rushing eased his previous unrest. He crossed the street bellow, without weapon.

The first bell screamed. Before the wide double entrance of the school, the animating students bunched together and like sand crowding at the neck of an hourglass, pushed into the hallways emptying the playgrounds.

Nathan was last. He entered the cavernous hallways, old, the school built in the 1910s. The students milled about in a fever of clanging metal locker doors—giggling, smelling of warm humanity, pushing, , shoving, touching, and pulling on toward first period classes beginning at the fast approaching second bell.

"Hey, Coach," someone yelled to the football coach making his way through the activity.

Nathan's emotions were quick, ranging widely. Now a deep sadness took him. He wanted so to be accepted, even popular, like the coach, and like Ted Cockrane, Red Ted.

Nathan opened his locker to get his schoolbooks wishing at that moment that he could be freed of his feelings yet despairing at the same time that their burden would always weigh him down.

He moved his hand to pinch a pimple on his chin and somehow a pack of loose notebook paper dropped to the floor spreading there like an oversized deck of cards. Nathan stooped to retrieve the paper. At once he felt bone and flesh slam into his body.

"Watch yourself!" exclaimed Red Ted Cockrane falling farther onto Nathan.

Nathan pulled out of the way as best he could.

"Damn!" said Red Ted. Hard profanity was not allowed at PCHS. Mild profanity was not spoken around nice girls, mothers, mothers' friends; and bathroom slang was slack even among males. "Damn. Damn."

Nathan rolled away, retrieved the papers quickly. Red Ted stood. Nathan at low eye level saw Red Ted's leg pull back as if to kick him and just as suddenly restrain itself against the impulse.

Nathan stood. "I'm sorry," he said.

Ted Cockrane with his shock of wiry, red hair, his muscular body, his great confidence and hasty grin, PCHS's quarterback and the most popular boy in school, glared at Nathan.

"I'm sorry," Nathan repeated.

In the beginning days at PCHS, Nathan had craved Red Ted's friendship. He had gone out of his way to please, smiling, picking up his pencils that seemed to fall with increasing frequency. Then things seemed to go awry. At first Nathan noticed that the more he tried to please, the more scorn he perceived in Red Ted's face. Recently Red Ted had begun to call him "goat" and to trip him in the hallways.

"Gettin' back, goat?" said Red Ted to Nathan. "Wouldn't do that if I was you. You're too puny."

"No," said Nathan, but there was no apology in the tone of the word. Nathan felt too bad.

Ted sensed a different Nathan. "Wait a minute, goat. You weak-kneed . . . you trying to get tough? Huh?"

"No," said Nathan positively. Let Red Ted kill him. He did not care.

"Aaah—" But Red Ted did not finish the swear. "You're making me late for class. I'll get back to you." Abruptly he hurried away to a nearby classroom.

Nathan himself hastened to arrange his schoolbooks and climb the big stairway to the second floor and his own first class. On the windowed landing that broke the stairway, he passed one of the two school janitors carrying a wastebasket smelling of pencil shavings. Above, the other janitor had just begun to sweep now that the students had emptied the halls. He sprinkled an oily sawdust over the wooden floor and pushed the resinous cleaner with his long broom. Both janitors were black. The hired only blacks in the school.

Nathan's discomfort worsened during first class. He remembered that he had not taken out the kitchen garbage at home as Norwood Pankum had ordered. The thought of his father's impending disapproval seemed to affect his breathing. When called to read aloud a poem by Poe, he made the dancing, rhythmic words a dirge.

On the way to second class he passed the boy's bathroom smelling permanently of old urine spilled over the many years. Red Ted would share second class with him.

The roll was being called as he entered the room. The boys were answering "here." The prettiest and prissiest girls were responding with a "present." Red Ted seated in the front row scowled at Nathan as he passed to his own seat in the back row.

Nathan did not participate in the class. He could not bring himself to learning. Near noon, Nathan was listening to his own digestive disorder and the stomach rumblings of the boy in the desk before him when the boy turned and passed him a folded note. Nathan opened it.

> *You are the worst pest in school. Meet me after classes at the foot of the front steps.*
> *Ted Cockrane.*

By first afternoon period, word had gotten to Nathan that Red Ted had challenged him to an after-school fight.

At last he felt nothing, not fear, not hate, not sadness—nothing. He passed the afternoon peacefully, like a sleepy lamb.

The last bell rang. Nathan copied the assignment from the blackboard and placed it with the first period assignment, a reading of Edgar Allan Poe's "Cask of Amontillado." His numbness continued as he left the classroom and headed through the dispersing students toward the foot of the entrance steps to meet Red Ted. At the top of

Sally Bolding

the entrance steps Nathan paused. Through a haze he saw Ted's face lifted toward him. Below his red hair, Ted's eyes were steady on him. A crowd of boys had gathered to watch the fight. Nathan's feelings awoke at a start. He was afraid. But he continued down the steps.

"You tripped me on purpose," said Ted shoving Nathan's shoulder.

"No," he responded, but the word trembled this time. He backed away. A boy behind him pushed him forward.

"Coward, coward, coward," chanted the crowd.

Ted swung at Nathan hitting his chin with a hard blow. Nathan tried to sink into the ring of the boys. He was propelled toward Ted by a student.

"See, he won't fight," said Red Ted. "He's a sneak. He trips you up on the sly, but he won't fight fair."

Nathan straightened. He put up his fists and approached Ted. Ted laughed. A few titters rose within the audience of boys. Nathan and Ted circled. Suddenly Ted struck and struck and struck. Nathan was on the ground. He flung his arms around his head for protection. The blows kept coming. Pain.

He heard someone say, "Enough, Ted."

"Enough, Ted," someone else repeated.

The blows stopped.

Ted began to laugh. "Sure, fellas. Sure. Look at him, though. You think there's a brave bone in his body?" He began what he did well, hollering the Ol' Miss Rebel yell "Hoddy Toddy!" following it with a howl of laughter which in turn led the crowd to more modest laughter.

Nathan remained on the ground as the crowd and their laughter drifted away.

The Trailways bus stopped to let Nathan off on the highway before the Pankum Nursery and Greenhouse. He had missed the school bus. Exiting Nathan bumped his nose. A drop of blood fell and soaked into his shirt already bloodied and disheveled from the fight. But. But he felt no pain. Again he felt *nothing*.

"You forgot the garbage, damn it, Nathan," said his father before looking at him. Then he saw his son. "What on earth has happened to you?" he demanded.

"I got beaten up," said Nathan.

"Beaten up? Well, damn, I hope you did some beating up yourself. What does the other guy look like?"

"He's okay," answered Nathan.

"Well, hell. I hope to God you didn't cry. They would have had to carry me away knocked out before I would have cried."

"I didn't cry," said Nathan dispassionately.

"Well . . . well . . . I don't know what to say to you. Go wash up!"

Before supper, Nathan began to read Edgar Allan Poe's "Cask of Amontillado." "The thousand injuries of Fortunato I had borne as I best could; but when he ventured upon insult, I vowed revenge." The short story told of how Fortunato, lured by the promise of a cask of Amontillado wine was sealed alive in a damp catacomb, where he died. The method of murder brought to mind Nathan's own claustrophobic tendencies. When he had finished the reading, he realized that something within him had been drawn to the protagonist of the story, who, without passion and with skill, had trapped his victim.

Supper approaching, Nathan went into the soil supply garage, which he had feared to enter since being locked in there overnight. Now fear did not enter his mind or body. On a shelf he found some arsenic. He knew from Hollywood movie-making that a few grains each day would make for sickness and eventually death. As he sprinkled grains of the poison into Norwood Pankum's hot tomato soup, he thought, someday Red Ted's turn would come too. Watching his father eat his soup at suppertime, Nathan Pankum continued to feel numb.

Fourteenth Sequence

"I am white. Out. Let me *out*. I am white." Arorah Hannah beat her head against the barred window before darting back into the sun and shadow striping the somber concrete of the cell floor. Frenzied, she moved like a wounded and fluttering bird breaking the meager sun stripes of the dark cell into fragments. In the corner by the ugly bunk, the open toilet was stained and unsightly. "Aaaa," she screamed.

At a desk outside the cell, a young deputy raised his head from a pornographic novel to find Ham Vance standing in front of him.

"She's so fucking noisy, I can't concentrate," complained the deputy.

"Listening to her is better than reading your book," said Ham.

"Yeah. Some imagination. Thinks they're gonna poison her at Whitfield. Keeps yelling about her stomach being eaten up and her intestines melting. Ugh," said the young man. "I hear she was Claude Hannah's whore."

Ham nodded.

"Rumor has it," continued the younger man, "he left her too much money, lotsa money, but Mrs. Hannah's lawyer fixed it. Mrs. Hannah 'bout had a fit."

"Elia 'bout had a fit, too."

"Who?"

"Elia Hannah Marshall, his only daughter," said Ham.

"I don't know her."

"I do. Know her *well*."

Big Ham Vance with his ruddy skin and blunt features, his youthful handsomeness growing puffy, thought now of Elia Hannah as she had been in Port City High School. He had been a football hero and an A-student. Elia Hannah had loved him. When she became pregnant, he had been anxious to marry her, but Claude Hannah had intervened and arranged an abortion. They had thought to elope, but the day he went to pick her up, she was gone. His heart seemed to have been torn out. Claude Hannah would not reveal Elia's whereabouts. A best friend told Ham that most abortions, illegal, were performed in Memphis. Ham borrowed a car, drove to Memphis, searched randomly one city street after another. He made wild visits to the doctors' offices listed in the telephone book. One doctor called the police. A kind policeman sent him home.

His senior year, his high marks plummeted, and he was often too hungover to play good football. There would be no scholarship to college. Out of high school, he took a menial job.

Claude Hannah had claimed his objection to the marriage rested on Elia's youth, but Ham was not fooled. Claude Hannah, a rough man at birth himself, did not consider a dirt farmer's offspring, the son of a widowed seamstress, worthy of his only daughter. Claude Hannah had sent Elia to Europe that summer and to boarding school the next year. When she returned, she hardly knew Ham Vance.

Elia lost, his future derailed, his hurt had turned to gnawing bitterness. Once he had watched his mother weep and had been astonished at himself that he was totally unmoved. He believed a great scarred cave had been struck into his body, replacing his heart, his heart thrown aside.

Then ambition grew and it steadied him. He would get back; he would be good enough. Positioned for a decade now in law enforcement, he had been able to extend courtesies and cover-ups to the prominent. He had built a healthy savings account of due favors banked for his future.

Ham picked up the circle of keys from the young deputy's desk. He unsnapped a pair of handcuffs.

He approached Arorah. "It's time," he said. He unlocked her cell. "We're going to Whitfield."

Arorah rushed to the corner of the cell and grasped the rail of the bunk. Vance spread his arms and crossed to the corner. She slapped at him. He jerked her up by her arm and with sleight-of-hand quickness, cuffed her. She tried to bite his hand, but he knocked her away, offsetting her aim and stunning her.

Arorah allowed him to lead her from the cell aware only that she was approaching sunlight. She looked up at the sun. She looked over to the man who imprisoned her. The sun and the outside air seemed to promise freedom and a new energy empowered her. Suddenly she

Sally Bolding

struggled away. The ex-football player let her break free for a few yards. Then he sprinted forward and tackled her.

A passing officer watched but did nothing.

Ham righted himself and picked up Arorah. She still struggled kicking the air, her legs seesawing, but he carried her away with ease and locked her into the back of his police car.

Outside the city limits, Arorah began to wail. "Aaaaa."

Vance roared out the opening lines of the popular song, *Stardust*. "Sometimes I wonder. . . ." His voice overtook Arorah's screams.

Defeated, she hushed then began to whimper.

"No used crying," he said. "I got no heart especially for Arorah Hannah."

For years an urge for retribution had blighted the hours of Ham Vance's existence. He harbored a terrible need to harm Claude Hannah for the losses the old man had inflicted in his youth. Vance had winced at each successful step of Elia's social and financial advance and used the pain to charge his own determination to get ahead. He would have his own winnings someday.

But now, now he would take a measure against the dead Claude Hannah.

On his left, he drove past One O'clock, the plantation of Elia's husband, Mumford Marshall. On his right, across the highway, he drove by Marshall House, followed by Norwood Pankum's business. Just beyond the far boundary of the Pankum property he pulled the car into a cave of brush growing at a grubby ditch bordering a nursery field lying fallow.

"I'm gonna do it to you. I owe a debt, and my wife's been holding out for weeks. I'm good and ready," Ham said, stopping the police car.

He got out of the driver's seat and spoke to Arorah through the side window glass. "You like white pricks, huh? Well, my peter's white, and it's a big 'un. I once wrote my name in the snow over a 1930 Ford with it."

She saw him outside and coming toward her door. Why had he stopped the car? She squeezed herself to the opposite door, turned, clawed at the outside window, broke a fingernail, felt him at the same moment grab her.

He pulled her out of the car, forced her to the ground.

"Aaaaa. Don't touch me. Your thing is poison."

Ham pulled her dress up. She pushed her knee forward but missed his erection protruding in a slant from his unzipped fly.

"You kick it," he said, "you're dead."

Vance seized her arms holding them back, pried her legs apart with his knee and plunged his penis at her. She screamed. He stuffed a pocket handkerchief into her mouth, excess fabric overlapping her lips like a flayed stopper.

"I'm gonna poison you with my poker." He thrust his member at her genitalia. She was dry. He shoved his fingers inside her, searching for moisture. He found blood. He had torn a vaginal wall. He rubbed her labia until moisture and blood mingled, then entered her. Arorah's eyes, wild and animal, widened and rolled backwards as if he had pushed life from her.

Up. Up. Down. "God damn, so good," he said. Up. Up. Down. "You black whore." Down. Down to the bottom of the earth, sliding up, down, up, down. "God damn. Good. Ugh. Ugh. Ugh." He rolled away.

His grip loose, Arorah scurried out between earth and Vance, and quickly righted herself from a squat. Away from him, she linked her arm to a firm branch, with the other hand jerked the handkerchief from her mouth and with it wiped repeatedly at her crotch.

Ham Vance wheeled himself over the ground, grabbing for her ankle.

She was quick.

Arorah ran from the thicket and crossed the open nursery field. Vance, on his feet, pulling up his zipper, chased. He stopped at the end of the tangle of brush, rushed back to his police car, and sped toward the road that bounded the other end of the field and led to the customer parking area of Pankum's Greenhouse and Nursery. He lost sight of Arorah in the field as he drove.

Before the entrance to the greenhouse-nursery, Vance jammed his foot on the brake, stopping the car abruptly, skidding it over gravel, and jumped out. He leaped toward the direction of the wide field and blindly stumbled at the edge of the greenhouse into a black man pushing a wheelbarrow.

At quick glance, the black man seemed not to have a nose and his eyes did not match. His skin was spotted pink where black skin had been burned, and he limped. He was a grotesquery.

"Can I help you, officer?" said Wash Bibbs.

Fifteenth Sequence

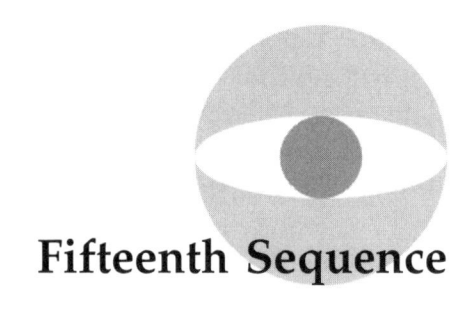

People came to the Lewis Brothers' Clinic from all around the Mississippi Delta and as far away as Jackson, Oxford, and the Gulf Coast. The three Lewis brothers, all doctors, had founded their clinic five decades ago and staffed it with specialists before there were any other specialists in the Delta and few in the state of Mississippi. The clinic thrived over the years. Now only Prather Lewis survived of the three founders.

On Monday afternoon, Verda Soper and Ladyree sat on hard chairs in the clinic's immense waiting room preparing for the usual long wait. Spreading from the full waiting room, wide halls led to the individual specialists' offices. In the halls, an occasional dark antique table or breakfront with a vase of fresh flowers contrasted with clean, light gray walls. Across the street, the hospital used by the clinic was visible from the waiting room through the lead-glass transom topping the entrance doors.

"Mrs. Verda Soper for Dr. Lewis," a nurse called from the hallway. Verda Soper and Ladyree followed her to Dr. Lewis's office. The nurse seated them in the old doctor's smaller, still spacious, waiting room.

"The doctor will be with you soon," said the nurse and left.

Verda Soper rose and began to scrutinize the old Port City pictures lining Prather Lewis' walls. Her late husband, Edward Soper, sat in a bleacher beside the three young Lewis doctors surrounded by half the white males of the town. Two men held a banner reading *Port City Baseball Club*.

"I can't remember the names of the two men holding the banner," said Verda Soper.

"It was a long time ago," said Ladyree.

"Come see. It's Edward."

"Daddy?" Ladyree stood to look.

"I was thirty-eight and pregnant with you when this was taken."

"Daddy looks so young," said Ladyree. "Did you want to be pregnant?" She knew the answer.

"Heavens, no. I was too old. I wanted Prather to abort you. But I'm glad your father wouldn't have it," said Verda Soper. She smiled at Ladyree. "God was right. Always, God is right."

"When did you realize he was right?"

"When your father died and my own family dwindled," her mother answered.

"Oh, God," said Ladyree.

"What?"

"All those years of the first decade of my life, I was unwanted."

"I didn't say unwanted."

"Yes, you did!"

"Oh, hush, Ladyree, you're being a brat. I had no intention of aborting you. I'm glad you're alive. I should think you'd be grateful to me for giving birth to you. My labor was terrible, terrible."

"Excuse me, Mother, I have to go to the bathroom."

"Rest room," corrected Verda. "You should have gone before we left. I always tell you to go before leaving home, but you never do."

Before Ladyree could get away, Prather Lewis opened his door. He nodded at Ladyree and said, "Come in, Verda."

Ladyree hastened into the hallway. There she saw a distraught woman. The woman yelled something Ladyree could not understand.

The clinic manager, a neat, colorless man said, "Shh," to the woman. "Dr. Lewis has a patient."

"Another one to kill," said the harried, middle-aged woman.

Three women, nurses, clustered in the big hallway nearby and looked on. The clinic manager maneuvered the woman away and into his private office. Ladyree pretended not to hear, tried to disappear, turned away toward a breakfront and rearranged flowers in a vase, listening all the while.

"I never," said the youngest nurse.

"It's all over the hospital. All the doctors are worried about it," said the oldest woman.

"What's all over the hospital?" asked the third woman, a redhead.

"Shh," said the oldest woman. "Haven't you heard anything?"

"I'm always the last to hear things," said the redhead.

"Me, too," said the youngest woman.

"Dr. Lewis is performing unnecessary surgery, and some of his patients aren't surviving," said the older and most experienced nurse. "He just lost it after his wife died."

"He's a hundred years old," said the youngest nurse, exaggerating.

"Dr. Lewis is going to get the clinic in trouble if he isn't relieved of his practice. You can't have a doctor who's lost it cuttin' on you," continued the older nurse.

"Well, what can be done to stop him?" asked the redhead. "He owns the clinic."

"His nephew is a doctor at Mayo's. The other doctors called him this morning. He's flying down next week to stop him," said the older nurse.

"Next week! Suppose he operates before then?" said the redhead.

The older nurse shrugged.

Ladyree ducked into the rest room off the hall for a moment and returned to the hallway. But the conversation of the three nurses had confirmed what she had heard in the lobby of the Majestic Theater.

As soon as she reached Prather Lewis's waiting room, he opened his office door and led Verda into the room.

Verda gestured toward the pictures on his wall. "All these people in these old photographs are dead, Prather. I can't believe it, but then I guess I'm pretty near the end myself."

"Nonsense, you're a young girl. You'll live to be a hundred like your aunt." He picked up Ladyree's hand and stroked it. "Your mother needs an operation. I'm going to take out her—" He stopped. "No, no, no. I'm going to perform a hemorrhoidectomy on her."

"When?" Ladyree asked.

"Next week," he said.

"I can't get off next week. It must be this week," said Ladyree.

"Thursday then, Verda," said Dr. Lewis.

"I can't possibly get ready by Thursday," Verda Soper protested.

"I'll help you, Mother. I absolutely can't take time off next week."

"Thursday it is, Verda," said the old doctor. "Check in Wednesday night. I'll reserve a bed for you."

Verda Soper made a grumbly noise, but she followed it with an affirmative nod.

Ladyree held her mother's elbow as they left the clinic by the wide halls.

Sixteenth Sequence

"Can I help you, officer?" repeated Wash Bibbs to Ham Vance.

Vance had come tumbling toward him with the full impetus of his strapping body, his arms askew, hurdling. The heavy metal of Wash's wheelbarrow had broken the force of his fall. Then the moist soil, straw, and nutrients filling the scoop of the barrow had overturned onto the grass, and Vance had rolled side-faced atop it.

Wash reached to help Vance up. Vance waved away his help, rose without aid. The soil mixture spread on his cheek and chin and smeared the coat of his uniform. The hiked coat revealed a belt twisted in its loops and a half unzipped fly.

Ham Vance scowled at the black man. Wash Bibbs sensed the white man's temper triggering.

Norwood Pankum arrived. He had started to run outside on hearing the first thump of the wheelbarrow when it bumped and shook the frail boarding of Greenhouse One.

At the sight of the nursery owner, the officer's chest heaved with a suck of his breath and his threatening anger steadied and seemingly vanished.

"What on earth!" said Norwood Pankum.

Ham Vance towered over the greenhouse owner, but the officer seemed vulnerable to the smaller man.

"She escaped," said Vance.

"Who escaped?" demanded Norwood Pankum. "A convict?"

"No. Claude Hannah's black woman."

"What! His servant?"

"No. *His woman.*"

"I don't want to hear about such things, Vance," said Norwood. His strict rearing in the Piney Woods and the Baptist teachings from his mother's workworn Bible did not allow Norwood Pankum to recognize some of the Delta's looser common practices.

"She's harmless," said Wash Bibbs to his employer.

"Yes," affirmed Vance. "I'm taking her to Whitfield. Not bad crazy."

"Harmless," repeated the black man.

"Well, you look awful, Ham Vance. Anybody'd see you would think you hadn't sense enough to protect Port City," said Norwood.

Vance frowned. Then, remembering his political ambitions, he defended himself. "I'm a first-class officer, Mr. Pankum. I've helped a lot of people."

"Okay. Okay. Go find her, but don't disturb my customers. And move that damned police car out of my entrance. The sight of it might make them nervous."

Once within the police car, Vance took a moment to assess his appearance. He would never get the vote of someone seeing him now. He called to Mr. Pankum. "Sir, that woman's not dangerous. She can't go far in open fields." He managed a polite smile. "It'll be better for you if I come back after your closing time. It'll still be light."

Wash Bibbs lifted a shovel of soil into the righted wheelbarrow as Vance drove away. "She's long gone, Mr. Pankum. There's no worry."

"If you say so, okay." Norwood watched the police car turn onto the highway. "Lout," he said, still annoyed. "Something funny about that Vance."

"Yes, funny," said Wash Bibbs.

Norwood glanced at the black man in the uncertain way he often did. How could you tell what any man, black or white, was thinking—with a face like Wash Bibbs'? But the town people were used to his ugliness, and the black man was a horticultural marvel. Norwood turned away from Wash and, without comment, went back into the greenhouse.

"Yes, funny," Wash Bibbs repeated under his breath. A facial muscle twitched and a strange motion, stopping and starting in odd places, crossed the twisted mass of his face, expressing unreadable emotion. No one could ever accuse this black man of too much smiling. No white teeth in a wide, dark grin. Where was his smile?

Wash Bibbs felt certain the officer had abused his charge. Arorah Hannah's image crossed his mind. How could such a black goddess mask her beauty so absurdly in white powder? Still, the image in his mind pleased. Wash Bibbs wished her well in her escape over the flat countryside.

He finished wheeling the soil, dumped it, and spread it out to dry in the waning sunlight.

"Yes, funny," Wash repeated aloud. The same fitful muscle of his face roused. He was thinking of the appearance of the uniformed Ham Vance, wound up too tight, toy soldier-like, and desecrated with soil mixture. He was reminded of William Winston Milledge's private remark that the uniformed Vance strutted like a German baker.

Wash needed to empty his bladder. He parked the empty wheelbarrow and limped across the rutty fields toward the outhouse near the levee. The outhouse, jerry-built of sturdy weathered wood, measured no more than five-by-five and lifted to eight feet high in the flat fields. It had swept onto the land during the great 1927 flood, lain in brush for years, and been resurrected by Mr. Pankum for Wash to use. A piece of old lattice nailed at the top of the entrance door allowed in small parallelograms of sun. Opening the door threw more light inside, revealing a crude bench with a round hole to sit upon and a deep, limey pit below. Getting used to this primitive facility had taken Wash time. In the Milledge household, Wash had been accustomed to the large, modern bathroom provided there for black help.

Wash pulled the rough knob of the outhouse door shut behind him. In the fetid air above ground, his urine made a strong rushy sound. But this was not the only sound in the outhouse. What did he hear? An animal? A snake? What? He reached behind him to shove the door open and let in a flood of western sun over his back and into the darkness of the outhouse. He stopped to peer into the round hole.

"Aah!" screamed Arorah Hannah. "It is the Voodoo Devil come for me. Aaah."

"My God," said Wash. The door swung shut, and the dark hid his disfigurement. "My God," he repeated. He discovered that he could lift up the seat board from its frame. Only the light coming through the lattice eased the night in the outhouse. Wash extended his hand into the pit. "Come," he urged.

"Nooo. Ugly. Voodoo Devil," she answered.

Wash heard her thrash against dirt and plank walls.

"Don't!" he yelled. "I won't hurt you. I am a *good* Voodoo Devil."

There was silence below. Outside, Wash could hear garrulous rice birds making a late sweep across the fields.

"Arorah," he said soothingly.

"You know my name," she whispered.

He paused a moment. He must be careful.

"Did Claude send you, Voodoo Devilman?" said Arorah.

What should he answer? "Yes," he said at last. "Come," he urged again.

"Send Claude to me, Voodoo Devilman, and I will come."

Wash sighed, discouraged. "Stay, Arorah. The white policeman looks for you. Do not speak when the door opens unless I speak first."

"Send Claude."

"I'll try."

Outside, crossing the still sunlit fields, he ruminated. Whitfield would not help such madness. He did not know what to do, knew only that he could not turn her over to Ham Vance. It was a time like this that he sorely missed William Winston Milledge.

At day's end, Ham Vance returned with another officer, almost as big as he, white and male like all Port City policemen.

Wash volunteered to help search.

"Where do you stay, Wash?" asked Vance.

"In a couple of rooms between the Pankum quarters in the main building and the big greenhouse. It's attached to the breezeway." Wash's words were soft yet precise, dissimilar to the ungrammatical vernacular of most blacks and many whites. It irritated Vance to hear him speak so well.

"Check his place, too," he snapped at the other officer as he started toward Norwood Pankum who had just come outside. "Mr. Pankum, will you show this officer inside? Wash and I'll check the fields. This won't take long."

"I hope not. I've got plenty to do besides this, Vance," said Norwood.

"Let's go, Wash, over to that gully on the end of the field east. That's where she escaped. Could have doubled back. Plenty bushes to hide in there."

Wash followed Vance. Both seesawed and wobbled at times in the clod-rough fields, stepping around and over the nursery plantings on the mounds near the greenhouse where Vance had stumbled into Wash earlier. They reached the fallow field. Wash shot a glance over his shoulder at the other field west where only the ruin of an old shed and the outhouse rose above the flatness of the land.

Could he divert Vance from the outhouse? Would Arorah heed his words to remain mute if Vance entered the outhouse?

In the brush at the gully, Wash picked up a handkerchief from freshly disturbed ground, scratchings of bared dirt within thick scat-

The Cyclops Window

ters of old leaves.

"Some animals been carrying on here, don't you think Wash?" said the officer with a smile.

Wash held up the handkerchief, revealing the Port City Police laundry mark.

Vance snatched the handkerchief away. "Didn't you see me just drop this, Wash?"

Another black man might have smiled. Wash's eyes, one wide, one narrow, stared at the officer momentarily before turning away.

"Hell, Wash, I can't tell nothing about you with that damned face," said Vance. "Come on."

In the west field, Ham inspected the ruin of the old shed. "Nothing," he said. "Ought to tear this junk down." The boards were gray with age. The floor was dirt. The shed was roofed, but open on two sides, window-height, and unprotected from the weather.

"What's that? Let's check it," said Vance pointing to the outhouse. "It's a Chick Sale?"

"An outhouse."

"I want to look."

Vance strode to the outhouse door. Wash limped behind as quick and nervous as a spider. He started to ask to use the outhouse—to warn Arorah—but he decided it might confuse her. He would take his chances. He must not let her hear his voice.

Vance pulled the door open. "God, you use this thing?" Wash nodded. The big man had to duck to enter the door. He looked into the hole. The sun gave only puny light.

"Damn, what a shitty place," he said. "Phew. Stinks."

For a fleeting second, Wash considered how the white man thought an outhouse should smell, then he felt relief for the silence inside and the officer's swift exit. One quick leg up, one quick leg down, Wash hobbled away with the uniformed man.

Vance and the other officer conferred in the parking lot before Vance approached Norwood Pankum at the entrance door of the nursery.

"She's gone, sir. I'll get her, though," said Vance.

"Well, you better not inconvenience Mumford Marshall next down the road. He hasn't the patience I have."

No, thought Vance, and how in the hell would I approach him about his father-in-law's black mistress? "She'll go back to Redbud Street, Mr. Pankum. Can't go any place else. I'll just wait. We'll get her."

After the police car disappeared, black geometric shadows formed behind the buildings and outbuildings of the nursery fields as the sun closed down. The sunset, like a sorcerer, had cast its last lights in an iridescence of pinks.

Wash carried straw to the ruin of the old shed and made a rough bed on the bare ground of its floor. The shed would house Arorah until he could think up better. He turned toward the outhouse.

The sun had gone.

Inside the deep, pitch-dark privy, Wash called Arorah's name.

"Claude?" answered Arorah.

"Yes," said Wash, overcoming his reluctance to answer falsely. "I am here." He lifted up the toilet seat board. "Come."

Wash was unprepared for what happened next.

Arorah grabbed his extended hand and held on. She scrambled over the ledge. On firm floor, she threw her arms around her benefactor.

"Nooo." He pushed away.

"Why?" she asked in the darkness surrounding them, puzzlement in her voice.

"The . . . the Voodoo Devil says we must stay . . . apart or . . . or he will send me back," improvised Wash.

She stepped back to her side of the space. Wash heard her breathe deeply. "Oh, and I am so dirty, too." Indeed, she had been inside the closed privy so long, its smell had permeated her clothes.

Wash took her hand and led her out into the night and toward the shed. The air outside soothed, refreshed, cleared their nostrils, and swept away bad smells.

He led her to the shed ruin. There he found a rusty faucet and cleaned Arorah's feet and hands and face. Later he stooped by her, and she, holding his hand, fell into the comfort of a deep and infantile sleep. Her clasp loosened. Wash removed his hand. He chose not to leave her but to sleep outside the broken wall in the weedy grass. Before daylight he would go for their breakfast. His sleep, unlike hers, was restless. From time to time he stirred and awoke to wonder if his disfigurement would impede his helping the beautiful and childlike woman sleeping near.

Seventeenth Sequence

On Thursday morning, Ladyree adjusted the draperies of the hospital room to let in morning light yet not allow the bright eastern sun to fall on Verda Soper's bed.

"Is that better, Mother?"

"Yes, but I wish I had breakfast."

"Not before surgery."

"I know, but I want it." Verda Soper's head rested on four pillows. "Maybe I shouldn't have this operation. I'm so old."

"You'll live another twenty years like your auntie Maude, Mother, but you have to maintain your health as you go."

"Maybe not another twenty. But I agree that you must keep yourself up. Anyway, I'm here now." Verda Soper had had second thoughts in the days before, but Ladyree checked each one, promising to give her much care and attention.

From the window five stories high, Ladyree observed the diminutive figures of hospital employees crossing the grounds. Most wore white uniforms bright in morning sun against the cool and dewy green grass. But her mind barely registered what she saw. She was thinking of her own reservations about the surgery.

"Mother, you've said you . . . loved me . . . all these years. . . ."

"Of course," said Verda Soper mindlessly. She pushed one of her four pillows deeper behind her head. "The Bible is a study in love, and I am a Christian. It is the most natural thing in the world to love your own—and for a daughter to love and honor her mother."

"I'm . . . not sure anymore, Mother."

"Nonsense. I raised a good Christian daughter." She rearranged another pillow.

"I'm not so sure."

"What do you mean?"

"I find it hard to accept the purpose of my life," answered Ladyree.

"Purpose?"

"To care for you in your old age."

"Yes, well . . . Ladyree! Plump my pillows. I wish we'd brought our own. These are so skimpy."

Ladyree reshaped one pillow at a time, smoothed each case, returning the pillows carefully behind her mother's head.

A nurse and orderly entered. They began to lift Verda from the bed to the stretcher.

The nurse spoke. "Leave your glasses, Mrs. Soper. If you got any bridges in your mouth, you better give 'em to Miss Ladyree."

Verda handed her warm, spit-wet bridge to Ladyree. Ladyree grimaced, found the bedside glass where they had been stored overnight and dropped them into the tepid and slightly unclear water. She caught up with her mother's stretcher and squeezed her mother's hand encouragingly as they wheeled her through the doors of the operating room. Ladyree chose a nearby wooden chair to sit in outside the operating room rather than in the solarium where families usually waited.

As she sat, her mind wandered. She could not imagine herself in Verda Soper's womb. She thought of her father, a vague figure in dim childhood years, a figure bloodless and spermless, but warm and loving. Edward Soper had been very old when she was young, as gentlemanly as his best friend, Will Milledge. She thought of how Verda Soper had sought to snuff out all her fight with frills and sissiness, shaming Ladyree at the least indication of anger or aggression, emotions she identified to her daughter as unchristian. Somehow passion and power had survived in this child who had been oversweetened like the iced tea on so many Southern tables.

Passion? Power? It was hate which had brought both to her. Her plants in the "good room" and her fantasies at the Majestic had been a weak lifesource, only enough to make the days go by. Strong hate had sustained her to this moment.

This moment. This moment Prather Lewis was cutting on Verda Soper.

What would Verda Soper have thought these past weeks of the forces throbbing within her daughter's psyche in such mercurial intensities as to leave Ladyree exhausted trying to sort or pacify them?

Now in her straight chair, a hard wood at her back, Ladyree felt eased. She rested after a storm. She felt as if she might have been spoonfed a warm macaroni and cheese dish.

So she sat for an hour. Then suddenly a nurse rushed out of the operating room.

"Find a doctor. Any doctor in the hospital," the nurse said in a voice of desperation to a passing aide and went in haste to search herself.

"Anything the matter?" Ladyree said when the nurse returned with a very young doctor.

"No, no, Miss Ladyree," said the nurse and disappeared into the operating room as at the same instant, Prather Lewis stumbled past her and into the hallway.

Ladyree stood and helped seat the old doctor in the wooden hall chair.

"Are you well, Dr. Lewis?" she asked, standing over him.

He looked up at her, his colorless eyes watery. "Ladyree, I lost my wife."

"Yes, I know," she said. "Some time ago."

He muttered. He was inaudible. Then he spoke louder. "I'm so old, Ladyree, so very old. I never thought I'd get this old. I used to be a young man." The old doctor looked up and around the hallway. "I used to walk these very halls with a skip in my steps." He stared at his old feet.

"Yes," said Ladyree, unable to think of more words.

A nurse came to lead him away. Ladyree reseated herself, waited. Soon a young doctor came into the hall.

"There's been a complication, Mrs. Marshall," he said in an unctuous manner.

"A complication?"

"Dr. Lewis became ill. I finished the operation," he said.

"The hemorrhoidectomy?"

"The hemorrhoidectomy? Well, there was another problem. Dr. Lewis found gall stones," he said.

"Gall stones?"

"Yes, and Dr. Lewis ran into trouble while he was doing the cholecystectomy."

"Was it serious?"

"Yes. Very serious. Especially at her age. The new intensive care unit is unready, so I'm sending her back to her room. You go there. I'll send an R.N.," he said. "I understand you're very close to your mother."

"Yes," said Ladyree.

"Mrs. Marshall," said the young doctor, turning to leave. "I want you to be prepared for the worst."

Ladyree and the registered nurse sat alone in Verda Soper's room, awaiting the patient. From the shaken and outraged nurse Ladyree learned what had happened in the operating room. Dr. Lewis had tried to perform an appendectomy instead of a hemorrhoidectomy and, finding no appendix in the patient, had begun a cholecystectomy to remove the gallbladder. There was a tremendous amount of bleeding At this moment, one of the attending nurses realized his befuddlement and fled the room to seek another doctor. Seconds later, he made the deadly mistake of clamping off the common duct.

"I'd sue," said the nurse. "No one ever sues doctors, but you should."

"Oh, I couldn't. Dr. Lewis is like family."

"Dr. Lewis should have stopped months ago," said the nurse. "You poor woman. I'm afraid you're going to lose your mother."

They wheeled Verda Soper back into the room.

The R.N. closed the draperies. The room darkened. Verda Soper was not conscious. She was attached to several tubes.

After two hours of silence, seated side by side with the nurse, Ladyree grew restless. She rose and moved to the window, sandwiching herself between drapery and window glass. In the dark of the room she had felt herself in a dream. She had become uncomfortable fearing her mother might awaken and pull her back within her control. She stood for a long time shaking the dreamlike scene away, turning in the flood of sunlight.

In a little while she felt the tap of a finger through the drapery material. She drew back into the cavernous room.

"I want to go to lunch," whispered the nurse. "She may awaken. Someone will check from time to time. Can you manage?"

"Yes," said Ladyree.

When the nurse had gone, Verda Soper stirred. She awoke.

"Ladyree," she said, barely audible. "I feel so weak." She moved. "There is pain." She touched her mouth carefully. "My bridge. Give me my bridge." Ladyree lifted the bridge from the glass of water, shook it, placed it in her mother's mouth. Verda tried to turn.

"Can't they give me something for pain?"

"Soon, Mother."

Ladyree stood over her mother—studied her. Verda Soper opened her eyes.

"Mother, you are going to die."

Verda Soper looked surprised for a moment, then shut her eyes, opened them, gripped the sheet.

"Do you want to know why, Mother?"

Verda Soper's eyes widened. She nodded.

"Do you know that Prather Lewis lost a black patient at the black hospital to butchery? I heard it in the dark of the black balcony at the Majestic. I heard at the same time in the lobby that he was so infirm he was butchering black and white patients. I knew about all this last Sunday when he came for cake."

Verda Soper closed her eyes. "I don't understand," she whispered.

"Yes you do, Mother. You are dying. Dying. You are dying because of me."

"Whyyyy?" Her word was like wind through brush.

"You gobbled up my life. You stole my soul."

"No."

"Yess," Ladyree's word was a hiss. "And burn as in an oven," she said.

Suddenly Verda Soper grabbed the worn sleeve of Ladyree's print dress. Ladyree jerked away, pulling Verda Soper and her tubes with her. Ladyree caught her mother's fall floorwards and shoved her body back to the bed. Verda Soper's other arm came around and circled Ladyree's neck like a noose. The old woman's face was a contorted mass of pain and rage.

"Aaah," said Ladyree, trying to shake herself away. Verda Soper hung on, half off, half on the bed. Ladyree leaped away. Still, the patient hung on, dragging the floor after her daughter, gasping, drowning, and clutching at life.

"Aaah," said Ladyree. She struggled to the door. She heard a clatter. Her mother's bridge hit the hard floor and the false teeth danced out into the hallway like a skipping rock. In the hall, the returning R.N. rushed to them.

"Get her off," said Ladyree. "Please," she begged.

The nurse grappled with both patient and daughter, managing to get Verda Soper back into bed. "There, there, Mrs. Marshall, I believe your mother is dead. Some people do strange things when they are dying." The nurse took Verda Soper's arm from around Ladyree's neck and straightened the tubes.

"Aaah," said Ladyree again, once free. Her mother's mouth was a grim ridge, open enough to reveal the great gap in her teeth. The whites of her eyes were visible in narrow slits. Her empty hand still formed a clutch.

The nurse pulled the sheet over the dead Verda Soper. Ladyree began to shake. The nurse led her to a chair.

"Sit for a minute," said the nurse, "then I'll leave you so you can say good-bye."

"No, don't. I want to go now. I'll wait in the hospital solarium for the doctors to do what explaining they can. Then I'll go directly home."

Eighteenth Sequence

On the levee behind and above the shed where Arorah Hannah still slept, Wash Bibbs sat among spring weeds and watched the sunrise. Occasionally he looked back toward the mighty river then turned at once to the sun and the shed before its splendor. The sun, a golden apple color now, would in minutes magically clear over the just-tilled fields. Wash waited for Arorah to awaken and rise in the opening above her that once framed a window.

The odors of last night had been dissimilar to the pungent scents of broken weeds, mostly wild onions, circling now around him in the breezy air. At intervals in the dark hours, he had awakened to a female smell and the sound of Arorah's cat-purr sleep. How long had it been since he had slept so near a woman? It had been since Lois.

Lois, his mother's age, had worked in the Milledge household, living in its servants' quarters on the far boundary behind the poet's colorful garden.

Early in his puberty, Wash had been caught playing with his member by Lois in the azalea bushes banking her house. That day she had reached into the shrubbery to clasp his hand and lead him into her house and into her bed.

"I need you," she said, "and you need me."

A few years later, Lois had a stroke.

"If I die," she had said, "you can't be shy about women. You're too ugly to be shy. You'll scare 'em, but you gotta let 'em turn you down till you find one who won't."

"I can't do that."

"Then ol' Lois'll be it for you, fella," she had answered.

The sunrise was complete. Wash drew out from his back pants pocket the collection of T. S. Eliot's poetry from Will Milledge's library. He chose to read aloud this morning the "Death by Water" section of *The Waste Land*. He recited aloud as was his custom when he was alone. He knew this poetry almost by heart. He often dreamed that he was dead and floating in a deep of water.

After a sea current had picked Phlebas' bones in whispers in Eliot's poem, Wash stopped reading. His mind turned to Arorah and from Arorah again to Lois.

The hour of Lois' funeral, Wash had remained in the empty, whispery house of Will Milledge. As a rule, he managed to hide emotion in the scars of his face, but this day he hid himself, fearing that unchecked tears would expose his grief.

In the servant's bathroom, a large room of red and white tiles off the back porch, Wash hurled himself from one tiled wall to another. He was a deformed, mad man bounding in erratic motion within the red-white room. He lost track of time. The bathroom door opened. Will Milledge entered.

In time, the old man stopped the young man's fury. Afterwards, Milledge stood in the middle of the room, holding Wash. Quiet tears finally came to Wash, gradually subsided, ceased. The poet then faced Wash to a mirror hung on a toilet door.

"We all have what you look like within," he said. "Yours is without. We are good and bad. You can balance how you look keeping the inside of you good. Then guard your worth because the bad seek company. This way, unsuspected, a precious jewel in the head of a toad, you may be like Flaubert's St. Julian and the few, and be able to reach whatever God is."

He turned Wash around. "Come with me," said Will Milledge. "Let us go into the library and read a few good poems."

And Wash had conducted his life as well as he could according to the lights of William Winston Milledge.

He broke off a wild onion spear from the levee weeds to suck. He wished, as he so often did, that the poet were here to advise him. Arorah, beautiful, simple Arorah, what must he do about Arorah? He ran his long fingers over his scarred cheeks. No woman, certainly not Arorah, would ever see again beyond the ugly ruts he touched. Wash ruled out being loved, but not loving.

Suddenly, below, Arorah rose within the rough boarding of the opening. Wash Bibbs got up. She ducked down when she saw him approaching.

"What do you want, Voodoo Man? Where is Claude?" she mumbled, hiding, crouching within the weathered wooding.

"I . . . I am Claude," Wash lied.

"Ugly man," she whispered.

"I . . . disguised . . . a mask . . ." He was confounded. He faced the empty space above the curve of Arorah's back.

She remained huddled and silent. Wash did not move. At last she spoke.

"You talk like Claude . . . like a white man."

The diction of blacks was hindered by segregated and unequal education, but Wash's diction surpassed Delta whites.

She stood. She looked at him, quickly looked to the fields, backed away, but remained upright.

"I will get breakfast. Wait. Do not leave the shed," said Wash.

She nodded, eyes now on the dirt floor.

Over the uneven fields between the shed and his rooms, Wash limped, his body rocking as his feet hit higher, then lower levels of land. The symmetry of Arorah's body made Wash more aware of his dissymmetry.

In a little while he returned from his rooms with toast and a jar of milk and coffee. As he made his way back to the shed over the fields, his mind worked.

Would his deformity keep the comely Arorah from accepting his help?

The citizens of Port City had long accepted him. The mothers of their children had explained him as just Will Milledge's "Ugly Wash" who helped the great man grow the beautiful flowers that showed up on Sunday-morning altars. Wash had overheard the explanation on the streets while bicycling by on the household bicycle, a wedge of layered tire strapped to his twisted foot to provide length. Always when he heard, he noted the deference in their voices when speaking Will Milledge's name. Port City denied the reality of Milledge's unacceptable sexual preference in order to accept a man who brought nationally notable figures into his home and provided many benefits to the community. Thus, they had accepted Wash because of the poet becoming accustomed to his unsightly body and face. But, thought Wash arriving at the shed, Will Milledge is dead, and Arorah Hannah is child-*like* and not a child.

At breakfast she fidgeted as she ate, but at meal's end, she began to deny in the same fashion Port City had Will Milledge's sexuality. She cautiously called him Claude.

"Now you must stay hidden and quiet here. Do you understand?" Wash said before leaving. She nodded, but he could only hope that she would comply.

He worked the day at the nursery, breaking only once to take her lunch. She seemed pleased by his brief reappearance. She remained in hiding. At day's end, he returned.

"Come, let us go to the levee top," he proposed, "and watch the sunset." In the distance, Mr. Pankum and his son, Nathan, could identify him but Arorah would be only some woman. That in itself would make them wonder, a wonder he could satisfy tomorrow when he made a new living arrangement for Arorah. "Come," he repeated.

From the crest of the levee, the muddy Mississippi had become a molten flow of golden lava. The dying sun, still too high to set, remained a bright yellow in the treetops across the way in Arkansas. Wash and Arorah stood in silence, side by side, high above the river and the low land, around them a splendor of color.

Wash drew out his much-thumbed anthology of poetry. Timidity kept him mute as he read in Arorah's presence.

"Read to me," she said.

"Would you like some books of your own?"

"I cannot read."

He returned to his reading, but he found concentration impossible.

"Read to me," she said again.

Wash began reading Whitman's *Leaves of Grass,* from a page dog-eared by Mumford Marshall the day in the greenhouse he had recited.

Wash glanced at Arorah. He could not determine her reaction. She faced the weedy grass. He continued:

Wash was uncomfortable. He lost his place.

He could not continue.

"Go on," urged Arorah.

She touched the hand that held the book. He looked at her. He let her hand linger then withdrew his.

"I love to hear your voice, Claude. It makes me feel safe. Go on."

Looking for something simpler, he turned the pages of the anthology backwards. He found Thoreau.

Arorah moved nervously from one foot to another.

"You want me to stop?" asked Wash.

"No."

Wash turned the pages forward. He found Lewis Carroll's "Jabberwocky." He read.

Arorah laughed. "O frab . . . frab . . ."

"'O frabjous day Callooh! Callay!'"

"Yes. Read it again. It makes me happy!" she said.

The beauty of the sky and the river and Arorah's beauty and her visible joy in the repeated readings of "Jabberwocky" filled Wash with a drunken delight.

Nineteenth Sequence

"Go to Evelyn," said B. T. Haynes, owner of the Homecooking Cafe, to Thor the morning after the supper with Dr. Johnson, giving Thor foot directions to the Mississippi Department of Public Welfare.

On his way as Thor quickly stepped over the streets and dirt alleyways, the things that had filled his mind and turned it away from sleep during most of the night came back to him. His mother? What was she like? In jail? He could not believe it. His father? He had not known him. One letter from him existed. It was now in his breast pocket. Who was Claude Hannah? Thor would recognize neither parent in person or photograph. He had felt always a pride in his genes because he sensed the deference his foster parents had for both his father, a prominent white, and his mother, the granddaughter of a wise and revered woman in the black community around Port City. Yet his roots, important to him, were unclear.

And what of Dr. Johnson's suggestion? His prediction? Mississippi, the spotlight of the nation in the coming decades? Could he, Thor Hannah, really make a difference?

Here, he thought, here in Port City, there are answers.

He entered the jerry-built DPW offices and approached the receptionist desk. He noticed on the wall behind the receptionist two water fountains, one marked black, the other white. Do you get used to segregation? he asked himself.

"I'd like to see Mrs. Buffton," he told the receptionist.

"Mrs. Buffton? You mean Evelyn," said Catherine Vance frowning. Catherine Vance had a high school diploma, Evelyn Haynes Buffton, a master's degree. "She'll be in soon. If you'll tell me what your problem is, someone else may be able to help you with your case."

"Case?" Thor was offended. "I have no case. Mrs. Buffton is going to help me find my mother."

"Your mother, *boy*?" Catherine Vance was growing irritated.

"Arorah Hannah."

"Arorah something, not Hannah. Calls herself Hannah. Powders her face white. I know her. My husband said something about her the other day. She's crazy. Your mother? I didn't know she had a child."

Spring Marshall, who had come out of the white toilet and was heading toward the white water fountain, stopped to listen.

"Claude Hannah was my father." Angry, Thor did not care that saying it was unwise.

"Hush up, young man!" Catherine Vance rose. She then realized that she had given Thor more respect than she intended. She corrected herself. "*Boy*. Yankee *boy*!"

Spring moved forward quickly to meet the tension. The tone of her voice was commanding. "Evelyn will be here shortly. Come wait in my office. It's next to hers. Catherine sit down." Catherine Vance sat. She looked as if she had indigestion. Spring half smiled at her discomfort. Thor Hannah followed Spring Marshall out of the waiting room and into the partitioned area serving as Spring's office.

"Rumor has it that a new and fine office building is in the making. The agency has grown so fast," said Spring, making small talk. "We should have more privacy, but we don't. I'm Miss Marshall."

Both were now seated. "I'm Thor Hannah."

After moments, silent and uncomfortable, Spring said, "My grandfather was Claude Hannah."

Thor pondered a moment. Then a great laughter broke from him echoing into the neighboring partitions. Someone peered over Spring's wall. For a time Spring lost her poise then her half-smile emerged. She gestured in the direction of a peering intruder to remind him of their lack of seclusion.

Thor leaned forward. He whispered, "I am your uncle."

Again Spring's poise failed her. She frowned before her half smile emerged. All at once she found her own mirth. Together their laughter shook the partitions.

Two intruders, one a social worker, the other the towering DPW Agent Miss Taylor, now entered the office. The social worker smelled of Toujours Moi perfume and Ivory Soap.

"What on earth's going on, Spring?" said Miss Taylor.

Spring did not satisfy the two women. "Nothing," she answered.

As the intruders exited, Evelyn Haynes Buffton entered. She looked at Thor and Spring warily. "Something funny?"

"No," said Spring. "This man wants to see you about finding his mother."

"I know. You're Thor. I've just come from where your mother was." She did not say jail. "She's not there now."

Thor had gotten up from his chair. He extended his hand to Evelyn. She did not take it. "Such manners can get you in trouble in some places," she said cautioning him.

"Where is she?" asked Thor.

"Do you want me to leave?" said Spring.

"No," said Thor answering for both blacks. "No need."

"I'm not sure where she is," said Evelyn. "She was to be taken to Whitfield, but my source, a trusty at the jail, says something out of the ordinary has happened. He can't find out what."

"Whitfield?" said Thor.

"The asylum," said Evelyn.

"I'll go there," said Thor.

"She may not be there. It's a hundred and fifty miles away," said Evelyn.

"What do you mean not there? Where?" said Thor.

"Anywhere—or dead."

"Dead?" said Spring and Thor together.

"Maybe," said Evelyn.

Spring spoke. "I'll drive you to Whitfield, and I'll somehow get my father to find out where she is." Spring's mind spun searching for solutions.

"Just a minute," said the levelheaded Evelyn. "Get your facts first from your father if possible, Miss Marshall." She did not use Spring's first name as Spring did hers from lingering Southern inequalities and habits. "When can you do this?"

"Tonight, I hope," said Spring.

"Well then, do. Then call Thor at my parents' Homecooking Cafe. Then go to Whitfield if necessary." She turned to Thor. "There's nothing you can do until then but stay alive and out of trouble. You're a sitting duck in Port City." She turned to Spring. "Can you help him stay alive, you think?"

"Yes," said Spring.

"Well, I've got to get to work. I'm not a rich cat like you, Miss Marshall," said Evelyn.

"I'll sign out and take Thor home," said Spring.

Driving toward Redbud Street, Spring said, "Would you like to see Claude Hannah's grave?"

"Very much," said Thor.

In the Port City white cemetery divided into Gentile and Jewish sections, near the black community, far from black cemeteries, Spring drove toward the landmark knight-in-armor, larger than life, that centered the graveyard. They parked on a bend of one of the blue gravel trails barely wide enough for current automobiles, trails which wound throughout the cemetery. The cemetery remained wintry and was flat as Delta fields. The trees, heavy trunked, mostly still leafless, rose near tangles of old evergreen bushes and English ivy crawling over gravestones. Spring and Thor walked over a special plot for yellow fever victims felled during a late 1800s epidemic passing a grave that had caved in leaving a coffin-shaped hole in the hard ground. They reached the well-kept Hannah plot begun long ago by Jennie Hannah's family. The monument of Claude Hannah was big and simple and new in its surroundings.

Thor stood before the grave. Spring held back. He pulled his father's letter from his breast pocket and silently read.

When he had finished it, he said, "It's the only personal letter I have from him. I brought it to read over his grave. I don't know why. It really isn't personal. It contains only instructions about money. I didn't know him."

Spring stepped forward. "I can tell you a little. He was a rough man who did well. He could be cruel, could be kind, had his own set of morals and ethics. He loved my mother, his daughter, Elia, as I'm sure he loved your mother. My father and your father did not get along I think because they shared strong personalities and some similarities. Will Milledge admired Grandfather for his courage and intellect. They were friends, good friends. I think he probably named you. The knight that centers this cemetery is on Will's plot.

Thor remained quiet. He put the letter back in his chest pocket. "Why are you helping me?"

"I'm not sure. For a long time I've wanted to talk to Evelyn about some things on my mind, but I've never been able to gather the courage. Maybe I can talk to you."

"Talk," he said.

After a moment Spring said, "I visit black welfare clients on different plantations to determine eligibility. Some of the cabins, like on Will Milledge's old place, are well-maintained, and the system works.

But so many of them are wretched hovels, loose-boarded structures with cardboard sometimes at the windows in winter. I know the owners, the planters, who don't provide fairness to their tenants. I know these men socially, and I can't believe they are bad. Yet I can't condone their neglect. Last week I read the yearly statement of a nouveau riche Middle Eastern man who has done well here and is thought well of. It was a cheat. And few of his statements can be read either because of tenant illiteracy or their knowledge of legal language. He's the only one I know for sure who cheats, but who is to keep others in line if they are tempted? It breaks my heart."

"Breaks your heart? I don't understand," said Thor.

"I was taught that the tenant-sharecropper arrangement was a necessary step to get the South functioning after the devastation of the Civil War. It was, I think, because Will Milledge said so. But the South functions okay now, not great, but okay, and I have seen the evils of the system outright. My people are generous spirited, courtly, not Red Necks, educated, give or take, fair with each other . . . but . . . unfair . . . but why do my people not see what I can't help but see?"

"Profit," answered Thor.

"That's not all of it. Often you don't see the steps you go up everyday into your home. And change is hard for mature people, the people who could make the change." She paused. "I've wanted to discuss this with someone for a long time. I don't know how to change it. What to do." She paused. "Now I'm embarrassed. I barely know you."

"Don't be embarrassed," said Thor. "After all I'm your uncle."

"No not really. I'm adopted."

"You don't know your parents either."

"No."

Back in the car Spring said, "I'm twenty-five years old, too old to be unmarried around here, and I'm not sure what I'm going to do with my life. What about you?"

"I've a girl I'm going to marry. We start college together soon. No marriage until later. But the rest of my life . . ." He stopped. "Have you heard of a Negro doctor named Johnson?"

"No," answered Spring. They drove on. "We have a lot in common. Family connected, parents unknown in different ways maybe, undecided life paths. . . ."

"We've one big difference," said Thor. "The color of our skin."

"Yes," she said. "Listen, what do you have to do this afternoon?"

"I haven't decided."

"Let me paint you," said Spring.

"Paint me white for more in common?" said Thor smiling.

She smiled in return. "No. Your portrait. I'm a fair painter. My studio is home."

In a while Thor answered. "Okay, but I won't enter your home by the back door."

"No." She added, "Damn you're touchy."

"The sins of your fathers," he said.

She grimaced.

As they exited the cemetery through a wrought-iron gate, a black gravedigger noticed them and stared as they passed. Usually in Port City a black man rode in the backseat or chauffeured in the front, never side by side with a white, especially a white woman. The contrast of Spring's fairness and Thor's darkness was inescapable.

Thor was impressed with Marshall House. Spring led him into her private studio from an outside door. Inside her studio, he admired her work before settling into a chair for her to begin his portrait. Anger arose between them from time to time as they talked while Spring mixed paint on her palette before dabbing or rubbing the oils across the canvas. But they were both careful of their words and responses. They were seeking like continental explorers common ground, new ground, between their races for their first time.

Outside the studio windows in the distance on the levee, the figures of a woman and a deformed man could be seen. Neither noticed. The man, Wash Bibbs, was reading "Jabberwocky" to the woman.

Twentieth Sequence

It was tomato soup night again. Norwood and Nathan Pankum ate a light supper together after a main meal at noon prepared by the black woman who also cleaned the nursery. The sun was going down outside the dining nook window over the far right side of the levee. Nathan studied the stark image of a still leafless but budding tree, black and alone against the deepening yellows of the sunset. Norwood and Nathan had ceased speaking to one another except when necessary. In silence Nathan served the hot red liquids and some toasted biscuits to his father.

Out of the quiet, Norwood suddenly spoke. "I haven't been feeling well, Nathan."

"I'm sorry," said Nathan not feeling sorry, not feeling. He had heard his father's vomiting and bowel disorders whenever passing the bathroom door. There was peace in not feeling, and he had come to associate that newfound peace with arsenic.

Nathan watched Norwood lift another spoonful of red soup from the bowl. A sudden rage emerged within him. His fist still held arsenic. He suppressed the urge to bang his fist on the table and tell Norwood that this was what he deserved for being unloving.

Nathan's eyes followed the spoon up to Norwood's face. There he recognized Norwood's suffering. Nathan started to look away.

Stop, he said to himself. He was *feeling*. What did he feel? . . . His father's pain?

Nathan put his fist into his pocket and released the arsenic.

Norwood's arm came forward in a jerk. The soup bowl tilted, and red liquid curled across the table like spilled blood. Norwood shoved his chair back and stood up. He pushed away from the table stumbling toward the door leading to the bathroom. He caught himself on the door jamb. He threw up.

Nathan rose and went toward Norwood as if to help. He gagged at the smell of his father's vomit.

"I don't know what's going on," Norwood mumbled. "Maybe I should go to a doctor."

"Doctor?" said Nathan. A doctor might find Nathan out. He had not thought far enough. Should he stop? Was it too late? Might he go to prison? Be locked up? Yet would his peace leave him if he stopped the sprinklings of arsenic? "It'll pass," he told his father.

Norwood straightened. "I'm better now. I'm going to bed. Clean up the mess, Nathan, would you?"

"I can't," he replied.

"Damn you. Then ask Wash to help." His father staggered away. Nathan heard the slam of his bedroom door.

Nathan disposed of the supper dishes and cleaned the soup spill before making a halfhearted swipe at the vomit with a rag. He could not clean it up. He knew he would only throw up himself. He left the breakfast area and headed down the breezeway toward Wash's quarters.

He knocked on Wash's door. He heard a woman's voice. The voice of the woman he had seen with Wash distantly on the levee whom Norwood had explained as Wash's sister?

"Wash," called Nathan.

Wash peeked from the door's edge.

"Norwood," as Nathan called his father, "he got sick. I can't clean it up. Please help me."

Wash followed Nathan to the kitchen. Nathan retreated to a wall getting as far away as he could while Wash cleaned then took the soiled rags out of the room to the garbage can outside. Nathan watched thinking of his own time of such sickness which had been followed by the awful night enclosed in the soil supply garage. That time seemed long ago and he was a different boy. He did not know why he had not been repelled by his own spew as he was Norwood's. He was just learning about life.

"Your father has been sick for days. His skin is yellowish. He should go to the doctor," said Wash.

"No," said Nathan firmly.

"Nathan?" said Wash questioning the boy's tone.

"I hope he dies."

Wash scrutinized the boy. "He may be a difficult father, but he provides."

"I could run the business," insisted Nathan.

"No. No one would let you. No." He continued, "A bad childhood passes, Nathan. If you don't let it hang on and you accept that you've been gypped, you can find good ways in future years." Wash touched the boy's shoulder. "Mr. Pankum doesn't know how to love. He was probably never loved himself. You cannot ask him to do something he doesn't know how to do."

Later Nathan decided to stop administering arsenic into his father's food. The scare of having a doctor find out influenced him more than Wash's words, for he was unready for Wash's words.

Someday, he thought, I may use arsenic again. Someday, I may find another way. I will look as I go along.

In a few hours, before bedtime, he found himself able to maintain the strange inner peace that had come to him. The practice of quelling his feelings evolved from the days lived with his fundamentalist grandmother when he had squelched the parts of himself she disliked. The peace, the numbness, a new thing, relieved him like a blessing and he was thankful.

Tomorrow he would go to school and afterwards work in the small floral section of the nursery preparing flowers for a funeral. Just prior to supper, he had learned that Verda Soper had died that day.

Twenty-first Sequence

From the hospital, Ladyree had returned to the Cyclops House. The house had seemed empty and drafty. She had spread a pallet on the floor of the "good room" to get the rest she knew she needed. People would be coming soon with covered dishes and sympathy, and the telephoning would begin.

The phrases, "Mother is dead," and "I did it," had rung in her head like pleasant jingles as she had sunk into a sweet slumber.

"Ladyree!" Ladyree turned on the pallet. "Ladyree!" said someone in her sleep. "It is Marsie, Ladyree. I just came on in."

Ladyree opened her eyes. The stylish and slim Marsie extended her manicured hand to help her unkempt friend rise. Marsie hugged Ladyree.

"Thank God you're here," said Ladyree. "I was dreading everybody coming."

Someone knocked on the front door.

"They've started," said Marsie. "You go into the parlor. I'll manage everything."

Marsie smoothed the comings and goings of the long evening. Ladyree, seated in her mother's parlor chair, exhausted from long eventful hours, endured the milling people by relying on the mindless manners of the Southern-lady programming cored within her. At last the day ended. Spent, she fell to sleep while thinking of what remained to be done of her plan.

Morning came. She awoke replenished and surfeited with a sense of relief. Her bed felt unusually comfortable. She did not rise. A great euphoria took her. She felt free, free and powered enough to challenge God, the sun, or any mighty warrior. All the yesterdays had been Verda Soper's. Today was hers and a new beginning.

The clock, unset, still showed time before seven. She got up and went to the kitchen to put on the coffee. She noted that she made less,

Sally Bolding

for one not two people. The perking began. When made, the dark, steamy brew's caffeine lifted her already high spirits.

She danced as she gathered scraps from yesterday's bounty of dishes delivered by the crowd of sympathizers to the Cyclops House, the Cyclops House now hers.

She took the food to the feeding bowls in the backyard. A kindle of kittens and their parents, gray, yellow, calico, clustered around the bowls at her feet. She heard the tinkle of the Christmas bell of CAT's collar in the brush by the lattice and pitched the scraps, the best scraps she had saved for him, beneath the bushy branches growing against the open, layered woodwork. She stretched, like a happy cat herself, in the warm morning sunlight. Her shadow fell in parts across the steps behind her.

She must go in. She had made it clear to everyone yesterday that today she wanted to be alone, and have time to make arrangements for her mother's corpse. And, now was that time. She smiled. She had in mind a great ending for her grand plan. She stretched again, her arms lifted, saluting the spring sun, and went inside.

Ladyree, still soaring, chose to walk to Bill Border's funeral home. Long ago, Bill Border had been her classmate. The Port City National Funeral Parlor rose on Main Avenue a few blocks east of the Majestic Theater. The town's most prominent banker had constructed the building as a home in the early part of the century. Billy Border bought it decades later, turning it into Port City's best mortuary.

The old scrubs still graced the front yard. An ancient willow, a story and a half, grew in a cascade of delicate, arched branches at one side. Billy Border kept the yard perfectly manicured. The huge house, straight lined, two-toned gray stucco, had a magnificent mansard roof of red tiles that gave the grand house a slightly oriental look. Ladyree climbed the imposing front steps to the lead-glass doors, pushed, went inside.

She prepared herself to shock Billy Border. She recalled to herself that he had not always been the town's loftiest mortician, that once as her classmate he had been a pimply, unpopular boy of unremarkable parentage. What she would have him do with Verda Soper's body was not done in the South. It was a practice maybe in India, in old rituals, in California, but never, ever in the Deep South where remains were revered and spoken around in soft, awed voices.

On her way to Billy Border's office through the spacious hallway lined with sitting and casket rooms, Ladyree stopped to peer into

The Cyclops Window

each opened door, looking for Verda Soper's prepared body. She failed to find it.

Billy Border was noted for the contentment on his corpses' faces. Some said they recognized similar expressions on the folk depicted within the inoffensive English countryside landscapes on the funeral home's walls. The landscapes had been chosen and framed grandly by a Memphis decorator hired by the mortician to make up for a taste he rightly felt he lacked. Ladyree thought Billy Border must have found working on her mother's contorted face a difficult job.

His tie and conservative suit coat hanging nearby on a walnut rack, Billy worked at his office desk.

"Ladyree," he said, "I hadn't expected you so early." Flustered, he shoved his paperwork into a top drawer, quickly put on his coat, fumbled with his striped tie. "I hate for you to see me like this. It isn't dignified."

"It's all right, Billy," she said. "We're old friends."

He finished knotting his tie. "That's better, isn't it?" He beamed at her as he might have at his wife before realizing the impropriety of his broad grin. "Oh, I'm sorry. Sit down. I'm so sorry about Mrs. Soper, Ladyree."

"I didn't find her body on the way in."

"We put her in the main parlor like we do all the old citizens. I closed the door. I wanted you to okay her appearance."

"I'm sure it's fine. I came to discuss arrangements . . . arrangements for her cremation."

"Cremation!" he exclaimed.

"Yes."

"But we don't do that, Ladyree. Nobody does. It isn't proper."

"It's as old as ground burial, I think, Billy, and that's what I want done."

"But, Ladyree, people may not stand for that."

"Her burial is up to me. I want her cremated."

Billy was silent a time. "Is it because of the money?" he asked. "The price of a casket here will be less than sending her body east, west, or wherever."

"I haven't a fortune, but it isn't the money."

"Then *why*, Ladyree? I don't understand."

"I doubt anyone will, but this is what I want. People will talk, but then I've never benefited because people haven't talked about me. I want her cremated."

Even the word bothered Billy Border. He shook his head in dismay and fell into a silence again. He had never known this Ladyree Soper Marshall.

"I guess I'll have to arrange it," he said at last. "I can't see how I can refuse you. You'll want her service at the First Presbyterian Church, of course."

"No," she said. "A small service in your chapel will do—and as soon as possible."

He withdrew a fat manual from his bookcase. "California, I guess. We can get her to Memphis by ambulance and fly her to the West Coast." He added grimly, "Shouldn't be much expense getting her back. They might even just mail her back for all I know. Now, let's see." He began to study his manual.

Ladyree interrupted him. "You let me know. I'll go see Mother now."

In the main parlor, Verda Soper's body, lying on an armless couch mid-room, had been draped in a flowing shroud. Her expression was so saintly as to suggest that her soul had already reached heaven. Ladyree hoped not so soon. Who but the dead knew for sure?

She touched her mother's perfect hands, resting above a fold of the shroud. They were cold and rubbery hard. She glanced from her mother's expression to the folk of the English countryside landscapes lining the room's walls, finding no likeness. She lighted the dim room by switching on several sconces on the walls holding bulbs shaped like candles. She closed the open door and stood at the side of her mother's body.

"Mother, do you hear me?" she said. "I'm not finished with you yet. Do you know what I'm going to do with your body?"

Ladyree drew a deep breath. She began to shake. "I'm going to burn your body up. I'm going to surround you in fire until you are ashes. I pray you hear me. I want you to know about the fire."

For a moment Ladyree thought she might weep. Her nose dripped. She fumbled for a handkerchief in her purse, touching as she did a small Bible belonging to her mother, which she had tucked inside the pocket of the purse.

"When you grow older, Will Milledge told me long ago, you forgive your parents for being human. Even being cruel is human, Mother, but it is the ultimate cruelty you find unforgivable for a parent—not being loved at all."

Ladyree withdrew the small Bible from her purse and read.

"'For, behold, the day cometh that shall burn as an oven, and all the proud, yea, and all that do wickedly, shall stumble, and the day that cometh shall burn them up, saith the Lord of Hosts, that it shall leave them neither root nor branch.'"

Ladyree passed Billy Border's son as she left the grand mortuary.

Twenty-second Sequence

Junior Border, Billy Border's ten-year-old son, went to the lead-glass door of his father's funeral home to let in two of his pals. He had been allowed to invite them to spend the night in the living quarters.

In the opened door both friends, classmates who had never visited the home before, stood uncertainly in the fading light of the evening. Then the taller boy, Frankie, his straw hair unwashed, drew himself up, nudged the other boy's shoulder forward, and swaggered in.

"It smells funny in here," said the more timid boy, Herschel.

"Flowers," explained Junior.

"I was wondering," said Frankie. "I thought dead bodies would smell bad, not sweet."

"Not here," said Junior Border. "I think the flowers help. They probably don't smell so good later covered up in the ground."

"Ick," said Frankie. "Imagine rotting in a box under dirt."

Herschel said, "I've never seen anybody dead."

"That's why we're here. He said he'd show us, didn't you, Junior?" said Frankie.

"Shhh. My papa wouldn't like it if he knew."

They passed the room where Verda Soper's body lay and began to climb the great stairway toward the Border living quarters.

"I told my mama I was spending the night with Frankie," said Herschel.

"I told mine I was gonna do it with Herschel," said Frankie. "She don't want me to stay here."

"Well, why not!" said Junior with indignation.

"Well, it's funny living in a home with dead people, don't you think?" said Frankie.

"Not to me. Look around. See this fancy stair rail. See how grand my house is. Grander than either of y'all's," said Junior.

"Don't get mad, Junior," said Herschel. "You'll still show us, won't you?"

Junior nodded.

They reached the top of the stairway and entered Junior's living room where Billy Border and his wife, Mary Sue, sat in overstuffed chairs separated by a radio. Billy Border looked up over the afternoon newspaper. Mary Sue Border turned the radio off and rose to inspect the visitors. The faces of Junior's friends tended to run together for Billy and Mary Sue Border. They were busy people, up and coming, careful and acquiring pretensions. Frankie and Herschel seemed strangers, and they were Junior's first overnight stayers other than cousins.

"You're Herschel," said Mrs. Border to Frankie.

"No'am, I'm Frankie."

"And what does your father do, Frankie?"

"He works at the Yacht Club." The Yacht Club was a huge houseboat anchored on a horseshoe lake cut off from the River. All boaters had motorboats. The river's treacherous currents and logs and debris moving fast from the north toward Vicksburg and New Orleans made sailboating hazardous. Most members frequented the Port City Yacht Club to use its bar.

"What does he do at the Yacht Club?" said Mrs. Border.

"He keeps the bar."

"Oh," she said. She wrinkled her brow. "And your father, Herschel?"

"He's a banker," said Herschel.

"A banker? That's nice."

"He's a teller, Mama," said Junior.

"That's still okay, Junior."

"Mary Sue, stop interrogating the boys," said Billy Border. "You know Port City High School has people from all walks of life. Let the boys be."

"Well, can you boys guess what's for supper?" she said.

"Spaghetti," said Herschel.

"Right," said Frankie. "I can smell it, too, and it makes you not smell those flowers anymore."

After supper, they all settled in the living room and listened quietly to "Inner Sanctum" on the radio.

After the program was over, the parents prepared to retire. "'Early to bed and early to rise, Makes a man healthy, wealthy, and wise,'" said Billy Border. He was not a thinker; cliché wisdom worked for him, and he often shared his enlightenment with his family. The boys left the family living area and went down a wide hallway to Junior's room where pallets had been unrolled on the floor.

It took the boys a few minutes to shake off the fetters of the presence of the Border parents. Frankie and Herschel unpacked while Junior got out their towels.

"I don't need a towel," said Frankie breaking the silence. "I only bathe when Mama makes me."

"I know," said Junior holding his nose.

"Aaah, smarty," Frankie said to Junior. "Bet you don't know what I got in my suitcase."

"Pj's," said Herschel.

"Pj's and more," said Frankie. "Look see." He lifted a small bottle of Mogan David wine and a pack of Lucky Strike cigarettes.

"Wow!" said Herschel and Junior.

The boys put on their pajamas, sat on the floor before a saucer to use as an ashtray, and began to smoke. Frankie blew a smoke ring.

"That's neat," said Junior. "Teach me."

"Teach him later, Frankie. I want to see the bodies, Junior," said Herschel.

"We got to wait until my parents are asleep for sure," said Junior. "I've got a secret," he added.

"Tell," said Herschel.

"You won't tell anyone else?"

"Never," said Herschel. Frankie nodded.

"Someone's going to cremate a body."

"What's cremate?" said Frankie.

"Burning it up. They don't bury it. They put it in a great big furnace, fire it up, and burn the body to a crisp."

"I never heard of such a thing!" said Herschel.

"They do it in strange countries like India and in crazy California," said Junior.

"Movie stars live in crazy California," said Frankie.

"Crazy just the same," said Junior. "And Papa says Port City's gonna fall out about it. It's just not done."

Both visitors shook their heads.

Frankie uncapped the wine. "Let's drink." He lifted it toward his mouth.

"No!" said Herschel. "I won't drink after anyone, and I want some, too."

"I'll get us some jelly glasses downstairs. There's a big kitchen down there that the original owner used that Papa's gonna get rid of someday."

"None up here?" said Frankie.

"In our kitchen, but it's too close to my parents' bedroom. Better let 'em sleep a while."

"They're not gonna wake up after they fall asleep, are they?" said Herschel.

"Don't think so. Mama says Papa sleeps like the dead ones downstairs. She does, too."

"The dead ones." Frankie laughed.

They smoked, told off-color jokes, and complained about girl classmates.

Finally Junior said, "Let's go. We'll have to feel our way downstairs in the dark. No lights."

"In the dark!" said Herschel.

"No such things as ghosts, Herschel," said Frankie. "Now come on. Junior, you lead, and, Herschel, you come with me."

In the dark they crept down the hallway and stairs. Their eyes adjusted to the dark, and on the first floor the outside light at the entrance allowed more visibility into the main hallway.

"Go in the first door at the front and wait. I'll get the jelly glasses in the kitchen," whispered Junior. "Don't turn on the lights. Papa might go to the bathroom and see the light under the door. There's a flashlight on the table by the entrance. I'll bring it."

"Okay," Frankie whispered back. Herschel said nothing, seemed not to move. "Are you there, Herschel? I can't see you, and you're quieter than us both."

After a moment Herschel said, "I'm here."

"Y'all go on," said Junior. "I'll be there in a second. Gimme the wine, Frankie. I'll divide it up into three jellies and put the lids on to carry 'em better."

"Don't cheat," said Frankie.

Junior left the two for the kitchen.

"Come on, Herschel," said Frankie.

Frankie and Herschel slowly and silently moved toward the room where Verda Soper's body lay on the armless mortuary couch.

They went in reclosing the door. Herschel said, "I can't see anything in here, Frankie."

"Must be some heavy curtains. It's black as a coffin in here," said Frankie.

"Coffin?"

Frankie heard a knocking.

"What's that?" said Frankie.

"It's me. I'm shaking," said Herschel.

"Well, don't. Are you scared?"

"No," said Herschel. "I'm just shaking."

"Stop it."

"I can't."

Frankie stretched his arms forward into the dark and moved toward the sound of Herschel's shaking.

"Frankie, I'm shaking on something funny. I think it's a . . . d-d-dead body."

Frankie tripped on the edge of a rug. He pitched forward, caught himself on Verda Soper's body lying on the armless couch shoving it toward Herschel.

"Aaah," said Herschel jumping away.

Thump. The body fell.

"Aaah," said Herschel. It was not a whisper.

"Quiet. Quiet," said Frankie.

Herschel scrambled over the floor until he hit a corner so hard that it disturbed the English landscapes on the two walls. Herschel crouched.

"Where are you, Herschel?" said Frankie.

Herschel began to whimper.

"Don't cry for God's sake. You'll wake Mr. Border if you already haven't."

Frankie left the far side of the mortuary couch where Verda Soper had been laid out and located a wall. Feeling his way toward Herschel he passed thick velvet draperies at a window. He found Herschel sobbing on the floor. He stooped down to put his arm around him. "It's okay. Don't cry. Boys are not suppose to cry."

"I want to go home," said Herschel. "Please, Frankie, let's get out of here."

"Shhh. I hear someone, I think. Maybe it's Junior with the wine." He got up to go to the door.

"Don't leave me alone," said Herschel.

"Don't be a baby. I'm just at the door." He opened it hoping to let

The Cyclops Window

Junior in. Outside he could see a shaft of strong light across the main hallway from where he thought the kitchen must be.

"God damn you, Junior," roared Mr. Border into the hush of the house. "What the hell have you got?"

Junior mumbled something.

"Wine!" Mr. Border continued to roar.

The hall light came on; the kitchen light went off. Frankie closed the door quickly. He listened as Mr. Border dragged Junior up the stairs.

"You and those damned boys. I'll have all of your hides," said Billy Border.

Frankie heard them stepping up the stairway, heard slaps and Junior's, "Don't. Ouch. Ouch. I'm sorry. Don't, Papa, please." The hall light went off.

Frankie rushed to Herschel, grabbed his arm, and pulled him. "We're going, Herschel," he said.

Out into the night they ran for home, shivering in their pajamas.

"Good morning," said Ladyree Soper Marshall.

"Ladyree, good morning," said Billy Border at the door smelling of coffee and fresh shaving lotion.

"I've come with a cashier's check for the crematory, Billy. The banks will be closed Monday. I went yesterday. I wanted you to have it at once."

"Ladyree, I wish you wouldn't do this."

Ladyree smiled at him, shook her head. "It's my decision, Billy." He led her back to his desk, gave her a receipt and began to walk her back to the entrance.

"Do you want to see Mrs. Soper?" he asked.

"Yes, I guess so. Then I want her in her coffin and the coffin closed for the service—ready to go."

Billy sighed. "People are gonna be upset, Ladyree."

He opened the door to the main parlor.

"My God!" said Billy.

"My God!" said Ladyree.

Three English landscapes had fallen to the floor. The corner of the Oriental rug was upturned. Near the center of the room, Verda Soper's body, still perfectly arranged, her expression still fixed in saintly repose, lay on the floor.

155

"I don't understand," said Billy Border.
"I do. I do," said Ladyree Soper Marshall and fled.

Twenty-third Sequence

Outside spring had turned to summer.

Abner Owens had convinced Elia Hannah Marshall that he had the best qualifications to instruct her on money matters. Already he had given Elia what he thought to be satisfactory introductions to government subsidy programs and Delta banking practices. His lesson plan included taxes and real estate and stock market investments. He had, however, another plan apart from these lessons.

On the day after the fourth lesson in Abner's office, Elia folded her notes and tucked them between the pages of a book Abner had located for her. "I think that's all my brain will hold today, Abner."

"You're an excellent student, Elia."

"I have more of my daddy in me than I knew. Abner, you must tell me what you expect from me for your generosity."

Abner rose. "A glass of sherry to end the lesson, sweetie?"

Abner's calling her sweetie surprised and troubled Elia. She hesitated to respond but decided not to risk appearing ungrateful and answered, "Yes, thank you."

He withdrew a crystal decanter from the handsome credenza he used as a bar and poured sherry into a stemmed glass.

Elia took the wine. "Abner?" She proceeded carefully. "What is this 'sweetie' name?"

"Does it bother you?"

"It's too . . . familiar, I think."

"I remember having a crush on you in high school when you were a girl." He sipped his wine. "In those days you wouldn't have looked my way. You were too good for me."

"No, Abner."

"Don't play dumb, Elia. I'm not the best people. You are."

"You don't need to be from the best. My father wasn't. But he was the best," she said adding, "And so are you, Abner Owens."

"Yes, the best lawyer—sweetie." He took another sip of sherry. "Now why shouldn't I call you sweetie?"

"It sounds . . . sounds like the pet name of a lover, Abner. I wouldn't want people to get ideas." She took a sip of her sherry. "Has Ruby left for the day?"

"I let her leave early an hour ago," he said. Moving from a stand, he circled to Elia's back, placed his fingers behind her ears, and started to rub the skin there.

Elia jumped up. "Abner, no!"

"All right, Elia." He was certain she found him attractive, but he returned to his chair.

Elia continued to stand. She put her sherry down on the glass covering his desktop. "I must go, Abner."

"Sit down, Elia. You can't leave like this."

"I'll probably come for another lesson. Maybe? I'll call you," she said still standing.

"Sit down," he insisted. "We'll talk now."

Elia decided to sit. She folded her hands in her lap giving Abner steady attention.

"Elia, you are a smart and attractive woman." He leaned back in his chair like a judge considering a motion. "I could go on, but you wouldn't believe too many soft words. What you must believe is that you are wasted on Mumford. Do you think this?"

"I don't know. . . . Daddy felt so, but then he would."

"I'm not Daddy. And I'm very up front about the fact that I want you. "

"Want me?" she said.

"You wouldn't be wasted on me. You should have noticed me in high school. I was a comer and you were and are quality. I appreciate quality, Elia."

Elia could not speak at once. His words made her heady reminding her of less careful days.

"Mumford will lose all your money, Elia."

Elia drew in her breath before speaking. She had had no one to hear her complaints about Mumford since Claude Hannah's death. She spoke quickly. "He's such a dreamer. He makes money, loses money repeatedly, drives me to distraction. He's already lost some of my initial money or taken it or something. That's the why of these lessons. I must understand. I must stop this losing and making business before it's too late."

"He'll lose everything eventually, Elia. He really doesn't care for money like you and I do. He dreams, as you say, of turning the Delta into a big business. He is a wild card."

"Yes!" she said. "He gambles with our fields, with our lives. I think, for glory or . . . something. I don't know." She put her hand across her mouth momentarily to cease speaking, but she went on. "I couldn't stand to be poor. Daddy used to caution me not to become a hothouse plant—but I am."

"Elia, listen to me. I have made good, but I want more, and I will never be poor."

"I believe it."

"We share regard for money, the power and comfort it brings. We're alike."

"In some respects."

He laughed. "Not all, thank God. Elia, we could be the best team. I'm the best lawyer; you're the best helpmate in the Delta. Nellie Owens wouldn't lift a silver salad fork without your okay. I know dozens of other wives who are just like her. We'd be a magnificent team."

"Abner. Abner? What of Nellie? What of Mumford?"

"I'm a lawyer. You let me tend to that."

"This is silliness," she said.

"Elia, I know you're not the type of woman for a shabby relationship. You must know I'm not a rounder."

"Women are never sure which man is a rounder and which is not. Men talk of fallen women, but rarely mention the man involved."

"Well, I'm no rounder. I don't have time for such nonsense. With you it's different. I'll render Nellie and Mumford harmless. Mumford can be led into other alliances. I don't mean to hurt you, but he's strayed before. A good detective from Memphis or New Orleans could take him out as a threat to you."

"He's strayed before?"

"I didn't want to hurt you. It's necessary."

"Who?"

"I know of only once that he has strayed during your marriage. But another in the period while still married, but separated, from Ladyree Soper."

"Who?"

"I'm not sure you want to know all the details."

"I'll never rest until you tell me."

"No," he said. "And your unease is not the point of my argument, so I'll tell you, but promise you'll listen to me until I've finished what I have to say."

"I won't leave until you wish."

"A few years ago he and Ruby were friends."

"Friends? Yes . . . I never suspected." She took the blow silently. "And . . . within Ladyree's marriage?"

"Ruby had a sister. She died. She had an illegitimate child. A girl."

"Spring?"

"Yes."

"I've always believed that Spring might be Mumford's daughter. He was so insistent on adopting her. I couldn't get pregnant at first. I was afraid that I might be barren."

"Barren? Why?"

She waved away his question. "Spring was such a lovely little girl, and I would have walked on water for Mumford then. I was in love and Daddy was pleased with Mumford at first. Later he complained he had been oversold by Mumford's enthusiasm. Spring. My Spring. She's still my Spring." She shielded her eyes with her hand.

"Let me get you more sherry."

"No. I must go."

"Not yet."

"No. I did promise not to leave until you'd finished. It's just that I didn't mean to weep. It's not for Mumford. It was the shock."

"It's your pride, too. Wounded pride should be like a skinned knee, painful at first, but quick to heal. Aren't you tempted by my offer of an alliance? We might even go to Washington if discrete divorcing doesn't thwart us. If it does, we'll control who does go to Washington." Elia did not answer. "You'll be poor someday unless you do something, and I'm something good to do."

"Abner I am afraid."

"Afraid of what?"

"Afraid an . . . alliance will get out in Port City."

"Nonsense. You're a babe in the woods. This sort of thing goes on anywhere you have men and women and opportunity. We'll just suddenly be a *fait accompli*. Our prior relationship will never get out."

"Never?"

Abner sensed the time for a closing statement had arrived. "Elia, *never*. One must take risks if one is to advance. Careful risks, of course. With my money, yours and your father's, your breeding and social power, we'll be magnificent."

Elia turned her face toward him. He stood and moved around the desk to her. He bent down in front of her chair placing both hands on her cheeks and kissed her. He undid the catch of an antique pearl and gold pin securing her collar and began unbuttoning her blouse.

Abner called Elia at her home that evening.

"Can you talk?" he asked.

"Yes."

"I have your antique and pearl pin."

"I left it! How careless. That frightens me. Carelessness can lead to discovery, and I don't think I could survive discovery."

"You could survive anything."

"Our . . . alliance could lead to great pain," she insisted.

"Alliance?"

"The word seems right," she said.

"Alliance, yes." Abner laughed. "You know truth when you see it. You really have been wasted on Mumford. And what of love, Elia?"

"Love? I guess. . . ."

"What you must love is our thinking alike. I have no illusions about myself or you, Elia. We are a good pair. And I enjoyed our togetherness today."

"Hush!"

He laughed. "When do we have our next lesson?"

She changed the subject. "Abner, you spoke of tricking Mumford into an infidelity. But what of us? Mumford would have his own grounds."

"He is not looking for grounds. We are. You do not look for something unless you think it's there. And I will see that he does not imagine even such a possibility." His voice became less lawyerlike. "Again, when do we have our next lesson?"

"Soon. You know, Abner, it may be a dangerous sign but I feel . . ."

"Yes?"

"I feel less frightened, more optimistic. I'm certain I can handle any Delta notion that being a grass widow is declassé. I will make it the proper silver fork to use, so to speak, if I have to. I am slightly exhilarated. I feel younger. And I don't feel you can hurt me without hurting yourself. Am I right? Yes, I think so. And, Abner, you are a gentleman, I'm sure."

"A gentleman?" He laughed again. "By your lights, I suppose so. I'll call you tomorrow—sweetie." Still in his office, Abner Owens put down the telephone receiver. As he had talked he had toyed with Elia's pearl and gold pin. He hid it carefully behind books held by two bookends on his bar-credenza and doubly concealed it by covering it with an upturned ashtray. He was a rare man who did not smoke, and he allowed only his best clients to smoke. He knew Elia would be back soon.

Twenty-fourth Sequence

Something very special happened a few days after the Picture Show Lady returned to her job at the Majestic.

It was the last showing of GWTW. She had scheduled herself to work the second shift so as to see the remaining half of the lengthy movie. She came early because she was to train a new part-time employee at the concession stand during intermission. N. Nathan Pankum Jr. had been hired to work a few hours each weekday, his weekends left free to continue working for his father.

Ladyree tapped the shoulder of another usher on duty to let her know that her time was up. The other usher left, and Ladyree took her place at the partition behind the last row. The Atlanta fire scene had not finished. Ladyree was tired of thinking about fire.

The disarray of her mother's room at Billy Border's funeral home last week had terrified her. Had Verda Soper come back for restitution?

Ladyree remembered clearly a long ago conversation about death between Will Milledge and her father. Will had said that he did not subscribe to the harp-playing heaven a local minister had depicted in a sermon that Sunday.

"Nor do I," said Mr. Soper.

"Maybe our consciousness lingers, but I suspect it may eventually disappear into the eternal to be reused differently," Will had suggested.

"Who really knows but the dead?" her father had said. "The Biblical saying of Jesus that his Father's house contains many mansions comes to my mind often."

"How so?" Will had asked.

"Maybe mansions means dimensions of reality."

"Interesting. Let's hope we find a good dimension together to continue our friendship if that is so," Will Milledge had concluded.

Was Verda Soper in another dimension? *No.*

Billy Border had called later on the day of the incident explaining that his son's friends had somehow been responsible for the disarray.

"Somehow?" she had asked, and Billy had not been sure. Yet his call had eventually given her back her peace.

On the screen the fire scene ended. Scarlett O'Hara found Tara, her family's plantation, unburned, but in ruin. Ladyree fastened her attention to Scarlett's struggle to maintain Tara and her family and the blacks who had stayed. In the fields, hungry, she unearths some radishes, eats, vomits, and speaks: "As God is my witness, I'll never be hungry again."

The background music expanded, and the camera backed away from Scarlett's darkened figure against the lighter panorama of the Georgia landscape. The screen faded and abruptly the lights came on. The audience, thrust from 1865 Georgia to 1947 Mississippi, vaguely disoriented, stood and began to shuffle through the seats and into the aisles. Intermission had arrived.

Already Ladyree had left her station and crossed into the lobby where Nathan Pankum waited for her at the concession stand.

Ladyree knew the boy only slightly having seen him on occasion at his father's business. She thought him odd looking with his sallow skin and rheumy olive eyes and sensed his silent demeanor masked uncertainty and unhappiness.

Nathan did not look up to see her. Approaching, she studied him further. What little she knew of male adolescence she remembered from Mumford Marshall's stories of a too quick growth, new body smells, heightened interest in copulating dogs, and sexual fantasies. Mumford, who disliked smutty jokes, nonetheless had not been shy about discussing sex.

Ladyree noticed Nathan's dirty hair, that his shirttail was out, and felt a motherly impulse to wash him and straighten his clothing.

While Nathan waited he attacked a cricket on the top glass of the showcase with a trashed popsicle stick. He pressed on the smooth, brown back of the insect until it began to ooze from its belly.

"No, Nathan!" She must teach him to respect all life. What cruelties had he already endured to make him act so? She must teach him that cruelty begets cruelty. "Nathan!"

Startled, he glanced up. He had been caught. "Oh, Miss Ladyree."

Ladyree wiped the cricket away, mercifully ending its life. Below the glass countertop, dark, purple-brown Hershey Bars lined the first shelf. The smell of warm popcorn surrounded the stand, and Ladyree instructed Nathan on bagging and buttering.

A boy came and bought a bag of the popcorn for two young girls.

"I want to be just like Melanie," said one girl.

"Not Scarlett?" said the other.

"I liked Scarlett," said the boy.

The girls giggled and said in unison, "*You* would."

Most Port City girls, like their contemporaries, identified with either the saintly Melanie or the secular Scarlett.

"Nathan," said Ladyree. "About the cricket. . . ."

Nathan hardened his jawbone.

"Crickets are sometimes lucky."

He did not speak.

Unlucky boy, thought Ladyree, you need luck.

All the customers had been waited on when Tudor Jackson and his son, a few years younger than Nathan, appeared at the counter.

"Tudor, may I help you," said Ladyree.

"No, I don't need anything. I just wanted to ask you how you are," said the minister.

"Oh, it's good of you to ask." She could say no more.

"Well, I want you to know that I have no objection to your cremating your mother," he said.

"I suppose there has been a lot of objection."

"Yes."

"I want something, Daddy," said Tudor Jackson's son. The preacher handed the boy a coin, nodded at Ladyree, and left him at the stand to choose his own treat.

Nathan whispered to the boy, "Your father prays over plants."

"They grow more'n the ones not prayed over," responded the minister's son pointing to his candy choice.

Nathan handed him a Baby Ruth. "Goody-two shoes, Preacher's son," said Nathan. The boy frowned, paid, and fled with his chocolate-nut bar.

Ladyree looked at Nathan thoughtfully. "Nathan, what is the matter?"

He studied his oversized shoes. She was making him feel. He did not want to feel.

"Nathan," Ladyree said a moment later, "how are you going to get home in the evenings?"

"By bus."

"Do you wait long at the station?"

"A while," he answered.

"The white waiting room isn't always fun. It's a good spot for bums and winos to sleep. Wash Bibbs is going to be putting out some kudzu shoots for erosion along my bank of Town Creek this evening before dark. If you'll help him, I'll pay you and run you both home. Will you come?"

"Yes, ma'am."

When they had closed the concession stand, Ladyree returned to the theater to watch the second half of GWTW.

Scarlett continues her struggle to save her family plantation. She marries her sister's prospering beau to meet Tara's taxes. He is killed defending her honor. Scarlett, now marries Rhett Butler for his wealth, but she still loves Ashley as Rhett loves her. They have a child, Bonnie Blue. Bad times come. Bonnie Blue dies in an accident. Melanie dies. Scarlett comes to her senses, at last realizing that Ashley has always loved Melanie and that she herself loves Rhett. It is too late.

"I only know that I love you," says Scarlett as Rhett leaves their Atlanta home.

"That's your misfortune." Rhett continues his exit.

"Oh, Rhett!" She runs after him, calling his name. "But, Rhett, if you go what shall I do? Where shall I go?"

And Rhett answers, "Frankly, my dear, I don't give a damn!"

He leaves. Scarlett weeps, but at last lifts her chin, saying she will think about getting him back tomorrow. She will return to the land, to home, to Tara.

The movie ends.

The land was as important to Delta people as it was to Scarlett, thought Ladyree.

After the Majestic closed, Ladyree and Nathan walked the few blocks to the Cyclops House. The days were getting longer. A good hour-and-a-half of light continued. Later Ladyree would forget the walk home but not the rest of the fading day.

They arrived to see Wash Bibbs squatting at the side of Town Creek. The soil on the banks around the water's edge was wrinkled like ancient skin around old lips. Wash punched holes into the earth and plugged them with kudzu shoots from a cardboard tray.

Ladyree walked Nathan to the creek. "Your father says kudzu is hard to control, but that it will stop the erosion. Wash can keep an eye on it when he comes to clip my ivy."

Wash stood. Nathan and Wash nodded to each other.

"I took a Special Delivery package for you, Mrs. Marshall," Wash reported. When they had been a black child and a white child in Will Milledge's house many years ago, Wash had called her by her first name.

Ladyree left them to work. Beside the entrance door, the package leaned. It was wrapped in black.

"Mother," she said aloud. She lifted the black-wrapped box, thinking how small a package to contain the ashes of a human body.

She carried the box to the kitchen where she began to make iced cocoa for Wash and Nathan. Halfway through the chore she cut the gas off beneath the sauce pan of milk, sugar, and chocolate for it to cool and took the package to the back stoop. She watched the dying light in the western sky for a few moments before sitting down to unwrap the container holding the remains of Verda Soper. She opened the gilded jar and smelled her mother's ashes. She rubbed a pinch of grit between two fingers.

Something about the moment did not seem real. "It is over. Really over," she said aloud but she was not reassured. She did not feel the expected triumph. A heavy feeling, like sadness maybe, overcame her. Then a mighty anger returned. She threw the contents of the gilded jar into a nearby planter, half full of soil and broken. "Maybe I will plant something in you, you old devil. Fertilizer! Old devil!"

When Wash and Nathan came to the back door for iced cocoa, Nathan brought a shoot of kudzu he had in his hands when Ladyree had called them to come. When the chilly cup became too cool for one hand, Nathan freed the other by shoving the kudzu down into the broken planter. Ladyree barely noticed at the time.

Twenty-fifth Sequence

Arorah bent downwards, lifted upwards, threw her hands and arms heavenwards as if to hug the sun. The happy laughter sprang over Mumford Marshall's fields near the Pankum property. The laughter blended with a hushy wind and its rattling sound of play in the bare and sticklike cotton stalks broken on the long mounds. The summer had come and gone. It was fall.

A mighty rain had filled the furrows, and one furrow away from Arorah, standing in rainwater, Wash stopped reading, watchful of her, enchanted.

"A spasm of joy," he said.

Arorah showed no understanding of his remark. She swung both arms side to side, the long fingers on her elegant hands shook like slender branches in a swifter wind. "Read it again, read it again," she chanted, dancing about and muddying the water in the furrow next to Wash, the rhythm of her dance matching the scan of the poem. "Read it again."

They continued their walk in the furrows though it was hard for the lame Wash. He did it for Arorah who had always loved playing in the rain and wading in the full furrows outside her grandmother's cabin out on Jennie Hannah's place so many years ago. Again Wash read the nonsense of "Jabberwocky."

"Claude," Arorah still thought of Wash as Claude Hannah. "Do you remember that first lay-by when you came to our cabin and walked in the fields with me?" Lay-by was a short time off season when everyone on the places awaited the opening of the cotton. Arorah's grandmother had always used these summer weeks to pick and can fruit and vegetables for the family's winter food.

"No," said Wash.

"But you must remember the wonderful 'volunteer' we found later that summer."

"Volunteer?" asked Wash.

"You know—from a stray seed."

"Stray seed?"

"From a garden into the fields. So good to find growing, so sweet and juicy when you're so hot and thirsty picking cotton and dragging your sack."

"But," she said, "it was lay-by, and we were playing."

Wash read "Jabberwocky" again.

Earlier in this year's spring, before summer and fall's arrival, Norwood Pankum had demanded of Wash, "Who is that woman?" Wash had allowed no one close enough to Arorah to see the telltale talcum powder on her face.

"My sister," he lied. "She has left her husband and needs to hide from him."

"Hide? What has she to fear?" said Norwood.

"The man is not violent. It's just an end of a marriage," continued Wash. "No trouble. And I'll feed her and work a free day each month for her lodging."

"As long as there's no trouble, Wash. A free day and no trouble. Understood?" said Norwood.

The months had passed. Arorah remained out of sight. During customer hours she listened to Wash's radio in his room off the breezeway sometimes going outside and hiding in the broken lean-to in the fields. At sunset and in the morning, she and Wash walked in the distant fields on Mumford Marshall's place or above on the nearby levee. Before a morning walk, Arorah usually made breakfast carrying the fixings alongside the hobbling Wash to the levee top above the river west and the glow of the sunrise east.

In the room they shared under the guise of brother and sister, Wash slept on a floor pad, Arorah in the full bed. Arorah often teased Wash, pulling him toward the bed, but Wash, mindful that she knew him only as the Voodoo man's Claude, always resisted. He warned her that the Voodoo man might spirit him away if they became intimate.

Once Arorah coming naked out of the tiny shower Wash had rigged up into a corner of the room, had said, "I do not believe the Voodoo man will take you away again, Claude." She had placed her hand over his fly saying, "Don't you miss me, Claude?"

Sally Bolding

Wash had turned away.

Now in the fall fields, Wash stopped reading. They had come to the end of the row and the beginning of the lift of the levee.

"It's almost time to go," said Wash.

"Let's say good-bye to the river," said Arorah.

They climbed to the levee top. They stood in dying Johnson grass, the plague of summer fields, and beheld the river, snarling and bloated from recent and unexpected heavy rains. Its coppery color had dulled from the stir of mud, and its surface water spun with innocent cartwheels that masked below the raging currents. "Last night I dreamed again of the river," said Wash. "When I do I always think of a poem by Eliot that I love. In the dream I was playing in the river's depths with baby bream and other sunfishes. Have you ever had a tiny fish swim by your leg when wading in a creek?"

Arorah nodded. She stroked his arm.

"It is good to be able to tell you little things, Arorah," he said. "Now we must go."

"Oh, but it is always so long until you finish work, and we can come back to the fields."

"We must go."

Before them the trees lining Arkansas' banks were almost leafless and lifeless, a mere smudge of old green on their branches and in the brush.

"Good-bye, river," said Arorah.

Below the levee they waded back.

At the broken shed marking the beginning of the Pankum property, Arorah shook the rainwater from each foot before she slipped on the shoes she had left there in the autumn-brown grass. Wash struggled with his shoes and then led her on toward his room.

They approached the breezeway. Above, the wet clouds of yesterday had vanished. Behind them, the sun from the east, now up a full hour, cast long shadows westwards across the ribboned mud of Mumford Marshall's fields, brown again with stalks and gray with gauzy cotton remains.

"I have a surprise for you," said Wash. He wanted to tell her before they entered the breezeway leading to his room.

Arorah looked at him expectantly.

"We are driving up to Memphis today," he said.

"Memphis!" She had never been out of the state of Mississippi.

"Shhh. Yes, Memphis. Mr. Pankum has ordered some Christmas

plants for the Yacht Club. But you must do something for me before I can risk taking you in the truck."

"Yes?" They entered Wash's room.

"You must clean off the white talc," he said.

"But I cannot," she said.

"You must." Wash asked her as he had often, "Are you ashamed of your black skin?"

"No. I have beautiful skin. I am beautiful."

"Then do not wear white powder today."

"It is safer to be white," she said.

"You must remove the talc if we are to go to Tennessee today," insisted Wash.

"Tennessee. Out of Mississippi," she exclaimed. "I will try to wash the powder." She grinned, moved close to Wash, touched his fly.

He left the room quickly for work.

Outside he was startled to see Ham Vance talking to Norwood Pankum near the truck which had been parked out front for the Memphis trip.

Wash approached them.

"Mr. Pankum, here are two tickets to the Junior Auxiliary dance. The MC lives in my neighborhood and gave them to me. My wife can't go. Maybe you and a girlfriend could go."

"I haven't a girlfriend," snapped Norwood.

Ham Vance knew many things. He knew of Norwood's affair with Ruby. "Oh. Maybe you and Nathan could go," he said.

"Nonsense. Why are you offering them to me? I won't buy them," said Norwood.

"Of course not, Mr. Pankum. I want to give them. I'm just sorry about that incident of the black woman escaping on your property. I wanted to make up for the inconvenience."

"It's okay," said Norwood.

"A lot of people in Port City think I should run for office," said Ham Vance. "I do a lot of good things."

"I guess. But you're not running now, and I'm not voting for you now."

"Well, I hope you will someday," said Vance. He turned to leave.

"Wash," said Norwood signaling for Wash to come. "Here're the keys. Nathan says you want to take your sister with you. It's okay." He dropped the jingling set of keys into Wash's palm.

Ham Vance turned back. "Sister?" he said. "I didn't know you had a sister, Wash."

"Yes, my younger half-sister. My father, Julius Bibbs, raised her in the north."

"Okay. I didn't know, Wash. Thank you for your time, Mr. Pankum."

Ham Vance got into his police car and drove toward the highway. Norwood Pankum went inside to open his business. Wash returned to his room for Arorah who for the first time had left off the absurd talcum.

As Wash and Arorah drove away in the truck marked Pankum Greenhouse and Nursery and onto the highway toward Memphis, he spoke glowingly of Arorah's appearance. "You are more beautiful than ever without the white powder." A mile later, he had another reason to be glad Arorah had cleaned away the powder. By the side of the highway in some brush, Wash saw from the corner of his eye the parked police car of Ham Vance.

On the trip north, the landscape of fields they traversed were strewn with vacant tenant and sharecropper cabins, vacant partly because black World War II soldiers were no longer content with the old feudal system of the Delta and many were leaving the area. The cabins reminded Arorah of her childhood out on Jennie Hannah's place.

"How old is our son now, Claude?" Arorah asked. Not many knew about the birth of Thor. Earlier Arorah had mentioned him to Wash.

"He must be seventeen or eighteen," answered Wash. "How old are you?" he asked.

"Thirty and more, I think. Our son is only a baby."

"Maybe he is older now," said Wash.

"No," said Arorah. She looked thoughtful before speaking again. "You are handsome, Claude, inside your mask."

Two hours later they drove into the shrubbery wholesaler's parking lot in Memphis.

A black worker winked and flirted with Arorah while helping Wash load the truck with gem magnolias, small almost dwarf trees.

"Magnolias for Christmas?" said Arorah. "Magnolias bloom in spring."

"They're Florida magnolias. Mr. Pankum thinks he can trick them into blooming for the Christmas parties. They'll be green anyway."

"Silly thing," said Arorah.

"Would you like to go to a fancy grocery store?" Once long ago he had driven Lois to this particular store, and she had loved it. It stocked gourmet goods and better groceries than any store in Mississippi.

Arorah nodded.

Driving east toward the store, Arorah watched the buildings pass. "Higher. Higher than Port City," she said. And a little later when the buildings became less tall, she said, "I think men like me. The Tomato Man even liked me, but he wanted to poison me like they did Mama at Whitfield." A few more blocks passed outside through the open window. "You know, Claude, if I lost you again, I won't care if they poison me."

"No one will poison you," he said. "We're here." He pulled onto the macadam of the grocery store parking lot.

Inside Arorah's pleasure was evident. She tossed her long crinkly hair in showy fashion as if to greet all the perfect fruits and vegetables neatly rowed before her. Much of the produce had been flown in by air cargo from other climates. At one bin, Arorah picked up one out-of-season cherry, matched it to her painted fingernails, and ran a finger tip over its smooth skin. She felt the fuzz of a peach from faraway in the next bin before noticing the high price of the cherries, whereupon she put the cherry back like a robin's egg into its nest. Seeing the high price of the bunches of cut, yellow chrysanthemums in pails of water in the wide aisle, she steered away to the cabbage bin where she lifted a head to smell its subtle freshness carrying the scent into her body.

A passing black man kept staring at Arorah even though he accompanied his wife, a domestic in a white uniform who shopped for her white-lady employer. Arorah returned his look and, with merriment on her face, glanced at Wash.

She strolled to the meat market. Wash followed behind with a cart. One package-filled hand balancing another, she weighed hamburger.

"It won't keep," she said to Wash. Skirting her reflection in the mirror of the custom meat case, she returned the white butcher's smile in kind, glancing again at Wash.

Down one aisle she found the racks of bread, so many varieties. She caressed the slick cellophane of a lovely and aromatic loaf and slipped it into their cart after catching Wash's nod.

She chose a box of cereal advertised by a brawny male model depicted on the carton.

Later, strolling toward the checkout counter, she halted and looked searchingly at Wash. He nodded. Joyously she returned to the produce bin and stuffed cherries in a bag modestly, then immodestly, and, sighting Wash and his second nod, reached back for two bunches of chrysanthemums.

Afterwards they placed the flowers in water in the truck bed and put the two brown bags of choice goods into the truck cab limiting the space between them. On the drive back Arorah watched the changing landscape like a movie, occasionally laughing for reasons Wash guessed were sheer pleasure. He was aware of her nearness. She smelled of sweet pomade and nature.

The sun had just set when they entered the Pankum Greenhouse and Nursery road. A great orange glow filled the western sky spreading over strings of cirrostratus clouds and making the universe seem afire.

Inside the room they put up groceries stacking the dry goods on the board shelves built by Wash. Arorah brushed his arm, looked to see if he had felt her touch.

"Come, Claude," she said.

He shook his head.

She placed her hand on his fly again.

He breathed in her scent.

"I will read you 'Jabberwocky,'" he said.

"No." She took his hand and drew him toward the bed.

He laughed, pushed away playfully, his little dribble of a nose flexing like a deer's sniffing a strangeness.

She began to undress.

"See, Claude." She swung out and danced a step still holding his hand. "I am a naked brown beauty." She danced another step. "I am good and beautiful."

Wash jerked away.

"Why?" asked Arorah.

"I cannot tell you. You would hate me someday if we loved."

"Never! Do you love me?"

"Yes."

"Why?" she repeated. "Why do you not make love to me?"

"I cannot tell you. Now go to sleep. I have much work tomorrow."

He helped her to bed. She was unhappy.

He snapped the light off.

Later asleep on his pad, Wash woke, Arorah's soft body at his back, her hands cupping his genitals. He had been dreaming that he was whole with straight unburned legs. Arorah kissed his neck, nibbled his ears, ran her hand down the insides of his legs before returning them to his erection. The dark denied his ugliness. He found it impossible not to respond. He turned and met her body. He could not name what he felt—a togetherness, a sense of living and reaching out, a strange gravity leading him back to the beginning of all life.

They rolled playfully a moment, Arorah's mirth, audible yet low, a breathy hum. Wash was careful to hold back. They explored bodies. He pulled her toward his erection. She rubbed her breasts across his chest and breathed deeply as he entered her. Slowly Wash began his rhythms.

"I love you," said Arorah.

The beginning was over. Trust there, bodies free and forceful, their rhythms one, their soft sounds commingled. They loved.

Afterwards Arorah fell asleep and began to breathe, more deeply than her usual cat-purr breathing. Wash held her, holding a dream into the night.

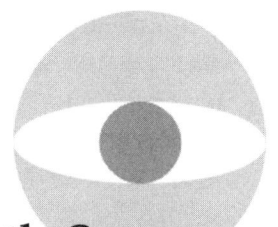

Twenty-sixth Sequence

In the kitchen of the Cyclops House, the Picture Show Lady prepared food for her cats out back.

"So many new kittens . . . and no CAT," she muttered.

The favored CAT had disappeared again during the fevered heat of the doldrum months of summer. She had often though she heard the tinkling of CAT's Christmas collar above in the twisting ivy where now the kudzu had begun to thrive. But since mid-September, *nothing*, and now she feared the early sounds had existed only in her mind.

Her mind? Who she was. Everything had changed these past months. The changes had come in daily descending slips and now felt unchangeable themselves. Where was the power she knew in the beginning after Verda Soper's death? And now . . . her mind? Could she trust it?

Outside in the backyard Ladyree placed the bowls of food about, and the cats and kittens, cur grays and calico yellows, rushed to and circled them, their pelts shoved together like great Joseph coats.

Inside the house again, she roamed the rooms. How quiet. How vacant. Was it better to hate than be alone? Passed by and now alone, too.

Ladyree entered the parlor. It remained exactly as Verda Soper had arranged it so many decades ago. Yesterday when she had come into the parlor, she had thought of Marsie's friend who had lost a child and kept its nursery the same for years. The friend had sealed the nursery windows to preserve the child's breath in the air of the room. Yesterday a draft from the parlor window had touched Ladyree's arm causing her a strange unease, and last night she had awakened thinking she could hear Verda Soper's breathing in the twin bed beside hers. Breath-in, breath-out, breath-in. She had risen from her bed to hunt for the sherry Verda Soper always kept, and Ladyree had begun to keep.

Now in the parlor a chill touched her, but she did not dare to light the fireplace. She turned away to leave the parlor and get a sweater in the hallway.

There in the dark hall, moving her arms upward into the soft sleeves, she remembered that Nathan Pankum would come to visit today. That should fill some of the too-much space of the house, she thought. She would see him in the kitchen and light the stove and pull its oven door forward to stand before and to warm the nearby space of the old kitchen table and its good, but worn chairs. The oven thermostat had not worked for years. The thought of Nathan's visit gave her energy to move on.

In the bathroom she smelled the Lysol she had used to scrub the basin earlier when her energy had been fresh. The smell always made her vaguely nauseous. Years ago Lysol had been thought to be a birth control method. Was the nausea because Verda Soper had used it after Ladyree's conception?

She glanced in the mirror above the basin. Her mouth had thinned; her jawbone was becoming lost in falling flesh. That mouth, that jawbone, is not me. Inside I am still a rose.

Already the day had seemed too long.

"I will feel better in the 'good room'," she said aloud.

The "good room" comforted her little. It felt like a stage empty or with ghosts for actors. She thought of the good times with Mumford in the room. She felt tears behind her dry eyes. She had known for years that it was dwelling on good memories which brought the most tears. Then she recalled that she had not been in Mumford's thoughts for all this time while she herself had continued to dream of him. Day by day passions seeped away. A corpse in a sweet dress, that was what she was.

She sat in an old rocker by the high windows looking north. Outside the fall light had faded leaving a lackluster gray which soon darkened.

"It is going to rain," she said. *No.* She must not talk to herself aloud. Last week her manager at the Majestic had called her in and revealed that she talked to herself. As she rocked, his words in her mind caused her pain.

"Miss Ladyree," he had said. Mr. Manager, as the Majestic employees called him, was forty-seven, his skin pale, his hair dark brown, his body already going puffy. He could be stiff or strict as he had been with the balcony ruling, but he had always been respectful to Ladyree.

She was fine old citizenry which he was not.

"Yes?"

"We've always been proud to have you," he said.

"Thank you, sir."

"But . . . I hated to call you in. I know you must be very grieved about Mrs. Soper."

Ladyree said nothing.

"But we are running a business. Our owner understands only ticket sales and overhead and . . . I guess the expression is keeping up appearances."

"Appearances?"

"Yes." He hesitated before plunging forward. "Miss Ladyree, you have always dressed . . . modestly. But you . . . have always been neat and clean."

"Am I not clean?"

"Yes, yes. I mean, I think, neat." He could not continue for a moment. He had never over the years spoken to her in such a manner or reprimanded her. "Miss Ladyree, please look at yourself." He pointed.

She looked down at her dress. A spot of catsup. She touched the spot.

"And, Miss Ladyree, the hem of your dress has come loose. It was the same last time you wore it. I said nothing then. I do consider our long relationship and that you've lost your mother."

"Yes," said Ladyree. Was she going to cry? Of course, not.

"And you should make sure your slip is not showing and that your stockings have no runs."

"I had no idea I had gotten this way." She was silent for a moment. Was she red-faced? Could a woman of her age blush? "I'm so sorry."

"It's okay. I mean . . . I mean. . . . And, Miss Ladyree, you must stop talking to yourself out loud."

"Do I do that?"

"Yes."

"Much?" she asked.

"Yes."

"I'm so sorry."

"Miss Ladyree, you've never taken time off to speak of. I think it'd be good for you to take a couple of weeks off to gather yourself."

"Am I fired?"

"Heaven forbid! What would Port City say if I did such a thing?"

"A couple of weeks? What will I do?" she said.

"You can gather yourself," he said.

"Gather myself?"

He did not explain. "Miss Ladyree, stay home a couple of weeks. Do it for all of us at the Majestic." It was a plea.

And that had been it.

She felt unbearable mortification at first, but now she was easier. Why should she suffer so. After all the years of finding pleasure and sustenance in movies, her mind had begun to wander too much to follow the storyline.

Her mind was no longer reliable. A few days ago the city had cut off her water because she had forgotten to pay her bill. She had managed to flush the toilet with a bucket of Town Creek water, but she had worried about her plants until running water had been restored.

Thinking about the water bill led her to thinking about her finances. In a few days she would meet Abner Owens in his office to complete the simple legalities of the small estate left her by Verda Soper. She must not forget the appointment.

She fell asleep in the rocker. The rain came. It grew stormy, and small hail hit the attic roof. Only when a strike of lightning exploded into thunder did she awaken. Dazed from the abrupt shake from dreams still unsteadying in her brain, she nevertheless went immediately to the back of the house to check on her cats.

The cats had found safety. She could only see one gray cur curled beneath the hydrangea bush, a shelter of dead blooms, big and shaggy, and wide, still green, leaves.

She sat on the back steps. A single tab-like roof jutted out from the house above her, below a back window of the attic, keeping her dry. High, below the windowsill, a hook held two outdoor torches not used since her father needed light to barbecue in the backyard on Fourth of Julys. A single drop of rain about to fall had collected on the low bend of the hook's curve.

A glass curtain of rain poured down in front of her from the edges of the little roof. The rain streamed across the bottom step falling at one side to form little puddles near the broken pot where Ladyree so many months ago had thrown her mother's ashes.

She looked down. A huge clump of kudzu blackening in the fall weather obscured most of the pot, and she could barely see its rim. Several black stems grew from the planter. They had attached themselves to the gray wooden grooves of the house and, growing upwards, had formed a crude, veined drawing against the pale wood.

"Kudzu in Mother's ashes? I must fix that," she said.

She watched the rain pooling on the backyard ground, filling the empty cat bowls. The single cat under the hydrangea bush was rounded and as still as death.

What had she been dreaming in the rocker of the "good room"? She had been dreaming of scrambled eggs. No. Scrambled brains. Brains and eggs? She had never liked the dish. What was that dream about brains she had had about her mother that morning so long ago in March when she had awakened beside her in her twin bed? She could not recall. It was not important now.

She laughed. "This is not *gathering myself* as Mr. Manager advised me." There was an edge to her laughter.

She tried to remember more of her recent dreams.

"They're gone, too." She continued to talk to herself. Mr. Manager seemed less important.

She looked up into the ivy. So much kudzu there from the shoots Wash and Nathan had put out along Town Creek. She must get rid of it before the dead of winter when kudzu became unsightly. She thought of the highway to Mississippi's capital, Jackson, where the Delta's flatness ceased and rolling hills began. The big trees along that way had become overwhelmed by kudzu planted for erosion. In summer the strangely beautiful landscape suggested prehistory and monsters. In winter the kudzu, black and leafless, caged the trees in heavy, ugly nets.

"Maybe Nathan will help me with the kudzu," she said.

She noticed that the strings of kudzu from the pot that grew on the house had reached the attic window. "It will break the glass," she said. She would uproot the kudzu from the pot, pull it away from the house before it damaged the wooden siding.

She dug her hands into the soil. Soil? Ashes. Gritty ashes. Her mother's ashes. She drew back at once. She grimaced before girding herself to continue.

Hands now through the mass of darkening, shriveling, huge leaves and into Verda Soper's ashes, she located an enormous root. She grasped it, big as an overgrown squash in a summer garden and white beneath the ash, and pulled. It would not come.

"It's gone into the ground," she said.

Wash Bibbs always brought his own gardening tools. If she owned them, she was unaware. She went inside to the kitchen to locate makeshift tools to do the unrooting. There she found a metal scoop and a heavy flat cookie sheet to use as a wedge.

Outside she struggled to cut the roots free with the scoop and to shove the cookie sheet beneath the pot. The kudzu held. She wrestled with the pot creating a minute crevice beneath it, the roots yet holding. She shoved the scoop under lifting the pot a half-inch more. She was tiring. She threw the energy she could muster into hacking the roots with the scoop. Finally she forced the cookie sheet under the pot severing the roots, separating pot from ground. She was exhausted. She retreated to the back steps.

The rain had stopped. A few drops fell from the eaves, but did not bother her. She heard the soft splats of raindrops falling from time to time from the sycamore tree and the bushes in the backyard.

"Maybe Nathan will help me get her into the attic," she said wearily.

She could not give up. At least she could pull the black stems from the house. Again she struggled. The clutching vines would not give. Now she really would wait for Nathan. "Nasty vines," she said.

But inside the kitchen, she saw on the counter the scissors used to cut twine from meat. She picked them up. She would clip around the attic window. She would get the awful vines out of her house. She walked to the door of the attic steps inside the hallway and, carefully avoiding a broken step, ascended the stairs.

At the top she dropped the scissors, her eyes wide, her expression incredulous.

When she went to the door to let in Nathan Pankum, sherry had steadied her.

"Come in, Nathan."

He was still timid around her after all this time. She could sense too that he must have heard something of her sudden vacation from the Majestic.

"Come into the kitchen," she said.

He followed her quietly into the dark hall. As they passed the "good room," she thought again about his timidity. He had been to the Cyclops House many times during the past months. Sometimes he had come to do little odd jobs for which she paid him well to encourage his return, sometimes with a ride home, a few times with a snack—she even paid him for a visit after work as was the occasion this day, a day now grown old. He had so few friends, as few as she. They reached the kitchen.

"It was cool, so I put the oven on to make us warm. I had planned to fix sandwiches and maybe bake cookies, but I didn't. Marsie sent me some homemade pound cake the other day to fatten me up. She worries I don't eat. We'll use what's left. Cocoa?"

"Yes, ma'am." He sat in one of the worn chairs at the table.

At the stove top she struck a match to one of the gas burners, old and charred. After a huff, little arms of blue flame shot upwards into the middle of the blackened, crusted insert of the burner.

What would she talk to Nathan about today? Marsie said some conversations were "uphill all the way." Ladyree often felt this way with Nathan, but his company to her was worth the fare.

Last week she had told him about dances at Ole Miss in her youth where her mother chaperoned, banquets before the dances where silver spoons, a third size less than demitasse spoons, were given as favors, dances where William Falkner's[*] brother had repeatedly cut in fancying the company of a so-called Delta Belle named Ladyree Soper. No such talk today. Young people could take just so much of the old days.

"I won't be able to give you a ride home this evening. I'm a little . . . tired."

"It's okay," he said.

She served him and, before seating herself, picked up from the counter a copy of *The Count of Monte Cristo* that had once belonged to Will Milledge.

"I think you'll like this. It is quite adventurous."

He nodded. Ladyree and Wash had been trying to lead Nathan into the world of books.

"Nathan, you know how ivy shoots out along the ground and catches to make new roots." She stirred her cocoa. "Do you know if kudzu does the same thing?"

"No. I'm not sure."

She lifted her spoon and paused it midair over the cup. "I mustn't take a chance."

"What chance?"

She put the spoon down. "I'm just talking to myself again." She rose. "I think I'll have a glass of sherry instead of cocoa. Have some more cake."

Ladyree went to the pantry. Behind a stack of canned goods, a row of sherry bottles stood like proud soldiers, too proud for hiding. She poured sherry into a stemmed glass, etched and gold rimmed, a wedding gift to Verda Soper in 1883. She placed the bottle, now empty, beside a special garbage tin on the pantry floor. Nearby lay the hammer she used to crush the empty sherry bottles before throwing the broken pieces into the tin. Even garbage men gossiped. Port City was a small town.

She was circumspect when she bought sherry at the bootlegger's just outside Port City's city limits. She never went inside. She blew her horn to signal for curb service.

When the black man came to take her order, she would always explain, attempting humor at the same time, "It's for several of us girls." Little old ladies in Port City sometimes referred to themselves as girls.

Fearing that Snatch Rosselli, the white owner, might look outside and see her, she would turn away her head. The nickname "Snatch" came from customers who snatched liquor furtively from within his great coat as he walked town streets during Prohibition.

Twice when her trips to the bootlegger seemed too close together, she had sent a taxi for her sherry purchases.

Ladyree knew she drank more, but it was . . . temporary.

"Nathan, what is playing next at the theater?"

"A western. It'll be Saturday."

"Of course. I lose track of time at home."

What will I say now? She was beginning to feel the effects of too much sherry. "I will say to you, Nathan, what is on my mind. Have you ever wished someone dead?"

Nathan jumped. He spilled his cocoa.

"What's the matter, Nathan?"

"Do you . . . know?" Did she know about the arsenic and Norwood?

"Know what?" she asked.

He did not answer. At last he said, "If you kill someone, and they find out, they will fry you, won't they?"

"Fry you?"

"In an electric chair."

"I think they still hang you in Mississippi, don't they?"

"No'am."

"Nathan? Whom do you want dead?"

"My father."

"Norwood is just a human being. When you get grown, you'll make mistakes and hurt someone and then you'll forgive him."

"No'am."

Ladyree lifted the delicate stemmed glass for more sherry.

"I don't know why I talk about forgiving a parent who commits the worst sin—not loving you. I didn't forgive mine." She suddenly felt nauseous.

"You didn't?"

"I killed Mother, Nathan." She got up. "I'm going to be sick." She rushed away into the hallway to the bathroom where she threw up into the toilet. When she had wiped her lips and rinsed her mouth, she tried to repair her appearance.

Ladyree returned to the kitchen.

Nathan seemed embarrassed. He wrinkled his nose. Did she smell of vomit?

She sat down.

"You didn't kill your mother," said Nathan. "She died from surgery."

"I did," said Ladyree. The nausea was gone. She lifted her empty stemmed glass and started for the pantry.

"Would you let me have a little sherry?" said Nathan.

"You're too young."

"I'm fourteen, and I've had all sorts of drinks."

"I guess a little won't hurt you."

She went to the pantry bringing back a full bottle of sherry and another of Verda Soper's glasses.

"Don't drink much," she said filling his glass.

"No'am." He took a swallow. It burned but stayed down.

"Sip it, Nathan. Don't swallow it."

"Yes, ma'am."

A little later, he said, "Did you really kill Mrs. Soper?"

"Yes."

"How did you get away with it?"

"Nathan, you must not harm Norwood." She must discourage Nathan from hurting Norwood and thereby himself.

Silences for thought, silences uncomfortable, halted the conversation from time to time.

"Wash read me a poem by a black man," said Nathan. "He explained it to me. It was about hate being a tiger and eating himself up."

"I know the poem," she said.

"I try not to . . . feel. It is better. But at night it comes back to me and keeps me awake. If I don't kill him, what I feel will eat me up."

"Slay the tiger. If you don't, a bigger hate can come or something worse."

Another silence.

"You won't get away with it. You'll go to a reformatory," she said.

"I'll think about it," he said. "How did you get away with killing Mrs. Soper?"

She would compromise. "I'll tell you about it if you promise not to harm Norwood for at least a year."

He had learned to sip wine. He thought about her warning. "Okay," he said.

Ladyree began telling him about the day she had seen the fire scene in *Gone with the Wind*. Her manner was spirited and quick as she described every detail until she reached the day of Verda Soper's death in the hospital. Then a terror came over her. In her mind she heard her mother's bridge clatter-clatter across the floor and saw her gappy, distorted mouth set in rage and death. Ladyree trembled. "Maybe I didn't get away with it."

"What do you mean?" he said.

"Come. I must show you. I think Mother is back."

He followed her out of the kitchen to the attic stairway.

"Watch the broken step," she cautioned him. She carried her usher's flashlight.

A small spot of light illuminated the dark stairway.

"Where's the attic light?" he asked.

"You can't switch it on. You'll see."

Nathan avoided the broken step.

"Look," she said from above.

Nathan reached the top.

Ladyree flashed light toward the dark.

"My God!" he said unaware of being profane.

"Don't go in farther," she said.

A wall of kudzu had met them. Hushed momentarily, stilled together, they stood before the wall.

"There's so much of her," said Ladyree. "You can barely find the stained-glass window in daylight, and the kudzu isn't even turning black as it should be this time of year."

"It's probably because it's growing inside."

"No, it's Mother."

"What?"

"I think it's Mother growing out of her ashes."

"That's not right," said Nathan.

"'In my Father's house are many mansions.' Nathan, the word mansions may mean dimensions. Mother's here. See. In the kudzu. We planted kudzu in her ashes and she's back. You think you hate. You should know how Mother hates." Ladyree's voice had been soft, almost a whisper. "She's going to strangle the house and then . . . STRANGLE ME."

"You think the vines are Mrs. Soper?"

"I know they are."

"No'am." The glow from the flashlight extended a short distance into the attic. Nathan was able to locate the light switch. Leaving the small light held in Ladyree's hand, he journeyed unseeing through the thick of vines toward the switch.

"No! Nathan stop!"

"They're just vines," he said pushing entanglements. He reached and flicked the switch and the light shot on. "Just vines."

Ladyree stood nonplused in the frame of the attic entrance. All that light into the night and into the vines was eerie, different from what she had seen in daylight. "I'm frightened," she said.

A green sea of kudzu took almost all the interior top of the Cyclops House. As Nathan scanned the cramped kudzu, he said, "Looks like something on a slide through the microscope at school, sort of like greenish shapes bunched together only. . . ."

"Big." She finished the sentence. "Bigger than normal."

"I don't know." Fighting the kudzu, he found the back window where the kudzu had entered. He cracked a space above the windowsill giving him a purchase whereby he lifted the window halfway. He grabbed a handful of vines and gave them a hard jerk. The pot came free and zipped up tipping at the sill until it dropped inside the attic. Nathan fell backwards into the mass of kudzu still holding one piece of uprooted vine. The heavy pot stirred a few inches until it lodged against a loosened and raised board of the flooring. From the pot some of Mrs. Soper's ashes scattered.

Ladyree began to weep.

"It's just vines," he said.

"Come out of the attic now, Nathan."

Nathan came to her hauling the bit of kudzu with its hairy, dirt-dotted roots. He handed it to Ladyree. "Feel it. It's just vines," he repeated.

She took the kudzu dragging it behind her as they left the attic. At the foot of the stairs, Ladyree's tears stopped. She squeezed the kudzu in her hand. "Maybe you are right, Nathan. It feels like just a vine."

On the way to the front door where Nathan would leave, she said, "Now that she's in the attic, it may bring peace if I just give her the attic and stay downstairs."

"It's just vines. If you want, Wash and I could clear out the attic," said Nathan. "We'd better get it outta the ivy, too. It'll ruin your house. Max Durham says it's foolish to leave it on its own."

"Yes. I think you're right."

She accompanied Nathan to the sidewalk and watched him in the brimming glow of the downtown streetlights until he faded into night as he made his way toward the bus station.

Going back inside, she stooped to pick up the morning newspaper she had earlier failed to bring into the Cyclops House. Still, she held the piece of kudzu.

"Is it you, Mother, or is it my mind?"

Inside she decided to put the roots in water and to take the sprig in the morning to Max Durham.

Twenty-seventh Sequence

In the night a November storm had chilled the Delta. Only gray bits of cotton survived on the dead stalks, down and broken on the mounds. The muddy fields spread low and far outside the window near Max Durham. The first frost in October had halted the growing season and lessened the pressures of Max's job.

Max stood in the sun and shadow created from filtering rays flooding down from a huge glass ceiling through the leaves of an orange tree in the solarium of Building #1 at the Delta Branch Station. The Delta Branch Station was an experimental agricultural farm created by the state of Mississippi in 1904 for the then good sum of three thousand dollars. Building #1, the station's oldest, once a pedigreed seed company, rose in a grove of wide-trunked oaks adjoining the original acreage.

Max liked old things. Max liked odd things. He preferred Building #1 to all the newer buildings. As chief superintendent of the station, he had been able to modify it with trusty labor from Parchman Farm, Mississippi's penitentiary, to structure the ceiling that had allowed him to grow the fine tree whose presence he now enjoyed. Orange trees did not grow in the fields of the Mississippi Delta.

Into the room came Max's redheaded secretary, the older sister of his football playing nephew, Ted Cockrane.

"Some people to see you, Uncle Max," she said.

"Drat!" Max Durham had appropriated the expletive many years ago from the script beneath a silent movie. "Who?" He pursed his lips. He had expected his day to be free.

"Some man from Washington with the Agricultural Department, and a lady just walked in. I think she's the one at the Majestic everybody calls the Picture Show Lady."

He put his water bucket down on the floor by a bag of fertilizer marked STATE OF MISSISSIPPI that he had planned to use. "M-M-Miss

Ladyree's very nice, but she can wait her turn like all of us. Send the damned agent in. I'll see him here instead of in the office."

"Uncle Max?"

"Don't call me Uncle M-M-Max at work. People will think I'm giving away state jobs. Call me M-M-Mr. Durham like I told you."

"Yes, sir," she said. "Mr. Durham, I was wondering if I could have a little time off this morning?"

"Time off?"

She smiled at him. "You're so good to me. Mama thanks you for my job."

"Shhh," he said.

She had on too much lipstick, her mouth a red cartoon matching her hair. "Look at my hai-ya. Mama says I absolutely have to go to the beauty parlor and get it cut and fixed."

He looked at her red hair. "You're lucky to have hair to cut," he said. As a child he had had hair as thick and red as hers and a sprinkle of red freckles on his pale skin. But he had stuttered and other children had taunted him claiming he spit on them when excited. He had not, but he felt his difference and gradually became at home with differentness. As a teenager he had purchased a little booklet by a California writer advertised in the local paper when ads were scarce and hype primitive. By its instructions and weights he had built muscles that made him as attractive then as he ever would be. Now, fifty, single, sex a stranger to him, Max had droopy flesh hanging where muscles had been, and his hair had almost vanished.

"Go to the beauty parlor. Leave a note for anyone coming in to use the buzzer and leave me be," he said.

"Yes, sir." She left.

Max straightened his red toupee for which he had paid half-a-month's salary. In back a fringe of real hair, still red, skirted the false. This morning Max had spent an hour at the bathroom mirror, another mirror in hand aimed at his head, arranging the toupee. When finished and satisfied, he felt young and attractive. Max had never forgiven the unkind remark made by someone that he looked like Humpty-Dumpty with a red mop on his head.

"Mr. Durham." Someone had entered.

Max went forward, hand extended. The bureaucrat was young. Max doubted he knew much.

The man, dressed in a conservative suit and tie, carrying a cheap briefcase, advanced and met Max's hand.

Sally Bolding

"I came, sir, to bring you a bulletin. We're getting them out personally across the South to anyone connected with agricultural research."

"We do that. Do it all. Experimental farming, crop diversification, insect control," Max bragged. He did not like to be disturbed by anyone from Washington. "Too dependent on cotton here, and the boll weevil nearly eats us up sometimes."

"DDT didn't eliminate the boll weevil?"

"Helps. Planes dust all summer, but the boll weevils are just resting, I think." Young people knew so little. "Chemical pesticides are the wave of the future, and all that development during World War II advanced 'em. We used calcium arsenate when we first started aerial application in 1928. I was the man who rode in back of the first biplane dumping the stuff over the fields from the side."

"Calcium arsenate as in arsenic?"

Smarty fellow. Of course. "Yes," said Max. "Let's see your bulletin."

The young man rummaged in his briefcase. "You familiar, sir, with what they do in Americus, Georgia?"

"Raise kudzu for erosion purposes."

"Well, yes. Americus, Georgia has been shut down."

"Good."

"Our bulletin details how kudzu has gone on a *rampage* in and around Georgia. It's taking over highways, houses, crops." He removed the bulletin from his cardboard briefcase.

"We know all about that, young man. Have for some time. Been trying to get a fella here in the county to be careful about it, too. He thinks to use it on the levees for flood control."

"We put a lot of care into this bulletin. It's our strategy to control kudzu." He tried to hand the bulletin to Max.

Max sighed. "Kudzu is not my main concern."

"Mr. Durham! That's why I've brought you this bulletin personally. The bulletin is important."

"Yes, I'm sure it's a good plan. I'll read it later." Max took the bulletin.

"Plan? Regulations," he corrected. "We're working on legislation."

"Too many laws. Then too many laws for the exceptions to the laws. A rampage worse than kudzu's. I'll keep kudzu at bay here. You keep it out of Washington, D.C."

"Mr. Durham . . ."

The Cyclops Window

"Going to Jackson, too? Better go. It's a long drive."

Max walked toward the solarium door. The young man followed. "Good-bye," said Max.

Afterwards Max fiddled with his toupee. It had a habit of moving. He looked through another window at the puny trees in front of the newer buildings. He caressed the old wood of the windowsill. Max collected what he thought were antiques. They were made of similar wood.

Max lit a Phillip Morris and sucked deeply into his lungs. As he smoked, he thought of what the planter, who recently had returned from Boston, had reported. The planter owned almost as much land as Mumford Marshall and could afford to travel for his health. In Boston he had seen the renowned Dr. Paul Dudley White for his heart condition. Dr. White claimed cigarettes were bad for you. What nonsense, thought Max. Everybody smoked. Everybody could not be wrong to do so. He himself smoked three packs a day—with great pleasure.

He had finished his cigarette and had mixed fertilizer into his bucket of water preparing to nourish his orange tree, when the buzzer sounded. "Drat." He scowled. His face collapsed. Then he remembered that Ladyree Soper was waiting for him.

He liked Ladyree. They had been classmates. In grammar school the boys rarely saw the girls since classes and recesses were separate, but whenever he did see Ladyree, she waited while he got his words together and never laughed at him. Once a decade or so ago, he had thought to ask her to dinner, but when he went to her house to ask, Mrs. Soper had quizzed him so that he left before Ladyree got home and never went back.

Max was proud of his waiting room. So spacious, he thought as he entered the room, almost like being outside without the November cold. In through its high windows the Delta sun swept the wide, old boarding of the floor with magical light. Across the room in one of its banker's chairs sat Ladyree Soper. Her name was Marshall now. She looked disheveled. Not like her at all, he thought.

"Did the storm get you last night?" he said approaching her.

She stood. "Max. I'm glad you're here. I put it on your secretary's desk."

"Put what? Where?" He turned to the desk. The kudzu lifted from a large jar of water and dangled over the corner of the desk. Through the glass of the jar, the kudzu roots floated like wet strands of hair.

Max walked to the desk. Ladyree followed and stood beside him.

Before he could examine the sprig, he wrinkled his nose. He smelled something stale and like a bus station vagrant. He realized it was Ladyree beside him smelling like an awakening drunk. He was suddenly glad Mrs. Soper had run him off.

"Kudzu," said Max. "I was just talking to someone about kudzu."

"What did he say?"

Max did not answer her question. He scrutinized the big leaves of the kudzu. "Interesting plant. Originally from the Orient. Japan, I think," he commented. "Still green in November?"

"It's different, isn't it?"

"Where did it come from?"

"It's growing all over my attic."

"Much of it?"

"Yes, very much," she said. She trembled.

It was growing inside like Mumford's in the greenhouse. He must tell Mumford how big it could grow inside and tell him, too, about the agent's report that the kudzu operation in Americus, Georgia had folded.

"It scares me, Max."

"Scares you?"

"I don't know how to tell you." She whispered, "I think it's Mother."

"What did you say?"

"You must tell me, Max, if it's just kudzu."

"I know kudzu. Of course, it's kudzu. You want me to show you a picture of kudzu in a book?"

"No. I know it's kudzu." Her words stalled in her throat. For a second the sweet Southernness of her voice sounded guttural. "Could it be more than kudzu?"

"M-M-More? How say?"

She swayed. "I think it's Mother."

Max did not understand.

"It's Mother, too," she said louder and clearer.

Still perplexed, he did not speak.

"Oh, I'm not sure. You tell me," she said.

"Cigarette?" said Max. He needed time to think.

"I don't smoke," she said.

"Okay for me?"

She nodded. "Don't get your match near Mother."

He lit his cigarette. He blew a silver cloud of smoke into the air over the desk. It curled and faded.

At last he had an inkling of what she believed. "It's not M-M-Mrs. Soper, Ladyree," he said.

"It's not?"

"I'll keep this." He picked up the jar of kudzu. "You go on home and go to bed."

"Help me," she said.

"It's not M-M-Mrs. Soper. I'll try to find someone to get the kudzu out of your house. Don't worry. Go home and rest."

Max took her elbow and shepherded her toward the door. As he guided her out, he was thinking that last night she may have drunk too much, but today she was crazy.

The night's storm had weathered the vines growing against the Cyclops House. The normal flow of growth had been disturbed giving the lower part of the house a crumpled look as if it had been dropped.

Back from her meeting with Max Durham, Ladyree prepared to enter her home. She looked up into the English ivy, black strings of wintered kudzu twisting in its green. Something was caught near the stained-glass eyespot of the attic. She hoped it was not part of the roof.

At her doorway she pulled at low ivy trying to dislodge whatever was caught. It remained in its high trap. No wind now, but when it returned, the something would probably fall.

Her hand shook on the doorknob. She went inside quickly to get warm and steady herself with a glass of sherry.

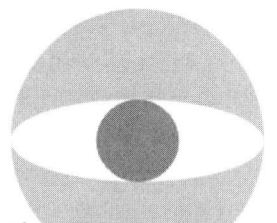

Twenty-eighth Sequence

Norwood Pankum pushed the swing door to enter Greenhouse Three. At last he felt well enough to work. The door hinge had squeaked. It needed oil. The high sun of summer had passed. The rowed plants before him appeared stunted. Worse was what he suddenly saw.

"My God!" he said.

Wash Bibbs was stoking a charcoal fire in a sportsman's iron grill beneath a large wobbling vat in a corner of the greenhouse. There was an otherworld expression on Wash's rutted face as if he had nothing to do with the stoking. Steam rose to gather at the greenhouse's clear ceiling. Mumford Marshall, too busy to notice Norwood, was lifting a twenty-pound sack of salt to stir into one side of the bubbling liquid in the vat. On the other side Nathan was scooping the boiling water and melted salt into a huge ladle and pouring the steaming mixture over the kudzu rows. The kudzu, its leaves medium sized, unweathered and still green, cringed bending from sunny ceiling to its roots in the soil.

Norwood wondered if he were awake. He had been so sick. Fleetingly he perceived something out of the ordinary in the tangle of pink scars and black skin that was Wash Bibbs' face. He thought of a happy saint he once had seen on the cover of a Sunday school program. The religious idea scared him. Had his grandmother's hardhanded God come to grab him up and taint his brain as he recently feared during his sickness?

No, he assured himself. This was real and in his Greenhouse Three.

"My God!" repeated Norwood in his anger. "Madness has taken over during my illness."

Mumford Marshall heard Norwood. He emptied his sack and said, "We're trying something. Will Milledge controlled his worst weedings with boiling water and salt. Wash just found out after a lot of researching. We're trying the damned stuff on the kudzu, one ladle here, one ladle there, to see what will and won't kill."

"Mumford, you're crazy," said Norwood. "Look at the steam in this room. It's like a bathhouse. You'll thwart the growth of everything else."

"Oh?" Mumford said. "I hadn't thought of that."

"Look at Tudor Jackson's experiment. It's wilting."

"Well, hell, Norwood, I didn't know. And Tudor can just probably pray a bit more over his corn."

"Wash! Nathan! Stop at once!" yelled Norwood.

Mumford, Wash, Nathan stilled.

Wash dampened two heavy rags. He lifted the vat, lowered it to the earthen floor, and began to put out the fire in the grill, snuffing charcoal piece by piece into gray ash by popping each with one of the wet rags. Nathan poured the last scalding liquid from his ladle back into the lowered cauldron.

Ruby Smith entered the greenhouse carrying a tray covered with a heavy cloth. "Honey," she said, "what's goin' on?"

Norwood wished she would not call him honey. "I hired Ruby to nurse me part time," he said. He wanted to explain.

"I brought your breakfast from home," she said.

"Hello, Ruby." Mumford Marshall acknowledged her presence.

"Mumford," she said.

Norwood moved beyond Ruby into the body of the greenhouse. "Nathan, you and Wash take that ladle and vat out of here. Cool them outside. I'll get this terrible fire out of here and the ashes to the river.

"But, honey, your breakfast?"

"Hang the breakfast. I got to get my business back to how it's supposed to be."

"Aaah, honey. . . ."

"And damn you, Mumford. You shouldn't have gone so far without me." Norwood led Wash and Nathan out of Greenhouse Three.

After Norwood's outburst, the greenhouse felt hushed. The steam haze at the ceiling was clearing

"You look well, Mumford," Ruby said.

"Been a while. You and Norwood got something going?"

"Yes. I think he'll marry me someday. Not soon, but someday." Ruby Smith never expected too much.

"You're a good girl, Ruby."

"I know. How's my niece, Spring?"

"A puzzle. Children are a puzzle, their parents are puzzles to them, too. Universal truth, I guess."

"Probably," said Ruby. "I need to talk to you."

"About what?"

"First of all, I think your wife and my boss have got something going."

"You're crazy," said Mumford.

"I don't think so."

"Elia and Abner? That's hard to believe." He offered a cigarette to Ruby. "You better tell me."

Ruby took the cigarette. Mumford lit hers and his own. "Months ago," she said, "Elia started coming to the office for some kind of lessons from Mr. Owens. Just before she came, he'd get me to bring in stuff on banking and taxes and other things to do with money. He started calling her on the phone a lot, and she'd call him a lot. It was too much calling for anyone not to notice. Then it sort of stopped." She puffed her cigarette. "I always go in early to check things out and make 'em orderly. One day under an ashtray in Mr. Owens' office, I found that real pretty pin Elia wears so much. Next day the office smelled of expensive perfume and the couch had been smoothed. She was leaving the pin to signal him she was coming for a lay. It's happened over and over."

Quiet for a time, Mumford continued to smoke. "It's a bit much," he said.

"I'm a good detective, and I'll say more about detectives later," she said. "You come to the office tomorrow around ten o'clock when Mr. Owens goes to Oscar's Cafe downstairs for his usual coffee break. I pretty much know their schedule, and I guarantee she'll leave her pin in his office tonight after work. And if you think all this is a bit much, it's more since yesterday."

"This is nonsense. She's there just learning to handle Claude Hannah's money, which still complicates things for me. My money is hers, hers is mine."

"It's legally hers."

"That's right. But women don't know beans about money."

"Apparently, she wants to learn," said Ruby.

Mumford took a long drag from his cigarette. "Damn," he said. "But Abner and Elia? I don't believe it."

"Don't let your wounded pride trip you yet, Mumford. You don't know the worse about them."

"What's any worse?"

"Hold on a minute," she said. "Do you know the salary I make?"

"No."

"Goddamned rich man. I make $200 a month, and that's a good salary. Do you know what $5,000 would do for me?"

"A lot, I guess."

"Right! And I'd take it if it weren't for Spring. Even so, I've been awfully tempted."

"I don't understand. Are you threatening to expose Abner?"

"No. I've known about Elia and Abner Owens for too long and have kept quiet even to you. It's the smart way to go if you're a small potato. As my sister's natural child and my only tie to the next generation, your Spring Marshall means much to me. A family breakup might hurt her. And Abner Owens is too greedy a man to be mixed into her family finances. If it weren't for this, I'd be $5,000 richer and you wouldn't be listening to me now."

Mumford nodded and waited.

Ruby paused. "I don't know how to tell you this. It's bizarre."

Mumford was grim. "Go on," he said.

"Ham Vance came for an appointment yesterday. People praise him, but I think he's nasty. He hinted he knew about me and Norwood being deep. Sort of quizzed me about Elia, too, and asked questions about Wash Bibbs' sister. I wasn't sure what he was up to, so I played a close hand. Let on to nothing. I flirted with him a bit to make things okay, and he didn't play it close like I did. He let it slip that Mr. Owens had asked him to come so he'd recommend *for a client* a detective in New Orleans or Memphis. About this time Mr. Owens buzzed and asked if Ham had come. He didn't snap at me for not letting him know at once, which I thought was unusual. Ham went in and came out soon winking at me as he left. Then Mr. Owens called me in.

"I'll try to tell you exactly what the bastard said. 'Ruby,' he said, 'how would you like to earn $5,000?'

"I gasped," said Ruby. "Then he went on, saying, 'It's a delicate matter. You must disclose nothing, no detail, absolutely nothing. You understand?'

"What he meant by understand was that my job would go if I said anything. Mr. Owens can be tricky, very tricky this time. I plastered a smile on my face and reminded him that I'd always kept his confidences.

"And he says, 'I know you can keep quiet. That's why I hired you and continue to pay you what some men in this town would think a munificent salary.'

"I changed my expression to grateful. Then he said, 'You and Mumford Marshall are friends, find each other . . . attractive.'

"'Mr. Owens, what are you saying?' I said. I knew perfectly well what he was saying, but not why.

"'I want you to renew your affair with him.'

"I wasn't sure what I heard. I said, 'It was my sister, sir.'

"He didn't even use the polite word girlfriend. 'Before your sister, you were his mistress.'

"Ham Vance keeps him up on every thing going in Port City. They're thick, sly about it, but thick. They arrange to take a long coffee break at Oscar's Cafe almost every day. Then Mr. Owens dropped his bomb.

"'Five thousand dollars is a lot of money. Would you consider helping me arrange grounds for Elia Hannah Marshall to divorce Mumford?'

"As I told you, Mumford, I wouldn't hurt Spring, but Abner Owens is a piss-poor father—excuse the expression, Mumford. I don't know why he had Dalton. Anyway, he just assumed I'd consider the money first. Intrigued, I said, 'Go on.'

"He started out with, 'Let me put it clearly.' Some nerve he had to put it at all.

"Abner Owens wanted me to screw you and let a detective get a shot of us with a camera."

Mumford roared with laughter.

Ruby laughed.

"What did you tell him?" said Mumford.

"I said I'd think about it."

"Damnest thing I've ever heard of. I'll remember this conversation on my way to dying. How you gonna tell him no?" said Mumford.

"I'm gonna tell him God won't let me, but that I can recommend someone else. And for now you, Mumford Marshall, better play it straight and narrow."

"Most of the time, I'm straight and narrow."

"When it pleases you to be, you are," she said.

Norwood returned. He was still disgruntled.

"Don't ever take over my greenhouse again, Mumford," he said. "You only rent out a part of this greenhouse! You don't own it!" he snapped.

The Cyclops Window

"Calm down, Norwood," said Mumford.

"Yes, calm down, or you'll be sick some more," said Ruby. "Come to breakfast."

"Mumford, Max Durham called early this morning. He wants to talk to you," said Norwood.

"About what?"

"Who knows," said Norwood. He continued to grumble as he followed Ruby out and toward the kitchen and breakfast nook.

Alone in the quiet and vast greenhouse, Mumford heard a slight squishy sound. He looked down to find himself standing in the overspillings of water and salt, now cooled and puddled on the ground. He had stepped so much on a wet earthened part of the floor that he had made it muddy.

"A mess," he said aloud. He wondered what Max had to report. He would talk to him soon. More importantly, he had to resolve the new development with Elia. He had planned to go down to Louisiana and talk to the rice farmers around Crowley and Jennings in a few days, but that would have to wait.

The door to the greenhouse swung inwards.

Mumford turned on hearing the squeaky hinge. What the hell? A black woman, her face pasted in white, stood in the doorway. She held up her finger. A drop of blood fell.

"Claude," she said. "Where is Claude. I need a Band-Aid."

Mumford realized who Arorah was. "Claude is dead," he said.

"No." She shoved the door behind her and fled. The door swung back and forward again and again, each time with the fierce squeak of its metal hinge.

So much for that, thought Mumford.

Mumford lifted the scalded leaves of a kudzu shoot. Salt and boiling water might work, but it was too cumbersome a method for controlling rampant growth in kudzu.

He paced the parameters of the greenhouse stopping to examine Tudor Jackson's experiment. He stood before it for a moment.

"Can't say I've got a closed mind," he said.

He walked back to the rows of kudzu. He knew a good bit about blasphemy, but he was not sure he remembered how to pray. He bowed his head. He would pray backwards and hope the Lord would protect him. "Goddamn, you son of a bitch, kudzu. The devil take your power. Not all of it," he amended. "Just some. You hear me, devil, Satan, Beelzebub?"

Spring Marshall dabbed her brush into color on her palette and transferred it to the portrait she was painting. She was tired. Also, pleased. The portrait had spontaneity, a quality she valued, but which at times she feared she lost in overwork. She liked the turns of cool and warm strokes she had managed. Spent, she stopped, put her paints aside but not away since getting set up to work was troublesome and her palette might suffer. She pushed the easel toward the wall opposite the studio windows letting in northern light. The almost completed portrait of Thor Hannah looked good.

After cleaning her brushes and her hands with warm water and soap and hanging up one of Mumford's old shirts used as a smock, she left the studio for the verandah to relax and sip a Coke.

On the verandah Mumford Marshall was seated in a cushioned wicker chair reading the afternoon newspaper. In a nearby wicker chair, Elia Marshall studied, a book and some paper on her lap desk, an antique fashioned similarly to Thomas Jefferson's "writing box." Mumford looked up for a second distracted by Spring's entrance before returning to his reading. Spring stood, Coke in hand, before the windowed wall looking out toward the Pankum Nursery and Greenhouse. In the distance she saw two figures, one recognizably the crippled Wash, the other a woman. He appeared to be kissing her hand.

"Who is that woman with Wash?" she asked.

"It is Wash's sister, I believe," answered Elia, not looking up.

"No, it's Arorah Hannah," said Mumford.

Elia lifted her head. She pretended not to know about her father's involvement with Arorah. Using the Hannah name was an anathema to Elia.

"How do you know?" Spring asked her father.

"Saw her. Saw her today. Recognized that white stuff she wears on her face. Norwood *thinks* she's Wash's sister. Ain't so."

"Excuse me. I've got to go call someone." Spring left hurriedly.

"She could have used the phone in here," said Elia.

"She's old enough to have a private conversation," said Mumford. "And so are you."

"What do you mean?"

"Nothing. Nothing right now," he said.

Twenty-ninth Sequence

At three o'clock Abner Owens finished his afternoon coffee break. He rose from the plastic cushioned seat of a booth, his coffee cup cold and empty before him on the table of Oscar's Cafe.

Oscar's Cafe, tucked between a jewelry store and a furniture store in the main block of the downtown, was like a diner with vinyl booths and four-chair tables, but larger and high-ceilinged. It specialized in early breakfasts for river fishermen and in business lunches. Business among businessmen and leading-citizen gossip transpired daily over coffee in thick-rimmed cups brought by brisk waitresses from huge hot-to-touch metal urns behind the counter. There a fat and aproned Oscar supervised.

Each work day Abner Owens religiously scheduled two coffee breaks in the cafe in order to stay abreast of Port City life and in touch with its power. "It's on me this time, Ham," said Abner. "Thanks for the information about the detective. You're a good fellow to know."

Ham Vance moved out from the opposite side of the booth. "You're good to know too, Abner. You sure Elia's right about Wash's sister being Arorah Hannah?"

"Absolutely. Her feelings were too strong. She wishes Arorah would just disappear."

"She may get her wish," said Ham.

Abner Owens lifted his eyebrows.

"No, Abner, I didn't mean I would kill her," said Ham Vance.

"Didn't think you would, Ham. Not smart to kill someone so noticeable, black or not. Much could go wrong."

The men separated each going his own way.

The next day when Ruby Smith came to work, she found a memo from her boss that an unexpected business had come up this morning at the courthouse. She worried. Mumford Marshall planned to make a secret visit to the office during Abner Owens' ten o'clock break at Oscar's. She worried the two men's paths might cross.

Failing to reach Mumford on the telephone, she turned to her job. She had papers to prepare for Ladyree Soper Marshall who was coming in to sign them finishing the work of her mother's estate. It came to her mind then that these two might also meet.

Ruby lit her first cigarette and smiled. *Interesting. Let 'em all come.* She was laughing when Mary Jefferson, Mary Tomato Man, entered the door from the outside hallway.

For years Mary Jefferson had worked for the building owner cleaning offices. In the doorway she struggled to control an unwieldy broomstick and a mop handle. She held a bucket and around her waist was a pouch of supplies and rags.

"You okay this morning, Mary?" said Ruby. "You don't look so good."

Mary smiled despite the fact that she also worried. Ham Vance who every day checked Arorah Hannah's house next door on Redbud Street had not come this morning. She worried that he had not because he had found Arorah. "I'm fine," she said starting toward Abner's office. She sometimes lingered to chat but not this morning. She left Ruby for the lawyer's office dodging the walls with the broomstick and mop handle.

In minutes, an agitated Mary Jefferson rushed back from the other office to Ruby.

"I never looked before. I found this under an ashtray." Mary held out her hand, in her palm a tissue wrapping and Elia's pin. She was breathless.

"Well, put it back," said Ruby.

"But I want you to see that I didn't take it. People in this building know I don't steal."

"Of course not, Mary."

"Well, just to be sure, you keep it, Miss Ruby. Everybody thinks blacks steal. I don't."

"I told you, I know you don't steal. Put it back. I'm busy, Mary."

Mary Jefferson stood silently at Ruby's desk as Ruby continued working. At last Mary carefully rewrapped Elia's pin and returned to Abner's office to put it back under the ashtray and resume cleaning.

Soon near Ruby, the door to the outside hallway opened again.

"Good morning, Miss Ladyree," said Ruby. "You come over here

The Cyclops Window

and sit at my desk to do your signing, and we'll have it all done." Ruby wanted Abner Owens' office empty for Mumford. The cleaning would be done soon.

"Everyone comes in today looks kinda' puny. You okay, Miss Ladyree?" said Ruby.

"I think so. I'm not sure."

"Your slip's showing, honey. You better stop in the lady's room in the hall and yank it up when you leave," said Ruby. "See. I checked the places you're to sign so it'd be easy for you."

"Thank you," said Ladyree seating herself in the only chair by the desk.

Standing Ruby checked the time. "Jeez! Coming up on ten o'clock."

Ladyree looked at her naked wrist. She had forgotten to wear her watch. "Am I early or late?" Her left hand shook. She grasped it with her right hand to stop the shaking.

"No. It's okay. The time's fine."

Someone gave the hallway door a powerful push, and again it opened.

"Jeez," said Ruby to herself. "I hope this all works out."

Mumford Marshall entered.

"You sit over there in the waiting area, Mr. Marshall. I'll be through in a minute," said Ruby.

Mumford sat down in one of the waiting room chairs in the far corner of the room. He began to flip through the pages of a *Saturday Evening Post*. The lady signing at Ruby's desk seemed familiar.

"There, Miss Ladyree, we're through," said Ruby.

Mumford rose. He had heard the name. "Ladyree?" He approached his ex-wife. "Been years . . ."

"Ye–es." A catch had risen from her gut to break the word.

"What are you doing at Abner's?"

"Mother's legacy," she whispered. "Mother's legacy," she said louder.

"Elia told me about—the mean old bitch. Excuse me, but you know how I felt about her."

"Yes." A tear threatened. "I've let myself go," she whispered.

"Elia said you had the old buzzard cremated. Probably nobody in the South's ever been cremated unless Sherman burned 'em up in a mansion in the 1860s," he said. "Anyway, I find cremation kinda suitable. Too bad she was dead. I wanted to burn her when she was alive."

Ladyree still sat. She looked down at her lap.

When the silence had lasted too long, Ruby said, "Why don't you wait in the office, Mumford?"

"Okay." He started away, halted. "Ladyree, the legacy, was it sizable?"

"No."

"Well, if you need investment advice, let me know," said Mumford.

"It's small."

"Yeah. Well, don't let anybody take it away from you. If it'd been big, I might have led you into trouble myself." He was the only one who laughed at his joke.

"You go on in, Mumford. Someone's cleaning in there, but she's almost finished. I need to show Ladyree where the hall rest room is. I'll be back to the office in a minute."

Mumford left the women and went into Abner Owens' office.

"Hello," said Mumford.

Leaning to dust a chair arm, Mary Jefferson stopped the sweep of her rag. She recognized Mumford as the white planter who now farmed the Hannah land where her parents had sharecropped. She and her brother had been born there. "I'll be through in a minute, Mr. Marshall," she said.

"No rush, auntie," he said.

The old name was demeaning to Mary Jefferson, but she doubted Mumford suspected his insult. She stood with her rag in hand and straightened her back revealing her perfect posture and at the same moment ever so slightly flinching from the unseen blow.

The office void of other distractions, Mumford Marshall watched as Mary Jefferson cleaned.

"You clean well," he said.

"Been working here fifteen years,"

"God, I don't think I could do what you're doing for fifteen minutes. Wouldn't have the patience."

"I guess it's woman's work." She was in the process of forgiving him a bit for his insult.

"My wife ain't worth a hoot at it."

"I expect she don't have to be," said Mary.

"No, but it'd be damned good for her."

Mary Jefferson laughed. A funny and pleasant man after all, she thought. "I'm going now," she said lifting her heavy bucket, broomstick and all.

"Mighty clean," said Mumford as she closed the door.

204

The Cyclops Window

Mumford waited for Ruby. Still standing he wandered about the room. Always he had considered Abner Owens a shyster of little consequence. Mumford prided himself on his good judgment of character. Now studying Abner's Ole Miss diploma from its law school, framed meaningless certificates of award from the Mississippi Bar Association, tennis and bridge trophies, he realized that he had not measured the full extent of Abner's drive. Everything about the office cried of ambition. And, Abner Owens had already come a long way.

Mumford searched the book shelves and found within Abner's law library a number of books on investments. He frowned. Imagine instructing his wife when he Mumford knew all about investing.

Ruby entered Abner's office. She went directly to the ashtray on the credenza, turned it over, and handed the tissue-wrapped pin to Mumford. "You got to get outta here quickly. Mr. Owens is off schedule, and if he finds you here, you better come up with an explanation or I'll just lose my job," said Ruby.

Mumford withdrew Elia's jewelry from the tissue. Suddenly he remembered unpinning it in the backseat of a car when he and Elia had been courting. He wadded the tissue and pin together and stuffed them into his pocket shoving the ashtray to a precarious balance at the edge of the credenza.

"Don't take it, you fool," said Ruby, pushing the ashtray away from the edge.

"I'm going to," said Mumford.

"No. You don't want to have to feed me if Mr. Owens finds you've taken it and that I let you," she said.

"You just play dumb. I'm taking the damned pin with me."

"What to confront Elia with? You're gonna get me in trouble."

"I won't let anything happen to you."

"God damn you! Then get out of here before Mr. Owens gets back." Mumford left.

Down the hall going to the elevator, he passed Mary Jefferson preparing to clean another office. He said good-bye to her not realizing that he would see her again before dusk. He did not encounter Abner Owens.

The afternoon sun had begun to fall casting its fading light on a large, leafless oak rising alone in a faraway field outside the verandah windows of Marshall House. Elia entered the veranda seeking her husband.

"Someone to see you at the side door, Mumford," she said.

"The side door? Who?" said Mumford.

"A black woman. Looks familiar to me, but I can't place her."

A curious Elia followed Mumford to the door at the side of the house. The woman waiting and standing by the steps of the stoop identified herself. "Mary Jefferson, Mr. Marshall."

"Do I know you, Mary?" asked Elia coming from behind Mumford.

"Yes, Miss Elia. My auntie worked for your parents when you were a girl. Cora."

"Cora. I loved Cora," said Elia.

Mary Jefferson thought, yes, in her place, you loved her. She said, "I've got business with Mr. Marshall, Miss Elia."

"Go on, Elia. Mary and I'll talk in my office." Elia withdrew down a hall. Mary Jefferson followed Mumford to his office just inside the doorway.

At his desk, Mumford said, "Sit down, Mary. What is it?"

"I lost my job. They let me go after fifteen years."

"Oh, my God!" exclaimed Mumford.

"It's either 'cause a pin got taken or because Mr. Vance, the policeman, is mad at me."

"It's the pin. I have it."

"I thought you might," she said.

"Why is Mr. Vance mad at you?"

"He hates my neighbor, Arorah Hannah. She's gone from next door, and he thinks I might know where she is. He missed this morning, but he's been coming by her house and my house every day looking for her."

"Why does he hate Arorah Hannah?"

"He hated Claude Hannah first and passed it on to Arorah," said Mary Jefferson adding with a meaningful look, "You wouldn't know. It was long after you were in high school. Mr. Hannah broke up Mr. Vance's high school romance with Miss Elia. My auntie said Mr. Vance went crazy, and Mr. Hannah had to send Miss Elia off."

"Off?"

"To Europe and a girls' school, and you know."

Mumford did know what the word *off* meant. So that was the reason Elia had trouble getting pregnant—an abortion. He was getting very angry at Elia when he realized how angry Mary Jefferson was. Had she told him about Elia to wound him? For a second he wanted to meet her anger with his, but he realized his anger belonged elsewhere, and he further realized that Mary Jefferson had cause and was brave to confront him.

"Mary," said Mumford, "I'm gonna fix it so you'll get your job back."

Mary looked intently at the white man. Mumford rose. She rose. He reached into his pocket for his wallet and from it handed her a hundred dollar bill. She had never seen a hundred dollar bill. Mary took it. "Thank you," she said.

"You got a way home?" said Mumford.

"My brother's waiting."

After Mary Jefferson left, Mumford pondered his situation and the new revelations into Elia's character. He had been searching his brain for the exact time to return to Elia her antique pin. He decided to return it to Abner's office at once. He'd get Ruby to say she had found it on the floor.

In his imagination he could smell and taste and touch Claude Hannah's money and see fields of rice stretching outside Marshall House next spring.

Mumford knew from Ruby the results of the detective search made by Ham Vance for Abner. He picked up the receiver of his desk telephone to make a long distance call to Bendleson's. A great sense of mirth came to Mumford as he thought of the irony behind the call. Bendleson's was the best private detective agency in New Orleans.

Thirtieth Sequence

Thor Hannah rode in the passenger seat of Dr. Jeff Johnson's Cadillac toward the Pankum Greenhouse and Nursery. Spring Marshall had alerted Thor to his mother's whereabouts and possible danger. Dr. Johnson had found time away from his exhausting practice and activities to drive Thor to an unannounced meeting with Arorah Hannah.

"Every young man of talent needs someone to take him in hand, a sort of mentor," said Dr. Johnson as he drove. "Much talent is lost for want of a mentor, believe me. And, too, for lack of the time or a worthy aim."

"Don't push me. I am thinking of all you've told me," said Thor. Dr. Johnson continued to urge Thor to choose a life course in Mississippi.

"I tell you again, something big is going to happen in Mississippi in the coming decades. It'll be a chance for you to make a life that counts, and you can do it."

"I can't really think in decades. You're talking about never to me."

Well, time'll pass to your never, believe me."

Through the car windows, the fields slipped by full of dead cotton and weeds. The sky was overcast, and the land was void of color. The passing scene behind the window glass was a movie, black and white dimmed to gray.

"I can't think of anything but meeting my mother. I'm not . . . prepared."

"Trust your senses. There aren't any guides here."

From the highway Dr. Johnson pulled the car onto Pankum property veering right toward the breezeway between the business and the greenhouses as Spring had directed.

It was early. The buildings of the business lifted up from the land into the gray, unstirred morning like grave markers. Quietly the two

The Cyclops Window

men exited the car and entered the breezeway. At Wash's door, Thor knocked.

"Yes?" someone said behind the door.

When Thor saw Wash's face in the crack of the door, he stepped back.

"Yes?" repeated Wash.

Recovered from the shock of seeing Wash's face for the first time, Thor said, "I'm Arorah Hannah's son. I've come to see her."

Wash came out of his room closing the door behind him.

No one spoke for a moment.

"You must let this young man see his mother," said Dr. Johnson.

"Does he know much about her?" asked Wash.

"I don't remember my mother," said Thor.

Carefully, Wash looked at the young man. "She's not like other people," he said.

"What do you mean?" asked Thor. He had sensed when Spring and others spoke of his mother that something had been withheld.

At last Wash spoke. "You must be cautious." He opened the door. "Come," he said.

Arorah Hannah sat on a stool before a mirror powdering talc on her face. Not turning, she said, "Claude, you had that dream again because you read me that bad poem about fish bones."

Nearby on the edge of a table a book of T. S. Eliot's poetry lay upturned on *The Waste Land*. Arorah liked the rhythm of the part "Death by Water," but she confused Eliot's bones of a man picked in whispers by the sea with ordinary bones.

The men waited.

Arorah turned.

She jumped up at once. The stool fell. She fled into the shower stall in the corner of the room and hid behind its canvas curtain.

Wash went to the stall.

"Come out, Arorah. It is safe," he said.

She peeked sideways from the limp canvas.

"Come," said Wash reaching out to her.

She took his hand and stepped from the stall.

"The white powder?" Thor asked Dr. Johnson.

He shook his head.

Wash explained. "She believes she is protected from whites if she looks white."

Arorah glanced at Wash. "Who are they?"

Thor stepped forward. Tentatively he offered to embrace Arorah. Quick as magic, Arorah vanished behind Wash's back.

"I'm Thor, Mother," he said.

The room was as quiet as death.

Arorah moved to Wash's side. "My Thor is a baby, a beautiful baby. You're too big," she said.

"I'm grown up."

"No," she persisted. "You're not my baby. I've known my baby all this time passed."

"Babies grow up in the time passed, Arorah," said Wash.

"No. Not my baby. You told me he would stay a baby in my heart."

"But only in heart, not in mind," said Wash.

"My heart is where my mind is. You told me so," she said to Wash, to Claude.

"Mother," said Thor.

"No. I am not your mother." She moved away from Wash and toward Thor. She raised her fisted hands.

Thor backed away. He felt the door behind his body.

"Stop, Arorah," said Wash.

She stilled.

Thor looked to Dr. Johnson. "I don't know what to do."

Arorah returned to Wash's side. "No," she repeated.

The room was as quiet as death.

The busy doctor spoke. "I can't see any use in staying. We can talk it out in the car later, Thor." Dr. Johnson turned around and took Thor's shoulders positioning him to leave.

Arorah took a step toward them. She puckered her lips.

Wash reached for her shoulder, touched it. "Don't spit," he said.

Arorah's lips relaxed. The visitors closed the door.

Outside no sunlight had invaded the gray of the morning. Dr. Johnson and Thor got into the Cadillac. The car rolled away and out onto the highway.

"What can I do?" said Thor.

"Nothing here. You must go on with your plans," said the doctor.

"I can't just leave her."

"Yes, you can. Wash Bibbs obviously loves her. He will see to your mother's needs better than anyone."

"She calls him Claude."

"She probably gets mixed up," the doctor said. "Get back to your education now before it's too late."

"I'm a semester late now," he said to himself.

Thor stared out the window to the passing landscape, still a dim and washed-out gray, black and white movie.

"I'll take you to the train station tomorrow, Thor," said Jeff Johnson. "And, I promise you will hear from me if you can help your mother."

Grim resignation in his face, the young man nodded.

An hour later Wash drove the Pankum truck past the same colorless fields toward the Port City Yacht Club. Arorah sat beside him. In the bed of the truck, evergreen magnolias bloomed unseasonably forced by false light and heat in Norwood's greenhouse. Rolls of cotton and plastic in and over the bed protected the greenery and its creamy flowers.

"Those crazy fish bones," said Arorah.

"What?" Then Wash realized that she was referring to Eliot's poetry. Concealing humor, his scars quivered.

Wash drove on to enter the misty downtown. Attempting to cheer up the modest daylight, the merchants, now busy in their closed stores, had left last night's decorations lighted. The bright strings of red and green Christmas bulbs swinging over the streets enchanted Arorah.

From the downtown they traveled up the levee. From its top and before them, the horizon was lost in gray sky and gray river. Everywhere a drab watercolor had taken the Delta. Below them, the giant houseboat that was Port City's yacht club floated out into the river. It was secured by an iron ring embedded into the girded concrete that centered the town's riverside. A fragile ghosty haze clouded the dark water. From the club's right extended a vast deck on pilings. The deck was bordered by boathouses and slips and made of heavy, weathered wood.

Wash drove the truck directly down toward the river.

"Are you going to drive into the water?" said Arorah watching as the car seemed to drop toward the River.

"Looks that way, but no," said Wash. "Can you swim?"

"No. Can you?"

"Yes," said Wash. "But I expect the water would make a cold swim today."

He wheeled the truck sideways and parked parallel to the water's edge. At the truck bed, Wash uncovered the gem magnolias. He reached beside the small trees and pulled out a fishing pole handing it to Arorah.

"There's a railed corner far on the deck where the members' children fish in summer. You may be able to catch crappie on a day like this." Then he lifted a tree from the bed to carry to the club.

Arorah followed Wash as he seesawed down the decline to a little bridge connecting levee to club.

"Is it safe?" asked Arorah when both of her feet were on the bridge. The segments of the makeshift bridge moved, and the water below sloshed.

Wash turned and reassured her, turned again and said, "You are my beauty."

"I am loving, too," she said sending back what she had seen in his eyes. Playing, happy, she stooped and stuck her hand low through the side of the bridge touching the river. "Brrr," she said.

Wash put the magnolia down beside the entrance door and led Arorah to the northern end of the football-field length of the great deck. There he layered plastic in the seat of a moist and unraveling wicker chair and settled Arorah. Summer gone, winter strong, the deserted dock was a hideaway hidden behind the boathouse covering the last slip.

"Catch us fish for supper," he said.

"I will," she said. "But don't stay far away too long."

"I'll check back."

Wash returned to the club entrance. The manager was unlocking the club door to open up for the day. Beside the manager, an aproned bartender stood with an aproned boy, his features matching his bartender father's.

"I've come with the magnolias," said Wash. "They need all the light and warmth they can get."

"Put most of them by the windows," said the manager freeing the door and leading the others forward. Tall windows and little walling structured most of the club's main area of bar, dance floor, tables and chairs. He switched the lights on. "Put two of them on the back porch if you think they'll make it through tonight's dance."

The manager strode over the dance floor and past the bar to his office in the rear of the big boat.

The bartender said, "Come on, Frankie, I'll show you what to do tonight. Don't let me down, or I'll box you."

"I'm not. You just pay me for my work," said Frankie to his father. The boy raised his shoulders to maximize his maturing height.

Wash placed the magnolia by a window and left to return to the truck and to complete the unloading.

Tree by tree he carried his load to the club entrance creating there a forest of flowering magnolias. The bringing had been an effort for Wash, but being surrounded by the beauty of spring and summer in dreary December touched the poetry within him. He paused to feel.

He heard a sloshing sound of swishing water at the bridge. Someone was coming. From the side of creamy blooms and leaves, so shiny in the dullness, he saw Ham Vance.

Wash pretended to be busy, low in the small forest, but it did no good.

"I saw the truck," said Ham Vance suddenly at his side.

Wash lifted a tree to carry inside.

"Where's your sister?" said Vance moving with Wash.

"She's gone back to her husband," said Wash.

"Really?" said Vance. "Gimme Mr. Pankum's truck keys. When you finish, I'm gonna follow you home and see that she's gone."

Wash knew that Norwood kept a duplicate key taped to the underside of the truck. He stopped, did not speak for a moment. He must somehow get Arorah to the truck and then away. Afterward he would think more. Memphis? New Orleans? He did not know where yet. Now they must escape. Wash put the gem magnolia down and handed Vance the keys.

At the bar, Vance said, "Coffee ready?"

Wash continued to work.

"Ready soon," said the bartender to Vance.

"You got some slugs for the pinball machine?" asked Vance.

The bartender gave him slugs.

"Gimme some, too, pops," said Frankie.

"No. And it's *sir* not *pops* around here. And you're here to work. Go help that lame black man," said the bartender.

"He's young to work here," said Vance leaving the bar for the pinball machine.

"He's big for his britches," said the bartender.

Frankie delayed.

"Now!" said his father. "Go on and help him, or I'm gonna backhand you."

Frankie approached Wash. "How you doing, Wash. I use to see

you coming by our house from Mr. Milledge's."

Wash nodded.

"You want me to lift those bushes? I'm strong," said Frankie.

"Bring the trees in from outside by the door and place them before the windows," said Wash. "I'll put this one on the porch." The porch extended from the rear of the houseboat, two walkways on both sides of the club coming forward to the front. "If you miss me, I've gone to the truck for more trees."

"Okay," said Frankie.

Wash hobbled past the manager's office carrying the magnolia, which brushed the ceiling from time to time. Out the back door on the porch he put his burden down, climbed the railing, and quietly lowered himself into the Mississippi to swim to Arorah.

Under water he swam outward toward the river's middle. There he surfaced and raised his head above the bitter water, colder than any he had experienced. He could see the last boathouse and knew Arorah's location. He would swim beneath the deck along the way catching breath in the slips. He began.

Under the heavy wood, the water grew inky, but he was able to spot the shapes of boats in the lighter dark of the open slips where breath could be gathered.

Ascending for his first gulp of air, Wash slid over accumulated slime on the bottom and side of the housed boat. He breathed. He was so cold. Should he get out and try to warm himself? He thought of a man once pulled from the river and warmed within a bale of cotton, and the thought brought him comfort. His wet head in the cold air seemed colder than his submerged body. He ducked his head under water and began again.

Dark. Cold. How much longer? He was not sure anymore. He swam. The cold had no mercy. He was becoming numb. He was becoming disoriented. Numb. Disoriented. Where? He must find the nearest slip at once.

Dark. Dark. His swimming slowed. His strokes shortened. It was cold? He could only dog paddle. Terrible fatigue. Must get out. His dog paddle slowed. Where was he? Cold? Yes. Arorah. . . . Slow. Slow. He felt no pain only the sense of slowness. Somewhere in the center of his brain was a shadow, a space there shaped by unclear boundaries, the shape becoming smaller, shriveling, tightening. A door in the shape flew open and what flooded out dissipated becoming one with the water rushing into his lungs.

That night as the white people danced before green and red lights shining around the magnolias at the windows, two logs from up north hit Wash Bibbs' body, crisscrossing and catching it, taking it deeper and south into the currents of the great Mississippi River.

Thirty-first Sequence

In the kitchen of the Homecooking Cafe, Thor Hannah sat opposite Spring Marshall at a metal utility table, spotless and shiny. Across the way near the doorway leading into the main area of Mattie and B. T. Haynes' business, a huge restaurant stove, black and porcelainized white, once belonging to a local hotel, was heating. Inside the oven, homemade biscuits baked. Beside the kitchen's double sink, coffee was making in an urn. The room was warm, and the smells of biscuits and coffee pleased.

"You could get into trouble meeting me like this?" asked Thor.

"Not as much trouble as you could."

"I guess not," he said.

They were quiet together for a moment.

"I will miss you, but I'm glad I had time to finish your portrait. It makes you look like the black equivalent of the Norse god for whom Will Milledge named you. Someone told me you had a reddish tint to a full head of wiry hair when you were born."

"My classmates teased me about my name. But you could say it's more like a tribal king from Africa born in Mississippi Delta Indian territory," said Thor.

The coffee was made. Spring got up and returned with two cupfuls. "I've been thinking, Thor. Our friendship is a new beginning for me."

"How so?" He took a sip of coffee.

"I remember the first time a black called me by my first name after I'd grown up. A black woman who kept the front desk of my dormitory during my freshman year called me Spring and not Miss Spring. Such a little thing, a tiny germ that started changing and shaking me from the comfort of not thinking, the comfort of the status quo. I've made steps with you. I'm sure I have to make bigger steps, but each step for me has been a big change."

Thor shook his head. "Dr. Johnson expects a lot more big changes pretty soon."

"I think so. Maybe not pretty soon."

"Pretty soon," insisted Thor.

"You know we talk freely now," said Spring. "We didn't at first. I think you have a mission to help your people. I envy you in that this is clear despite the fact that you will have to be brave. There may be bloodshed, mostly black, I think. But I'm unclear about my mission. Maybe it's in my paintbrush. I don't think it's the same as yours but it's certainly linked to yours. Maybe if you do come back to the Delta we can, whatever our missions, make some good changes."

He was thoughtful. "I think we're friends and I think together we'll try just that."

"Yes," Spring said. "Another thing I think. I'm as separated as you really. Not from the land or river, but within the community. Here you're an old maid at my age, twenty-five, and old maids tend to be left outside."

B. T. Haynes entered the kitchen. "Dr. Johnson is here for you, Thor," said the restaurant owner.

"Already," said Thor and got up.

Spring stood. "I must go," she said.

B. T. Haynes pulled the oven door down and checked the biscuits. The smell of the swelling biscuits took the room. When leaving, Mr. Haynes closed the kitchen door tight behind him. He did not want trouble.

Thor and Spring exchanged quick hugs. Spring immediately left by the back door. In the other direction Thor followed Mr. Haynes.

At a table in the cafe, Dr. Jeff Johnson glanced at his watch impatiently before looking up to see Thor.

"I didn't expect you so early. There's plenty of time before the train leaves," said Thor. "I'll have to finish packing."

"Well, hurry," said Dr. Johnson. "I'm gonna have to drop you off at the station. I've got to get ready for a full afternoon of surgery."

"I'll be as quick as I can."

Thor climbed the stairs to his room. B. T. Haynes went to the kitchen and returned with coffee and biscuits for Dr. Johnson. Customers began to enter the cafe.

"Where's Mattie, B. T.?" asked Dr. Johnson.

"She's in bed. This weather makes her rheumatism hurt."

"Anything I can do?" asked the doctor.

"No. She's got aspirin and, if worse comes to worse, your medicine. Evelyn's taking a day off from the department to help me in the kitchen today."

Two more customers entered. Evelyn Haynes Buffton, child welfare worker, was behind them.

"About time you were here," said Evelyn's father.

Quickly she sat beside Dr. Johnson. "Arorah Hannah has been found. She's in jail. Does Thor know?"

"No," said both Dr. Johnson and Mr. Haynes.

"Well, I'll do the telling," she said.

"Wait," said Dr. Johnson. "Just wait. I've come here to drive Thor to the train station to go back north. It's extremely important for him to get to his studies."

"I think he should be told," said Evelyn.

"Think. Thor cannot help his mother without sacrificing himself and will most probably get himself killed with his Yankee, imprudent ways. You leave this to me, Evelyn," said the doctor. "Please."

She scrutinized his empty cup for a moment, picked it up and walked silently to the kitchen.

Thor came down the stairs carrying his suitcase.

Evelyn returned with a full cup of coffee for Dr. Johnson. Her father was waiting on a nearby table.

"Thank you for your help in locating my mother, Mrs. Buffton," said Thor.

Evelyn stood still a moment. Dr. Johnson caught her eye. She looked to her father a few feet away.

Mr. Haynes stepped forward. "You haven't got time to dally, Evelyn. I got these orders to cook. You better get that other table." People in the cafe began to mingle and enjoy themselves.

Evelyn said to Thor, "You're welcome." She picked up two plastic-coated menus from the counter and approached the new customers. She called back to Dr. Johnson. "It's in your hands now."

Later Thor rode beside Jeff Johnson in the Cadillac toward the Illinois Central railway station. As they drove away from Redbud Street they entered downtown Port City.

Thor handed Dr. Johnson a card. "Would you do me one last kindness. This is a signature card for a little account I want for Mother. Would you give it to Wash Bibbs and have him sign it to make the money available to her through him?"

"Are the statements going to you or Wash?"

"To Wash."

"Why not me?"

"I hated to trouble you."

"Send them to me. I'll make sure she gets what she needs if she becomes ill."

"Thank you," said Thor.

"The things I've done for you are bread cast upon the water. I expect our people to have the returning bread."

"I hope the bread won't come back soggy."

"I'm certain it won't," said the doctor. He took the card.

"You will let me know if my mother needs me?" said Thor.

Dr. Johnson studied Oscar's Cafe out the window as they passed by it. The white cafe opened in the morning at the same early hour as the Homecooking Cafe.

Thor waited for the answer.

"Of course," said Dr. Jeff Johnson.

After Thor lifted his suitcase from the backseat of the car idling in the loading zone, Dr. Johnson reached outside to shake his hand.

"I'll keep you posted about school," said Thor.

"Do that for sure," said the doctor.

When Jeff Johnson pulled to a stop at his first red light, he took the bank card out of his breast pocket and tore it into small bits.

That evening the old and slow IC train stopped, started, and rumbled north outside Memphis.

In Port City, in Oscar's Cafe, apple pie a la mode in his belly, Mumford Marshall shoved a sticky plate to the middle of a booth table. At the entrance he spotted a man, his stomach protuberant, his nose prominent and bulgy, who appeared to be a Louisiana Cajun, a rare man in the Delta. Mumford signaled to him, and he came forward.

"You from Bendleson's New Orleans office?" Mumford asked.

"Yeah," said the detective.

"Sit down," said Mumford.

The investigator sat. "You got the key?"

Mumford handed him the key Ruby had made for him and gave the man directions to Abner's office. "I saw the elevator boy leave some time ago," he said.

"You sure they're up there?"

"I followed my wife's Packard from the house. She's there. So's he."

The detective delayed.

"Something else on your mind?" said Mumford.

"Yeah. I hear you thinking about growing kudzu on the levee."

"Who says?" Mumford was surprised that the detective knew.

"Somebody I know in our Memphis office has been making a dossier on you."

"For Abner Owens, I'm sure. We'll do him one first."

"I got something to say about your kudzu. I worked before this job for the Corps of Engineers for a long time 'til I got to drinking too much. You ain't got it figured right."

"How come?"

"You know what a boil in the levee is?"

"Sure I do. It's when a hole in the levee changes from muddy to clear. Means the hole has reached through to the river and a flood is imminent."

"You know how big a kudzu root gets?" continued the detective.

"Pretty big."

"Too big. They'll make boils, I guarantee you. You'll get more floods, not less."

"Thanks for your opinion. I'll tell your employer what a good guy you are," said Mumford.

"Thanks." The detective rose. "I'll get right back to you if I can."

Upstairs in a corner of Abner's office, Elia dropped the challis skirt of her suit to the floor. She picked it up and smoothed its black and white houndstooth check across the tobacco leather of Abner's high-backed chair. She unbuttoned her blouse. Naked, she stepped mid-room toward a naked Abner.

She waltzed her last steps.

"Your little dance is charming," he said pulling her to him. "There's a bit of honky-tonk in your waltz, you realize. All your fussy social friends would be amazed at their cool Elia."

"They need never know." Her manner was coquettish.

"Are you so playful with Mumford?"

"No. He'd think I hadn't been a virgin." She stroked Abner where he liked.

"Would he think right?"

"Of course not!" She feigned offense, then piety, then in his arms, danced a slow fox trot.

"Stop your fooling, Elia. Tell me."

"No."

"Don't you trust me?" He smiled, his breath warm on her face.

"Not exactly." Guiding Abner to her ear lobe, Elia turned aside her head, her carefully done hair moist with sweat.

All of a sudden she pushed away. "Do you hear something?"

"This old building can be creaky. The door is locked." Abner grasped Elia to him and kissed her hard.

"Ah," she said feeling passion she had inherited from her father. She drew back and placed her hand around his penis and started to lead him to the couch.

The door opened.

A flash.

"What!" said Abner.

Another flash.

Abner pushed Elia away, groped toward the door. The man behind the camera had vanished.

Abner ran through the offices toward the hallway.

Elia grabbed a pillow trying to cover herself. "You're naked, Abner," she screamed.

Abner rushed back for his pants, put them on, hastened once more to the hallway.

Elia dressed.

Abner again returned. "Useless," he said. "He's gone."

They sat on their trysting couch. Neither spoke for minutes.

"What a day," said Abner breaking their silence. "First my wimpy son Dalton comes home weeping like a girl and now this."

"Wimpy? I can't see that he's wimpy, but what are we going to do?"

"Well, by damn, he is just that, wimpy," said Abner. "And then this goddamned thing."

"What are we going to do?" repeated Elia.

"The question is what is Mumford going to do?"

"Yes," said Elia.

"I don't think he's going to do you the honor of killing me. He came after me with a camera, not a gun," said Abner.

Elia rose and prepared to leave, picking up her purse from Abner's desk. "You swore no one would ever find out," she said.

Sally Bolding

"Look, Elia. Didn't work out. That's all. The point is to win more than fifty percent, but the greater the gain, the more risk. This was risky."

"You convinced me differently."

"I'm a lawyer. I'm paid to convince."

"And to advise. What do you think I should do?"

"Well, our plans won't work."

"No," she said. "And you're saying in other words, 'My dear, I don't give a damn.'"

"Come on, Elia. Friends?"

"I'm never friends with old lovers."

Elia went to his desk, picked up his daggerlike letter opener.

"I wouldn't," he said.

She dropped the opener, point down, on the wooden seat of a client's chair. "No, but if I were my father, I would."

She left.

Downstairs at the building front before Oscar's Cafe, the detective hid in the backseat of Mumford's Studebaker, slant parked on the street. Mumford sat upright at the wheel of the car.

"Got 'em both bare, the lady leading the lawyer to the sack by his ding-ding."

"His what?" said Mumford.

"You know what I mean," said the detective. "Anyway I gotta get outta here and back to Nawlins before the bull comes running out that building."

"Abner won't come now. He doesn't want to chance meeting me. I'm waiting for my wife. Where would you think she parked?"

"I saw a big car as I was running out the back."

"Packard?" said Mumford.

"Yeah," he answered opening the back door. "I'll get you your photos right away."

After the detective had rushed away, Mumford left the Studebaker to stroll to the back of the building where he located Elia's car in a service parking space. He got into the driver's seat. He waited.

He began to hum "Jingle Bells."

On Christmas Day he would tell Elia he had given back her pin earlier as his gift. In exchange he would expect gift-wrapped full access to the inheritance from Claude Hannah. Tomorrow he would go see Max about the kudzu.

He heard the click-click of Elia's high heels. He could tell she was angry by the cadence of her heels against the concrete.

She stopped at the car door when she saw him.

"Get in the back, Elia. I ain't Sam, but I'll chauffeur you."

Silently the Marshalls drove to Marshall House, its magnolias unblooming but festive with Christmas tinsel.

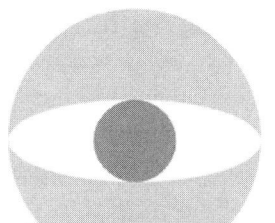

Thirty-second Sequence

Mumford woke early. Outside he walked his fields. His breath froze white in the gray air. The cold did not deter him. His stride was young as he crossed the drab fields, worn low, and his mind alive at the thought of promises sleeping in the soil beneath his feet.

"Hot diggety." He could see in his mind's eye springtime fields of rice. He saw great masses of slender sun-reaching lines growing in waters from low reservoirs, the waters held by dikes formed in great curves over the land.

He climbed the levee, beheld the river, soft haze belying its might, a drowsy snake not to be disregarded. At this moment in time, he felt he knew what it was like to be as powerful as the river. Atop the levee, atop the world, he gave the river a generous bow.

He loved the river below him, the land behind him, but he was tethered to neither. He was as elemental as both river and land. He did not understand people who lived as if they were tethered.

"The *Great Big Yes*, that's what I believe in," he said.

He breathed deeply pulling much air into his lungs.

He always breathed deeply.

Mumford turned eastwards to the land. There would be no sunrise. Dawn looked like late dusk. The dim light prevented his seeing across the highway to his second plantation, One O'clock with its Choctaw mounds, but he could see the whole Pankum operation abutting the Marshall place, and he recognized the greenhouse where his kudzu continued to grow

"Damned kudzu," he said. "Phooey." The thought tainted his enthusiasm. Then he reminded himself that Thomas Edison had met many failures within his successes, and his spirits revived.

"Kudzu," he said again. "I bet Max wants to see me to tell me more bad things about kudzu."

Mumford took another full breath of the cold, cold air. It stung his lungs, but the sting was a stimulant.

He began his descent down the levee to the fields, his steps wide and strong, a dare to the universe to cause him to stumble.

Back on the barren fields, he headed home. Along the way the light struggling from the clouds caught the water on his buffalo fish pond coloring it a tarnished silver. The reflection drew him. He stopped to stand before reaching the mud that rimmed the pond. In high season the edges of the pond had formed a clear rectangle of water set within the stripes of the furrows over the fields. But recent rainfall had swelled the pond past its banks, the shape of the pond now lost in overflow and mud.

Mumford took a piece of breakfast toast wrapped in one of Elia's damask napkins from his breast pocket. The cold toast had dried crispy and flat pressed so long against his chest. He stuffed the napkin back in his coat and took a bite of the toast. "Phooey," he said again. "I'm too nourished on life itself to eat such stuff." He crumbled the toast and threw it into the pond.

At once buffalo fish made a quick feast of the crumbs.

"I'll be damned," exclaimed Mumford.

A few crumbs became waterlogged and slowly sank. The fish continued to feed on the crumbs, both fish and food disappearing into the deeps as Mumford watched.

"I'll be damned," he repeated. "I think I'll feed you suckers grain like we do pigs instead of just letting you make your own way like river fish. So much fish poundage for so much grain measured like we do grain for pork. Maybe that'd change the equation."

He started to turn away, but turned back.

He spoke to the pond. "You buffalo are the wrong fish. You got too many bones. Catfish don't, and they're sweeter. Maybe Max could get the name changed so people wouldn't feel they were eating cat something."

He circled again and was off into the colorless fields, toward Marshall House, merry with red and green for Christmas.

"Sweet Fish, that's what Max ought to get them to call catfish," he said as he went reminding him at the same time that he must not to forget to call Max.

Before he reached home, he had willed himself to forget about raising catfish. He would make a success of rice growing first. He would somehow get the constipated farmers in the area away from being too cotton dependent, get them to move.

He opened the door to the glassed-in porch of Marshall House. There Elia sat in a wicker chair. She was on the telephone doing her favorite thing, arranging a social affair.

"Buffalo ponds and kudzu. Phooey," said Mumford. "But like the great Edison, I'm gonna have my share of success. Rice, yes. Catfish, later, maybe."

Elia put her hand over the receiver and glanced up. "What?" she asked him.

"Never mind," he said unaware that he had been speaking aloud.

When Elia finished her telephone call, Mumford tried to call Max at work. When he found it was too early to reach him there, he decided to go by Max's house and have a second cup of coffee with him.

He would drive one of Marshall Place's jeeps, U.S. Army surplus from World War II, each purchased for fifty dollars. Sam could make arrangements to pick up his Studebaker downtown.

Maybe Max would make him a piece of hot toast.

The clock beside the Picture Show Lady's bed read seven thirty. The alarm, set and rusted at seven, had been shut off since her work at the Majestic had been interrupted.

She awoke. Her sleep had been sound. Eyes still closed, she stretched her legs deep into the warm sheets touching with her toes to the down tuck. Her body seemed at peace, her muscles, her soul, relaxed. How different from her last days when her body had cried for any rest, when her brain, circling as in a squirrel cage, would give no quarter. She welcomed the curious peace.

Finally, reluctantly, Ladyree opened her eyes. She measured her whereabouts. The room's familiarity supported her comfort. She could hear strong wind. Outside a window, daylight was dull and the branch of a tree moved.

Abruptly she sat up.

The branch moved in slow motion. The slowness was no stranger. She knew the feeling from the weeks before she had decided to arrange Verda Soper's death. Then, the usher in her had seen the world slow and distorted as if rolling from a faulty movie projector. Now she knew the slow motion had been caused not by film but by a seething in her brain, a rage she had turned into the energy to do the deed.

And now? Why this sluggish motion in her world? She rose, went to the window, and studied the untimely branch.

Last night she had come to a conclusion. It would be her paralyzing fears that would cause her downfall more so than Verda Soper's transmigration into the kudzu, if that were the case.

Will Milledge had had a lot to say about fear. He said that there were too many things to fear in the world, that you had to choose your fears carefully letting go those of odd chance.. More important to Ladyree last night had been her memory of his saying that it took fear to generate courage. At this thought she had pushed away a glass of sherry and, seeking courage, had gone where she had been reluctant to go—into the cold parlor with its pervading essence of Verda Soper. Shaking she had lit the fireplace and when the flames came, pulled herself close in the rosewood chair. Then she had reached into a near bookshelf for one of her mother's genealogy books, *The History of the Soper Family*.

She reread her Grandmother Soper's story. Mr. Soper's mother had been the granddaughter of the governor of Alabama and the wife of a prominent Memphis cotton broker before the Civil War.

Ladyree's father remembered his mother as a strong person. A woman, he said, who could drive a six-foot wagon through a four-foot gate. He had laughed and said his mother nursed his wounded father on returning home from war treating him as if he were the most powerful man alive and she only a weak thing. Afterwards and secretly she had gone into the fields to pick cotton.

"She picked cotton?" Ladyree had asked her father.

"That's the story. You never know," he had answered.

Whatever. Ladyree had closed the leather volume determining that she must emulate such courage, fact or fiction. In her veins was the blood of many and different histories.

She had reshelved the book, put out the fire in the grate, taking from the mantel the fireplace box of matches. She had climbed the creaky steps to the doorway of the attic. There she stood facing the kudzu vaguely illuminated by downstairs light. She endured her fear, but she shook. She stepped into the dark attic, the kudzu now around her and started toward the back window. The pot was certain to be nearby. She would uproot the kudzu now that its roots were no longer embedded in the ground.

Outside a wind came up and seeped through the cracks of the attic making a sound like whispers in the kudzu. She could go no farther. She fled to the bottom step of the stairway and, panting like a nervous dog, paused to calm her breathing.

The going up to the attic, the coming down, the willing of herself to meet her fear, had enervated her. She went to bed at once and fell immediately into a blessed sleep.

An hour later again, she awoke. She avoided looking at the branch she had seen earlier moving slowly outside her window. She got up, went to the kitchen to make coffee trying as she made her way down the dim hall not to think of time. When the coffee pot seemed not to perk fast enough, she lifted it from the stove and shook it to hurry it in vain.

In slow motion she left the kitchen to get the morning's *Memphis Commercial Appeal* to read with her coffee.

Outside in front of the Cyclops House, last night's wind had blown dead twigs down from the two old oaks. She saw an almost imperceptible sway above in the limbs. She decided to leave the ground untidy. The wind remained and was erratic, and it would be better to wait for Wash Bibbs to clean up on his next day of yard work.

She picked up the newspaper. Turning she looked up to check the bundle she had noticed lodged up high days ago. As she did, the wind strengthened, and the something loosened, tumbled down, caught, tumbled again, and fell to the ground beside the front door. Slowly, slowly, she approached the vine-covered something.

"No," she said nearing it. "No," she said peering over it. She held her nostrils. She pulled back kudzu vines. She saw the tiny movements of worms and the decay below the dead fur of an animal. She touched the tiny Christmas bell of CAT's collar.

She stood covering her nose. The slow motion was gone. Again rage had righted her sense of time. "I still hate you, Mother."

Inside she cut off the coffee, left the newspaper spread unopened on the kitchen table, and dressed. It was too early to call Norwood's, but she would park in his lot and wait for Wash or Nathan. They would help her destroy the kudzu.

She pulled her old Buick out into the streets of downtown Port City and headed toward the Pankum nursery.

On her way she recalled that Verda Soper had disliked Max since that one time he had come to court her, disliked him as much as she disliked CAT. She must warn Max about the kudzu sprig. His house was within the city limits before the highway leading to the Pankum nursery.

She would stop for a moment at Max Durham's.

Mumford Marshall drove toward the new subdivision of GI houses where Max Durham lived. He steered off the highway into a circle of little toy homes finding Max's in the bend of a curve. Max's Ford filled the small driveway. Mumford parked the Jeep on the macadam beside the dull grass of Max's lawn. There was no sidewalk.

Mumford rang the doorbell. He got no response. He knocked on the flimsy door. It opened. "Max," he yelled.

Mumford entered. The room felt like a closet. The smell of new paint and sawed wood remained. Ugly "antiques" and an Early American couch and matching coffee table of shiny pine, purchased from Sears Roebuck, furnished the living room. Before him he could see into the miniature kitchen, plants on its window sill above the sink and through its window a backyard, sunless and barren of scrubs.

Mumford heard a moan coming from a narrow hall adjoining the living room. "Max?"

"Here," said Max Durham, his voice a different kind of struggle from a stutter.

Mumford found Max, his back against a wall, his feet akimbo on the floor blocking the middle of the meager hall.

Mumford stooped over him. "You okay?"

"Nooo. I'm sick. I feel terrible, M M M. . . ."

"Don't talk. You look as gray as outdoors today. The clinic should be open by now. I'll call you a doctor."

Mumford reached the clinic. On call, the young, new doctor, who had taken Prather Lewis' place when he retired, listened as Mumford reported Max's distress and said he would come at once.

"Bring an ambulance, too," said Mumford to the doctor. "I've seen heart attacks before, and this may be one."

Mumford returned to Max's side.

"You stay calm, Max, and, for God's sake, don't fight to talk."

"Hello in there," said Ladyree at the still opened door.

Mumford stepped slightly away from Max and into the hall entrance.

"Ladyree? Yes, it's Ladyree," he assured himself before explaining. "Something's wrong with Max."

Mumford returned to Max's side. Ladyree closed the door and followed him. She stooped to speak to Max. "Don't talk to him," said

Mumford. "He'll try to be polite and die."

Ladyree patted Max's arm and straightened up. Mumford picked up an overturned ashtray Max had dropped on the hall floor and lit a cigarette. He smoked standing by Max's other side. Max's eyes were closed. "Is he okay?" asked Mumford.

"I think he's just dozing."

In a minute or so, Mumford spoke. "How old do you think Max is, Ladyree?"

"About our age," answered Ladyree."

Mumford felt his belly which leaned down in his lap. "Damn, I ain't tough at the middle anymore." He smashed the tip of his cigarette into one of Max's ashtrays. "Somebody told me these were bad for you. I think too I'd better join the Y or maybe buy me some Tennessee Walkers to ride horseback. I promised myself I'd live to be one hundred."

"You will," she said.

"One hundred ain't as far off as it use to be," continued Mumford. "Can't deny it, Ladyree. We're closer to the Big Reaper."

They lapsed into silence.

Max stirred. "Shhh," said Ladyree.

"Do you still sing?" said Mumford.

"Did I sing?"

"Sure," he said. "Do you still read poetry?"

"No."

"Pity," said Mumford. "In college poetry was for sissies and something I had to do until you came along."

"Will Milledge taught me to love poetry," she said.

"I remember that. Do you remember that we were going to live in a bee-loud glade like in Yeats' poem?" An old bitterness had crept into his voice.

Ladyree shook her head.

"So long ago, Ladyree. Damn. You were the most beautiful girl I'd ever seen and so much more. It was worth it fighting your mother off to get you. You could make me see and think about things I'd never seen around me or thought about—the red in the color of wood, the blood in the clouds of a sunset, the sounds of Port City I'd never heard."

Ladyree could not respond.

Mumford continued. "You kept opening doors for me like some kind of magic. But your goddamned mother kept slamming them and praying over me."

Ladyree's breathing became labored.

"I was certain you'd follow me away from that house with its funny window and its god-awful witch Mrs. Soper, but you didn't. I stayed drunk for months. I'd even get maudlin and call you. Your mother'd answer, tell me to leave you alone, and hang up." Mumford stopped for a moment. "Terrible hurt. Didn't ever want any more of that, and ain't ever had it either. Women don't know how men can hurt."

"I . . . Mumford. I truly didn't know."

"Hush!" He looked into her eyes. "Your eyes . . . the same."

"Mumford."

"I always said your eyes were like opals. You'd laugh then and say I had called you glassy-eyed."

"I was glassy-eyed."

"Too late, Ladyree. All that's settled. I got to live with what is. I got lots to do with the time left me."

"You didn't recognize me, Mumford."

"Hell, no. You don't look the same. You aren't the same. I'm not the same."

"No," she said.

"Why on earth did you choose your mother and that negative stuff she was over me, over us?"

"I chose?"

"Who else chose?"

"I chose because . . . Florida. . . ."

"Florida?"

Ladyree thought. "I chose . . . I think . . . because maybe it seemed the Christian thing to do . . . and because it was . . . safer."

"A safe life is a small life. I told you that."

"I didn't hear you when you told me," she said. ". . . And it's small . . . *and* sad."

"Yeah, I guess," said Mumford. "We both lost, you know. I might be a different man, maybe a little more vulnerable and aware, maybe better."

"I lost more."

"Sure. It's a man's world. Men are bigger in size, and the body speaks."

They heard voices in the street.

"The doctor and the ambulance are here," said Mumford.

Ladyree jumped up. "I've got to do something." She ran to the kitchen sink and grabbed the sprig of kudzu on the edge of the windowsill. She jerked the floating roots and stem, still in her jar of water, out and onto a cutting block of wood on the counter. She grasped one of Max's knives and began to chop.

"What are you doing with that knife?" said Mumford from the kitchen entrance.

"It's Mother. I killed Mother. She came back in this kudzu. She'll hurt Max. She may already have."

"You don't make sense!"

In a fever Ladyree continued to chop.

"Ladyree, what nonsense!"

In fury Ladyree scraped the hacked vine into the sink and hurled the jar in at its remains.

The sound of shattering glass further astonished Mumford.

"Mother! Why didn't you let me talk to him? Why! Why! Why!"

"Ladyree, look at me," demanded Mumford.

She turned.

He saw the rage.

The doctor knocked at the door.

"I got to see to Max, Ladyree. Hold on. You're not balanced. I'll send Elia to you. No. I'll send Marsie. We'll do something." He left.

Ladyree had stilled. She looked at the broken glass and was shocked.

She listened to a few of the doctor's soothing words before, unnoticed, leaving Max's house and Mumford.

As she steered the old Buick away and around the new subdivision, she failed to see the decorated Christmas trees, cut from southern forests, through the clear glass of each house's picture window. When she reached the highway, she turned east and drove toward the Pankum nursery.

Nathan Pankum heard a loud creak from the swing door of his father's greenhouse. He looked over from the corner where he swept. The Picture Show Lady had suddenly entered the greenhouse.

The only other person around was Tudor Jackson. At the far end of an aisle before a divided row of corn, both parts diminished by winter but one more so, he stood with his head bowed.

The Picture Show Lady did not see Nathan. She rushed to the

minister. "Tudor, where's Wash? Where's Nathan? I need them."

Tudor Jackson, who had much experience with the strong feelings of his flock, seemed to recognize her distress immediately. He ceased his praying and met her midway in the long aisle.

"Wash left Norwood without notice a few days ago," said Tudor. "Nathan's on Christmas holiday and is around some place doing Wash's work. Can I help you, Ladyree?"

"Only Wash or Nathan," she said. "But no, no one can really help me."

"God can help you," said the Presbyterian minister.

"I'm not sure God recognizes me anymore. Tudor, do you believe in reincarnation, maybe in transmigration? Could Mother have come back after me?"

"After you? Sweet Mrs. Soper wouldn't hurt you."

"Oh, Tudor. She deceived you."

"Deceived me?" he said. "It happens, but . . ."

"You pray over plants, Tudor. You think they are like people?"

"No. I do think they have some of God in them just as people do."

"But *not* people?" she said. "I've got to know if I'm mad or not."

"Mad? Of course not. Just disturbed."

"Isn't being disturbed being mad?"

"No. I think madness is losing touch with what everybody assumes is reality, and we're all a little guilty of that. You're just upset," he said. "Now, Ladyree, I believe in a mysterious God, but I do not believe He'd let someone come back to harm you."

"Well, I do! You just don't know sweet little old ladies like my mother."

"Ladyree, be calm. Let us bow our heads and pray in silence for your peace."

She bowed her head, but she could not reach Tudor's God of love.

In trying to stay quiet and still while they prayed, Nathan dropped his broom.

Ladyree heard and turned to see him. "Tudor, tell Norwood I've borrowed Nathan. I won't keep him long." She rushed toward the corner where Nathan stood.

Tudor called, "Nathan, go along with Miss Ladyree. Help her." To Ladyree he said, "Come to church Sunday and afterwards we will talk a long time."

On the highway Ladyree pushed the accelerator low until the speedometer read seventy-five miles an hour. Neither Nathan nor

Ladyree spoke. The rattle of the old Buick, not use to such acceleration, seemed loud. Nathan liked the speed.

Inside the Cyclops House, Nathan asked, "What do you want me to do?"

"We're going to kill Mother again." Then she added, "But you mustn't kill Norwood, Nathan."

"No. I don't want to go to jail. And, Miss Ladyree, you mean get rid of the kudzu like we'd planned, don't you."

"Mother. Kudzu. Don't argue," she said.

She's crazy, not drunk, thought Nathan.

"We'll get those two old torches of Daddy's They're on a hook at the side of the house out back. Help me get them. They'll protect us."

Nathan was unsure how they could protect but he dragged a kitchen chair to the back side of the Cyclops House. From the bend of the big hook, he lifted up the two old torches, sooty rags wrapped foot-long on poles, and handed them down to Ladyree. Then Ladyree led Nathan to the attic stairway. Each held one unlit torch. She began to climb.

"You're not going to light these torches, are you?" Nathan asked.

"Of course, I am," she answered.

"Aren't you afraid of fire?"

"No. Mother's afraid of fire." She reached back. "Here are your matches."

He put them in his pocket and started up the stairs.

"Remember the loose step," she said.

Nathan stopped. "I don't think this is a good idea."

At the top, Ladyree struck a match, and the torch fired.

Nathan could see her outline against the kudzu. The great vines did seem spooky. In the torchlight the kudzu appeared to crawl, and the attic drafts in it made a rustling like faint voices in a far room.

"I'm going back, Miss Ladyree. I'm going home."

"I can't drive you home now," she said.

"I'll take the bus."

"Oooh," she said and fell from his viewpoint. "Oooh, Nathan, I've tripped over a piece of vine on the floor. I can't hold this torch much longer. Oooh, there it goes."

Nathan sprinted up the steps to aid her. Careless, he hit the loose step. It cracked, then parted.

Nathan dropped down. One board tore his trousers splintering the surface of his thigh. He landed in a bed of vines which held him aloft somewhere below the attic. He felt a strange panic. What if the kudzu were Mrs. Soper? Wherever he had fallen, a pitch black surrounded him, only above a faint orangy light and below a barely visible line of light, maybe under a door. Was there a closet beneath the stairs?

His body swung in space, one arm tight in vine. The arm throbbed, its circulation blocked. Panic rose again. He saw in his mind the arm black with backed-up blood. The other arm free, it swayed above him weighted by the unlit torch he still clutched in his fist.

"Help me, Nathan."

He was entrapped. How could he help? He butted his head low, tried to make a somersault of his body curling his shoulders back, his knees and legs forward, against the net of vine. Suddenly he dropped a short distance dragging both arms. The entangled arm grew numb, but in the other he had kept the torch.

"Nathan! Where are you?"

"I don't know. I think I'm in some sort of closet."

His arm pained, and he could hear himself breathing, his heart thumping. He felt as if both lung and heart were outside his chest, raw and exposed.

"Nathan!"

He must do something. Again he struggled.

He was now closer to the dim line of light below. It had expanded and become a rectangle. *A coffin lid?* he thought at first. *No. It was probably a door.*

Above the orangy glow brightened.

Mrs. Soper or kudzu, it did not matter now. Wasn't kudzu a weed? As Norwood's son, he knew fire could be used as a weedkiller. He must act.

He managed with his aching arm to unpocket a match.

Above he heard a crackling and a bumping as if someone was rolling on the floor in the attic.

"Nathan. Get away. Smoke."

He scratched his thumbnail against the match head again and again. He lowered the torch toward the match. Pain. He felt pain in his arm. He tried again. The match fired from a flick of his thumbnail. He touched the match to the torch. It flamed.

Slowly, carefully, he burned through the stem around his arm. He welcomed the release.

"Don't, Mother," said the Picture Show Lady above. "Nathan, get

Sally Bolding

away from this smoke. Get to the fire department."

Absolutely mad, he thought. The kudzu still held him in a loop. The torch remained in his hand. He burned away one side of the loop. Again he dropped. He hit a flooring. Yes, he was in a closet, but one matted in kudzu. He kicked through the mass of vine at the dim outline of the rectangle. The door gave and parlor light came. He began stem by stem to burn his way out into Verda Soper's parlor.

"Smoke!" yelled the Picture Show Lady.

Nathan looked up. He could see fire at the roof end of an attic beam. The beam teetered. It fell.

"I can't get up! Get help *now*, Nathan!"

"I will," he screamed back.

He could only hear her now in a faraway voice. She was chanting Biblical verses.

"In my Father's House are many mansions," she said. "And burn as in an oven."

The words faded He heard no more.

He freed himself and ran out and away from the burning house. In a few blocks he reached the downtown firehouse. He leaned on a shiny red fire truck catching his breath and tried to call up through the space around the fire pole. He could only manage to blow air. He heard the firemen recently made full-time talking upstairs. He smelled the bacon they cooked. At last his breathing righted, and he could scream.

"Fire!"

The water from the fire hose flooded the downstairs of the old house. The back part of the attic and roof were charred or burned away. Soon after the fire had been extinguished, one of the firemen and his volunteer helper found beneath a fallen beam the Picture Show Lady's corpse. She still clutched a huge kudzu root, and a fine dust of ashes covered her body.

The coroner listed the cause of death as smoke inhalation.

The following day a sad-faced Marsie Klingman and one of her servants could be seen around the burnt-smelling rubble of the Cyclops House gathering up Ladyree's cats and kittens.

On Monday of the next week, Norwood informed Nathan that

Max Durham would survive his heart attack. Norwood continued to smoke thinking Max's cigarettes could not possibly be a factor. Still shocked at seeing Max nearly dead, Mumford quit smoking.

That same week, Nathan packed up Arorah Hannah's few belongings and carried them out to her where she was imprisoned in Ham Vance's police car. Officer Vance was again transporting her to Whitfield.

Nathan put the cardboard box into the trunk of the car. He approached the opened back window which was cracked to allow in air. Inside the back seat Arorah Hannah made no move to escape. She stared in the direction of the breezeway. Nathan was reminded of a stunned cat he had once rescued from the mouth of a dog. When Arorah saw Nathan, she roused and spoke through the window crack.

"Where is Claude? No . . . ," she said, "I do not mean . . ." She seemed to mumble, then swallowed and cleared her throat. "Where . . . ," she said clearly, "Where is my ugly man."

Nathan shook his head. He watched as Ham Vance drove her away.

Later, in summer, Sears Roebuck, next door, bought the Picture Show Lady's house, demolished it, and paved the yard over for a parking lot. An out-of-towner salvaged the Cyclops Window and installed it in his restaurant where in the evenings, candles on the dining tables made the eyespot luminous until closing time when the owner drew across it a silvery curtain.

Short Feature

Nathan Pankum, president of the Mississippi Delta Bank, followed a back walkway through chilling air shortcutting to the bar of Port City, Mississippi's country club. Behind the club the sun had vanished. A spot of light, the moon, appeared near the cold wine sky in the west, at the horizon a stencil of dark treetops. Between the trees and the club stretched wintery riverbottom fields.

Nathan paused at the back door to take in the moonlit fields. Despite his piney woods origins, he had lived in the Delta long enough to revere its rich fields as much as any native Deltan. Nathan's bank figured as a controlling force in the flow of the area's monies, but he knew that the land before him and its bounty and the river really controlled Mississippi Delta life.

The silence and the stillness of the nightfall belied the approach of the evening's activity. It was New Year's Eve 1980. Only a faint crumple of a few old leaves surviving on tree limbs could be heard and only a vague wind stirred, too weak to shake branches but sending enough air up Nathan's sleeve and over his neat collar to remind him of the chill, the chill even in summer he sometimes imagined—as if his bones were cold.

He entered the club. A blast of hot furnace air enveloped him. The heating system hummed nearby and the smell of burnt dust dominated his immediate surroundings. All of humanity socialized and seemed to sway in the room. The only blacks were wearing white jackets and serving drinks. He had come too late. He had wished a quiet supper before the festivities.

He hesitated. What to do? Nathan Pankum, forty-eight, silver-haired, slim, tall, neat, so scrubbed-looking that his father-in-law, Mumford Marshall, insisted he smelled of antiseptic, Nathan Pankum, who courted a dignity so cool as to deny the behind-the-back remarks that if you scratched the neck of Port City's most prominent banker, you would find it redneck red, stood in the gush of warm air, nonplused.

People in the room looked over to acknowledge him. He stepped forward into the bar. A purple and yellow streamer hanging from a bunch of multicolored balloons at the ceiling touched his hair like an insect wing.

"Nathan, old boy!"

Ted Cockrane. Nathan suppressed a wince and raised his hand weakly.

"Why me?" he whispered to himself. His questions were never to God but to the something he did not know.

Momentarily Nathan wished for his wife, who had taken a holiday trip with her father, Mumford Marshall, to New Orleans. Her easy manners smoothed his social life. Like his wife, Ted Cockrane was dumb and cheery, the Port City High School's popularity king, who had beaten the hell out of him long ago, forgotten by all—all but himself.

"Nathan, old boy," Ted Cockrane repeated, extending his plump, no longer hamlike, hand, "come join us.

Nathan met his hand with the proper amount of pressure of his own drawing back quickly.

"Of course," said Nathan suppressing his reluctance and the irritation caused by Ted's extended familiarity.

As they crossed the room Nathan said, "I thought you'd given up the club, Ted."

"I have. I'm just a paying guest tonight. Come on now, Nathan, be merry. It's the holidays. Don't worry about my finances anymore." Then, mimicking a gangster voice from a 1930s movie, he said, "Ya' see, I'm going straight now, ya' see."

They reached a gathering of men standing and sitting around a table.

"Hey, fellows, look who's here tonight, Mr. Moneybucks himself," said Ted.

The men exchanged greetings. Nathan's eyes met and steadied on the hangdog eyes of Dalton Owens, the bank's vice president. Dalton had had too much to drink.

"Oooh, Nathan," said Dalton with a sob. He lowered his head onto the tabletop.

The gathering hushed. Ted fidgeted once before agitation overwhelmed him. "My God, Dalton, straighten up. *Nathan's here.*"

Someone sitting by Dalton Owens said, "It's okay, Ted. Keep your wits and leave him be. He's just crying, he says, 'cause his daddy didn't love him." Dalton's lawyer father had once been a guest speaker at an assembly in Nathan's high school days. Abner Owens had died of a heart attack a few years before Nathan's father had died.

"Well, it's kind of a hoot to cry about such things at our age," said someone.

"We're supposed to outgrow that, Dalton," said Nathan.

Dalton mumbled, "You get away from your parents, you get away from yourself."

The aged faces of the fifty- and sixty-year-old men turned solemn.

Ted Cockrane laughed. The nervous laugh sounded false in the circle of silent men, but Ted continued his levity. He began to bounce up and down, a rubber ball in clothing. He doubled over confronting Nathan with his fish-belly bald crown fringed in graying red hair, a roll of flesh at the base of his neck. Ted's body was a fat infant's. He lifted his head, and Nathan thought of an aging Kewpie doll with sagging facial planes.

"Hear this, fellas," Ted said like a carnival barker. He cleared space around himself with his arms. He pushed a decorative pot of mother-in-law plant to center stage with his foot. "No Christmas poinsettia, no Easter lily, no one red rose for love. No, sweetheart," he said in the voice of the movie actor Humphrey Bogart, "but the tongue of a mother-in-law." He shoved the potted plant toward Nathan. "For you, sweetheart, from my private jungle."

Nathan was not pleased to be kidded about his dislike of houseplants. Somehow such plants shook his sense of reality, and often he awoke from a dream in a sweat from work in his father's greenhouse so many years ago.

Ted whipped out his pocket knife and cut a long green spear from the plant of rising spikes and began to fence with it. "Am I Errol Flynn or Douglas Fairbanks Jr., fellas?"

Someday the bastard will go too far, thought Nathan as he watched Ted swing the makeshift sword. Nathan wondered about his lingering involvement with Ted. Port City too had been surprised at his employing Ted and forgiving Ted his money troubles. Nathan, through bank records, knowing of Ted's insolvency before Ted, had forgiven his imprudence because . . . because maybe Ted had yet to go too far. Too far? Nathan asked himself.

The Cyclops Window

Ted threw the spear aside and assumed a modest pose. In Jimmy Stewart's voice, he said, "Wall, I dunno, I just sorta' thought you'd like this plant, Nathan." He picked up the potted plant that then towered toward the ceiling like so many church spires pointing heavenward and stepped toward Nathan.

"Pop. Pop." The plants broke into a cluster of balloons.

Nathan grimaced and backed away. "That's enough, Red Ted," he said. He had not called him Red Ted since high school days.

Dalton Owens, reviving momentarily, raised his head. "You son of a bitch, Ted. We've heard that moviestar spiel a million boring times. You son of a bitch, you'll go to your goddamned grave believing in Hollywood happy endings."

"Awah, fellas. I was just trying to liven us up. Awah, Dalton, I don't like sadness," said Ted.

Ted lowered the plant to the floor. He searched the disgruntled faces of the other men. "Awah, fellas, it's New Year's Eve."

"Get off it, Ted," said one man.

Ted clenched his fist at this last rebuke. He said no more.

Nathan watched Dalton slip over to the table side and relax into a deep sleep. His attention suddenly focused on Ted's fist. He thought of their fight in high school.

Ted revived.

"We had some characters in Port City then, didn't we, Nathan?" said Ted. "Not run-of-the-mill."

Nathan frowned.

"Is there a lot of sameness in us? Like a McDonald's being the same in Pittsburgh as Port City? Are we blending even with Yankees?" said someone. "Yankees? I hadn't said that word since *Gone with the Wind*."

Another man directed attention elsewhere. "Nathan, you know everything that goes on in Port City. Somebody told me they were gonna demolish the old Majestic Theater."

"Yes," said Nathan. The magnificent Majestic had been boarded up long ago.

"Gee," said Ted. "That makes me sad."

"It makes me sad, too," said Nathan. "The new theater out at the mall is plain and functional."

"We got TV now anyway," said Ted. "What was it we use to call that old lady who ushered at the Majestic?"

"The Picture Show Lady," said Nathan. "Ladyree Soper Marshall,

241

Mumford's first wife."

People began to crowd into the bar. Too many people for Nathan. He made his excuses to the men and left without eating to exit the club via the foyer where he knew his sister-in-law, Spring Marshall, had just unveiled a new painting.

In the foyer he stopped to scrutinize Spring's work. The oil painting was the first of a series she planned representing Delta life, one painting for each decade of the twentieth century, this one for the 1940s.

Spring Marshall was gifted and unsocial, an opposite to her sister, Nathan's wife. The delicate-looking Spring had the brushstrokes of a wrestler. Once she had told Nathan her power came from Diego Rivera and the river. Her paintings usually depicted history in symbolic, specific events, and crowds of people pigmented in earthy colors, some of her people recognizable.

The painting was controversial. She had painted her crowds in emphasized segregation disturbing some members of the still all-white club who did not wish to be reminded of the broad injustices of the era and some injustices remaining. Port City citizens depicted in her crowds complained of their likenesses. Those not depicted felt slighted.

Nathan's image was absent from the painting. He was grateful. In the 1940s, he had felt himself as out of the city limits as his father's business, estranged from Port City's life. It was then that he had begun to build within himself an emotional armor.

A strange boy. Maybe now, a strange man?

The men in the bar, consumed by their own lives, probably had no recall of such a boy, the boy yet within Nathan.

He recognized the robust figure of Mumford Marshall in the painting. Spring's "brilliant, funny, outrageous father."

He recognized the figures of Wash Bibbs and the Picture Show Lady.

Why tear down the Majestic? We need to fix the old more, not spin and spin in making the new always assuming the new to be best. Damn, he said to himself. No. Bullshit and worse were the new words. Bad language had lost its place just as had the Majestic leaving no room between anger and gun.

He hoped his own thoughts were not like those of the older generation of his youth whose praise of their own youths spoiled their nows. The good of his own maturity was that it allowed him to accept questioning what he could never answer.

A multicolored image, a blur because of his lessening vision, caught his attention on the canvas. He moved forward. He recognized the Cyclops Window. Once in a while he still dreamed it was looking at him.

What a good painter Spring was.

The entrance door of the foyer opened.

"Come meet our banker," said an aging, obviously wealthy widow entering on the arm of an effeminate Memphis decorator.

Nathan's frown surfaced before he could check it.

A man's sexual preferences were his own business, but the economics of Port City were Nathan's. Club members, citizens of a debt-prone community dependent on chancy weather and shaky agricultural yield in a time when American agriculture was in a financial decline should not underwrite expensive redecorations. This year's crop had been good. A good crop brought euphoric spending as a bad crop brought gloom. Nathan wondered that the Delta survived its peccadilloes, its manic-depressive scenario.

"Nathan," said the widow moving toward him.

He liked the effusive lady, but he did not wish to be best friends. Before they reached him, he had determined to make his getaway.

"Don't go," said the widow.

Nathan shook the decorator's extended hand, muttered, "Must go," bobbed his head agreeably at the lady and hurried out the door into the cool and moonlit evening.

Driving home, the engine humming and the dashboard aglow, he was grateful when the dark cab of his Buick warmed. Outside the December temperature continued to drop.

At home, the house seemed less warm than the Buick. At once he shoved the thermostat lever up thinking as he did how expensive it was to heat the commodious house. His wife's grandmother had left the big house to her. One of the few things Nathan could not persuade his wife to do once their child was grown and gone was to move from this family relic. They lived he claimed among too many other people's lives and stories, dead people's lives and finished stories, theirs the only huffs, gasps and grunts in the ghostly house.

He went to the kitchen to make a sandwich then standing over the open oven door turned occasionally, sandwich in hand, to warm both sides of his body. Afterwards he picked up the *Delta Times* on the chair by the stairs and went up to the bedroom.

In bed Nathan read the New Year's issue of the paper In the 1940s the paper had been a weekly.

Changes. So many changes. They came now in decades instead of centuries.

He thought too about the glut of new sensations—too many vivid colors, music every minute, news and information escalating, sex as common as a handshake, things to taste from all over the world, the aroma of baking bread overcome by multitudinous perfumes found even in cleaning agents and the flush water of toilets.

The *pop-pop* of firecrackers in the night irritated him. *Pop-pop*. He threw the newspaper on the floor beside the bed, the act too forceful.

He was angry. Goddamned, motherfucking whatever angry.

He breathed heavily. Why such anger? It rose to rage. He cut the light, tried to sleep. The anger continued to gnaw.

At two o'clock, Nathan's sleeplessness hung on. He got up and went to the bathroom to swallow one of his wife's Valiums.

On January 2, the bank reopened.

From the spears of the mother-in-law plant atop his credenza-shaped stereo, Nathan shifted his eyes to his office window with its Levolor blinds. The early January sun and shadow striped his face. A stratum of light struck his olive eyes bleaching them clear. He glanced away and back to the sharp tips of the mother-in-law plant beside a roll of posters and a card.

The card was from Red Ted. "The fellas say I irritated you New Year's Eve at the club. I'm sorry. I bring you five of my best posters from my collection as repentance." It was signed Humphrey Bogart.

Nathan touched the point of one green spear of the plant, and fury swept into his heart like river water over a levee. Leave it alone, Ted. You will go too far.

The banker touched another spear fighting to squelch his emotion. The power of it astonished him. He turned to his bookcase beside the stereo. His books had kept him sane so far, but he knew he could not read now. He switched on the stereo shoving the release lever which dropped an old 33 record onto the turntable. The sound of Bach's *Toccata and Fugue in D Minor* overwhelmed the office. His rage unleashed and swelled with the crescendoing organ music. He quickly cut the volume and, trying to retreat from such strong emotion, moved closer to the window. He grabbed a cord at the side of the window and zipped up the Levolor blinds flooding the office in high sun. Light flashed on the glass of his desk, and he saw his image.

A trick of mind? He saw not himself but the Claude Raines Ted often mimicked from the old *Phantom of the Opera* movie, which had featured the Bach music now filling the room.

On the glass the image of Claude Raines, a mask jerked clear from his face, revealed Hollywood acid scars and grotesqueries. Nathan moved. The image vanished. Had it mirrored the phantasm of his rage?

The music took him. The rage abated. The cool banker prevailed.

Nathan unrolled Ted's posters. *Gone with the Wind*, *Mildred Pierce*, *All About Eve*, *Jaws*, *What Ever Happened to Baby Jane*. In the fierce window sun, the banker listened quietly until the record finished its spin. He stood, and in the silence, decided. He walked back to his desk.

Red Ted had gone too far.

Seated in his chair he flipped a switch on his intercom calling his secretary, Willow. "Send Ted, please." Willow, a spinster, plain, her pear-shaped bottom always in a tailored skirt that was topped by a mannish jacket, would be quick.

A cool draft leaked from the bare window and crossed Nathan's back. He waited.

He had always known that this time would come. He opened the storage drawer of his desk. He searched through paper clips, rubber bands, touched a small first aid kit and his Colt 38, moved a box of staples and at last pulled forward a manila folder. He placed it topside. The draft at his shoulder rose, dipped to play at the paper edges protruding from the folder and passed to stir the door of his private bathroom.

He got up to empty his bladder. As he shook the last yellow drop from his penis, he noted Ted's shaver on the back of his commode. When Ted overslept he asked to use the plug to shave because no other bank bathroom had one. Always Nathan allowed him to do so holding in his irritation at the familiarity of the request.

He heard Ted's knock.

Nathan zipped his fly and reentered the office. Ted bounced in, grinning. He swept his arm in the direction of the gifts he had left on Nathan's stereo and stood, grinning, glowing, expectant, waiting for Nathan's response.

"I stole the plant from my jungle, you know," Ted spoke in the gangster voice of the movie star Edward G. Robinson. "You reckon

Sally Bolding

they'll send me to Sing Sing?" he said in his own voice. Ted met Nathan's unresponding expression and his mirth vanished. "I don't know why people don't laugh anymore."

"You've been brainwashed by movie tinsel and false sentiment. No happy ending, Ted, just death, is the real ending."

"I know."

"You don't, Ted."

"Yes, I do."

"Sit down." Nathan's fisted hand now across his desk appeared to relax on the manila folder. He continued, "How is Amanda?"

Ted brightened. "My wife is her old steady self." Ted said. "Holds me up like she used to. Gone back to teaching Sunday school. Got the house in tip top shape again. You know she's really sturdy. Always the strong one. Nobody knows about that collapse—that's what the shrink called it. She was crazy, Nathan. You wouldn't believe it. My Amanda, the most popular girl in Port City High School. But, God, you can't imagine how hard it was for her being dunned by creditors. She stopped going to the front door. Like a ramrod she moved about the house. I kept saying, 'Amanda, help me.' Amanda always helped me. Never a better wife. Never a better mother. And that damned boy of ours. Wouldn't lift a finger. Had his own problems, he said. And fifteen-year-old Lisa, bless her heart, shaking her pretty head, crying, not going to school. She kept saying, 'Daddy, do something.' Didn't ask her mama. Lisa's so smart. Musta known her mama wasn't well. I didn't know. I kept thinking Amanda was angry at me. God, no one helped me, Nathan. All those people I'd loved and tried to make laugh all those years." Ted stopped. "I ramble, Nathan," he said. "You helped, Nathan, the only one." Ted became aware of Nathan's absolute stillness. "Nathan? Nathan, are you okay?"

Nathan nodded.

Ted continued. "I can talk to you. No one else. I can't even talk to our minister. He's as crazy as Tudor Jackson that Presbyterian preacher who prayed over those plants until he got involved in the Civil Rights movement and got booted out of his church taking up for blacks. I can't talk to anyone else, Nathan, who understands? Just you."

A heavy silence sucked away what warmth the drafts had left behind in the room. Ted searched Nathan's face looking for friendliness. Nathan, familiar, always reserved, seemed steady to Ted.

"I'm cold," said the bank teller. Ted pulled his elbows in and crossed his arms for warmth. His unease prevailed. At last, he said,

"Nathan?"

"Ted, I'm going to have to fire you."

Ted got up. He turned one ear to Nathan, unsure of what he had heard. The little movements of his body ceased. "Oh," he said finally, "you're joking back like I joked about the plant."

"I'm sorry, Ted. Particularly sorry about Amanda."

"You aren't serious."

"I am."

There was a catching in Ted's throat as he sought air for his lungs. "But, why?" Another catch. "Because of the prank?"

"Ted, I know you've been short at your window."

"No, Nathan!"

Nathan opened the manila folder and pushed the paper toward Ted.

Ted glanced at the top page, looked up. "I never did it but once. It was at first. I needed the one shot to get up."

"Tomorrow's bank exam will show it."

"No. You must have covered it before. It's been so long. You can cover again," said Ted.

"I can't explain it again and keep you. The examiners will be satisfied if I fire you."

"Nathan, we're like brothers. *Try.*"

"Go and clean out your desk, Ted. Don't beg."

Ted walked away, returned to stand over the seated Nathan. "I can't get up again. I thought I'd solved the money problem. Help me. God, help me."

"Of course, you can get up, Ted. Life's a getting up and a getting up." Saying this, Nathan rose. He had done it. He had fired Ted. Something like a mild euphoria turned the tone of his voice lighter. "That's it, repetitious problem, and no life problem is solved but temporarily." He moved toward Ted. "I've always thought it's a question of the temporary solution lasting or the temporary you lasting."

"You don't make sense, Nathan. I'm not a philosopher like you. I leave that to God and smart people. Help me, Nathan."

Nathan stopped beside his desk. He let the euphoria subside. "I'd like to, Ted. We go back a long way—to 1947 about when I moved to Port City. Do you remember those days?"

"No. Not now. Not the football, the making out, the not making out. Not now. I can't remember. Help me, Nathan."

"I can't."

"You won't."

"Go now, Ted."

"Nathan, I'm begging."

"Don't. You're no coward. Remember how cowardly I was in high school. Not you, Ted." Nathan opened the storage drawer for his car keys kept near the clips and bands and remembered that he had walked to work and now must walk to lunch. "I have to go to Rotary for lunch. Clear your desk after the one o'clock closing."

Ted started to protest.

"Don't beg again. You dramatize. It isn't that bad." Nathan shepherded Ted toward the door.

Halfway Ted stopped. "Damn it, Nathan, you can't do this."

Nathan, practiced in ending loan denials, kept the motion doorwards. "Go on, Ted."

In the outer office, Nathan and Ted passed Willow while she typed. Ted clutched at his heart as if to calm it at each *click, click, click* of the typing. The two men entered the hall, and Nathan walked on leaving Ted stalled at the doorway.

Down the corridor from behind, Nathan heard Ted ask, "Can I get my razor?"

"Of course," Nathan called back.

From the hallway leaving the new part of the building, Nathan emerged into the opening of the greater body of the bank, the old part built in the 1920s. He felt a wholeness as if he had held the unattractive Nathan of the 1940s in his arms like a beloved son, a son he had never had, and comforted him at last.

His steps quickened. He paused to nod or chat a moment with customers and the tellers behind the curlicue bars and within the cool marble of their cages. He looked up to the cathedral ceiling and to the tall windows stretching down. The sun through window bars similar to those on the teller cages struck a gridiron pattern on the marbled floors.

This part of the bank reminded Nathan of a church. Its spirituality came from an essence of Port City past. He could see in his mind's eye ghostly banking queues, lines of the Port City people of his youth, each person's story now almost complete or complete, each person almost gone from mind and memory leaving only essence.

Nathan heard a noise. It sounded like World War II battle noise from the sound track of all those propagandist war movies of the mid-1940s. He circled around, saw Willow rush out of the hall entrance. Her anguish drew him toward her. He stretched his arms out making and keeping a path through the stirring, alarmed customers. Inside the hall, past Willow's desk, into the office, he felt his face going long and Lincolnesque.

Entering his office, Nathan felt it hushed like a sanctuary, hearing only the soft sound of moving water, distant, like a faraway running creek in a valley. On the tan carpet, he saw the toe mark of Willow's shoe in red. He saw a constellation of rubber bands and paper clips littered from his storage drawer to the bathroom door. Chill returned to his bones. *I'm so cold*, he thought.

Ted's skull had butted the bathroom wall before sliding to the commode, his head now in the bowl. On the wall lines of blood ran from smears of brain and skull, on the floor lay his Colt 38. Ted's collar had snagged the toilet handle, and a continuous flush, swirling, coming pink, circled his torn head. He had faced the mirror as he pulled the trigger.

Nathan stepped over a pool of blood, its perimeter compromised by the stamp of Willow's shoe. He pulled Ted's head from the bowl by a fringe of red hair. The bullet gap seeped new blood. Nathan lost his grip. The head made a thud on the floor tile. Nathan stood fixed over and within the kneeling body.

Behind Nathan, Dalton Owens had quietly entered the office. "Is he dead?" he asked.

"What? . . . Yes, I hope so," said Nathan. He could not move.

"Get back. Close the door," said Dalton to other employees gathering at the office entrance. Willow had retreated from the area. Nathan heard Dalton talking to a doctor over the telephone. Dalton completed the call. The doctor would handle any other necessary calls.

Dalton spoke to Nathan, who still stood over Ted's body. "Come out of there, and sit down."

Nathan started to lift the Colt 38 and return it to his storage drawer.

"Leave it alone," said Dalton.

Nathan complied and disentangled himself from Ted's body. "Red Ted is dead," mumbled Nathan before sitting in his desk chair.

Dalton studied Nathan. "Why don't you go home? I can manage."

"Yes, I think I will, Dalton. Thank you."

Nathan left the bank by a rarely used back door. Outside the noon sun was merciless.

As he walked home, he tried to find meaning in what had happened. He realized that a past wound had reopened. He wished he were more like Mumford who seemed never to let the past trip him, who overcame all failures and, undeterred, succeeded in many other endeavors. His rice fields and grain-fed catfish ponds thrived. Greater was his national success with fried catfish making him a king of fast food franchises. But Nathan could not shake the past.

Nathan turned a corner entering an old area where old homes had been remade into doctors' offices and real estate firms. There was Dr. Thor Hannah's offices. Nathan remembered the first time he had seen Spring's portrait of Thor, learning at that time about him and his mother. Thor had returned to Mississippi during the 1960s to work on civil rights issues. He had several times been arrested, once for integrating a lunch counter in a drug store, once for integrating the white library in Jackson, Mississippi. Now he and his wife, also a physician, and old Dr. Johnson continued to work on behalf of their race.

Arorah Hannah was gone. She had disappeared into the state bureaucracy of Whitfield never to be for certain found. Thor had managed in the 1960s to find a Whitfield employee who remembered a catatonic black woman who occasionally would break through her living deadness and talk about a Voodoo man, a white man, and a baby born to a clap of thunder. One year the woman had wandered away into some woods near the asylum and never returned. Some years later in the same woods a skeleton was found of someone who seemingly had died of exposure.

Nathan wondered what had happened to Wash Bibbs, Wash Bibbs who more than Norwood Pankum had left something of himself to Nathan.

Norwood had died suddenly of heart failure in the late 1950s. In his mind, Nathan saw his father's corpse stiff against the soft white satin lining his casket. He saw the powdered folds of Norwood's neck. He remembered the curious sympathizers leaning over Norwood's body. Norwood and Norwood's strict mother had cheated Nathan, but Nathan had long realized that he had to accept this fact and had taken what he had left.

Norwood had willed Nathan an investment in bank stocks and to Nathan's stepmother Ruby his nursery business. Nathan had avoided working with plants after his encounter with kudzu in the Cyclops House. Ruby had sold the property and taken the money to move to San Miguel de Allende in Mexico, where modest money could provide a good living, while Nathan had used his stock to build a banking career.

Nathan passed the City Hall. A sign hung from a ledge above the first floor: HAMILTON VANCE, MAYOR.

A few blocks more and Nathan had finished his walk home, the home a grand old house among grand old trees. A neighbor had discarded a plastic pot of a dying Christmas poinsettia near his curb for garbage pickup. Inside the still empty house, his wife expected home today from her holiday trip, he sat in his favorite rocker in a sunny window on the front glassed-in porch remodeled after the porch at Marshall House. The windowed area by the rocker was the warmest part of the house at the noon hour. Outside he could see the poinsettia.

Ted had called him a philosopher. He was not, only a thinking layman who read the books Wash Bibbs and the Picture Show Lady had led him to. Looking at the poinsettia his mind turned to the rows of plants he had once tended at his father's business, turned again to the kudzu twisting in the attic of the Cyclops House. "In my father's house are many mansions," the Picture Show Lady had repeated, meaning many dimensions of reality. He believed the Picture Show Lady had been mad at times, but he was unsure. All mystery, of course. And he, Ted's so-called philosopher, was not even sure he knew the questions mystery generated.

He knew Ted's suicide had shaken him. He had not hated Ted. Instead he had hated not being loved, just as the Picture Show Lady had hated the same—and Ted had gotten caught in that hatred. He grieved for Ted.

Outside he looked again at the failing poinsettia, symbol of the season of love.

Love. He believed love was passed along like genes. And Norwood? How could he pass along what he did not have? Had he, Nathan, passed any love along to his daughter? He doubted it.

Nathan went outside and retrieved the dying Christmas plant. Inside he watered its dry soil and placed the pot beside him in the sunny window. He longed to change the thread of unloving in his family as easily as he had brought the poinsettia inside.

He sat for a long moment in the quiet. Some unfamiliarity within him so comfortable that he thought of rest, a letting go, like a gentle death, stirred in his depths and brought forth a vague memory of a forgotten mother, of a soft breast, of a melded scent, sweet and faint, of tepid milk and delicate face powder.

When his daughter came into the house later with his grandson, Nathan took the warm boy in his arms and rocked him.

About Sally Bolding

Sally Bolding was born in Greenville, Mississippi, on the banks of the Mississippi River. She lived a of number years in Cleveland, Mississippi. She attended Rollins College in Winter Park, Florida and was graduated from Delta State University in Cleveland, Mississippi. She has taught Mississippi history and written a history column for state weekly newspapers. She has owned a bookstore, is a former airline attendant and water-skier. She and her husband live in Pensacola Beach, Florida.

Before publication, this book was a semifinalist for the James Jones First Novel Fellowship. She has written a full-length play, *Luke Soldier*, and is working on a second play and a novel, *River Currents.*

Her writing has been described by Cecilia Bartholomew, a writer and teacher at the University of California, as being "in that wonderful old tradition of the fine women writers of the South.